How Long Is Forever

A FLEETWOOD FALLS NOVEL

How Long
Is
Forever

DANIEL THERIOT

Paperback ISBN: 979-8-9873337-2-3

Chapter 1

Simultaneous with the stopping of Mason Chadwick's car was a flinging open of the screen door, followed by Mom racing across the lawn. The separation of a year since his last visit was evident, with prolonged hugs and watering eyes to follow. Not far behind was Dad, with a failed attempt to conceal his emotions. Whoever said grown men don't cry didn't know what they were talking about, Mason concluded as waves of emotion flooded him.

Up to the point of his recent discovery of cancer, his memory failed him as to the last time he'd shed a tear. A brush of his sleeve wiped the moisture from his cheek as he took to the steps leading into his parents' home, with Dad lingering a few paces behind, probably to compose himself.

"I've got fresh coffee made. I'll bring some into the living room." Mom hastened to the kitchen with a wide grin, revealing the joyful spirit she displayed during his visits home from Boston for the holidays. The yearly tradition being the single most important time of the year Mom and Dad looked forward to. Regrettably, he'd canceled the last trip back for Thanksgiving and Christmas due to pressing deadlines of editing and the release of yet another novel. A decision he now lamented.

Mason examined a partially assembled recliner lying on its side in the center of the living room. "Need some help with this, Dad?"

"You still remember how to work a wrench, Mr. Big Shot Best-Selling Author, with a possible movie deal on the table, your mom tells me?" Dad held out a ratchet with a five-sixteenth socket and smiled.

"Not holding my breath on that long shot of a movie deal. But as far as this recliner goes, I still know how to do things other than write, you know. Everything you taught me about working on cars, carpentry, and remodeling—still up here." He tapped his temple, dropped to his knees, and set the ratchet on the bolt. He couldn't recall Dad having slivers of graying hair on his last visit. Or perhaps he hadn't noticed.

Dad held the swivel pedestal in place while Mason bolted it on. The clicking of the ratchet came to a stop for a second, then continued. Kneeling in this room brought on recollections of twenty-plus years prior, with many such moments with Dad. Whether setting up a train set or putting together a new mountain bike, it was always with Dad. A given constant he could count on. But him returning home to Boone, North Carolina, for visits the previous few years, outside the holidays, was not something Mom and Dad had been able to count on.

"So your mom mentioned you'll be staying at a bed and breakfast in Fleetwood Falls." Dad dropped another bolt into Mason's hand.

"Yeah. Worked out a deal with Charlotte, the owner, for an extended stay. She was honest enough to mention that business had been a little slow the past few seasons. It's an arrangement that will benefit both of us."

Mom placed their coffee cups on the end tables. She removed her spool of yarn and needle from the couch and sat. "Wish you were staying here, of course, but I am excited about you being less than an hour away. Your doctor friend David mentioned six months of treatments, right?"

"Yeah. He suggested I remain close to family, especially if things get . . .you know, worse. The new treatment center in Fleetwood would administer the same meds and care as any other facility, with the latest cutting-edge technology. We both thought it made sense."

Mom's and Dad's eyes met. Mason disguised his detection with a twist of the ratchet. A pang turned his stomach at the flash of distress in their eyes. He hadn't given much thought to what they were possibly going through, given his diagnosis.

Dad walked to the kitchen and called back, with a shaky voice, "How about a slice of pecan pie, Mason? You're looking a little thin there."

"No thanks. Stopped for a bite before getting into town. Couldn't hold out any longer." Dad was right. Weight loss, as well as frequent migraines and night sweats, had become the norm over the past month, up to the point of the diagnosis of stage 4 lymphoma. Additionally, the cancer had spread throughout various organs and the spinal area, leaving him to wonder how it took so long for symptoms to manifest.

Mason stood up the completed recliner as Dad returned. "Go ahead, Dad. Try it out."

"I can't. You go first." He took a step back.

"What do you mean, you can't? It's your chair." Mason gestured with his hand for Dad to take a seat.

"It's mine only because you're here. I've been asking your mom for one of these for two years. She was so excited about you coming, she'd have bought me anything. I should have asked for that old Chey truck in the antique yard down the road. Been eyeing that beauty for half a year now. I just know it's calling out to me." He shot a sideways grin to Mom and shook his head.

"Would you stop. Besides, I think rust is the only thing holding that truck together." Mom laughed and fumbled through a stack of old photos on the end table next to her. "Ever since we found out you were coming, the memories of our summers at Morgan Falls Campground keep flooding in. We miss those days. Your dad and I took a trip to Fleetwood a couple of months ago, only to find the campground locked up and shut down. Couldn't help but take the picture box down to look through all those old photos when we got home. I guess these pictures and occasional trips down memory lane are all we have now. In one way, it feels like it was only yesterday."

She was right. As a teen it was a place of his best memories, taking trips to Morgan Falls Campground with Mom and Dad. Unfortunately, it was also the birth place of what would result in years of lingering regret. Despite the years that had gone by since visits there, it was a reminder that time didn't always heal all wounds. He, for one, would know. And if history had a chance to repeat itself, he'd make certain it wouldn't end up the same way. But regret had made a home in his heart for far too long and had every intent to stay.

Mason took a seat next to Mom on the couch and kissed her cheek. She squeezed his hand and smiled. His eyes fastened on a wooden plaque with a carved Romans 8:28 verse hanging above the archway to the kitchen. *And we know that all things work together for good to them that love God, to them who are called according to his purpose.* How could anything good possibly come out of sickness and disease? His "leave nothing to chance" creed of preparedness in all aspects of life had sprung a leak and the ship was sinking. The devastating news of cancer had been nowhere on his radar. Not on any wall calendar amassed with sticky notes or goals and dreams for the future.

Mom passed a photo to Mason and shook her head. "Look at that handsome boy. I don't think anyone would recognize you today compared to that graduation photo. How much you've changed."

"Yeah. Guess I have."

"Soo. . ." Mom's eyes hinted a sparkle. "Speaking of handsome . . . any female friends I should know about? I seem to remember you mentioning a Sherri."

Right. Ulterior-motive Sheri, with a desire for a more "committed" relationship. The commitment part being a promise to not deprive her from frequent world travel and its associated lavish lifestyle. To do so would potentially cause irreparable damage to their meaningful one-date relationship, as well as deem him a monster, or so she'd unequivocally stated. Monster.

"And here we go." Dad flung the leg extension open and clasped his fingers together behind his head, lacking only popcorn for the feature matinee.

"What? Can't a mom have a say as to whether a woman is good enough for her son? Now tell me, Mason. Does she have extravagant tastes? Like, break-the-bank taste?"

And there it was. The way out. The truth, and the name Sherri would be banned from Mom's vocabulary. There'd be no interrogation session on why things couldn't be worked out. "As a matter of fact, yes. Unimaginable, extreme extravagance. And she called me a monster. Me. A monster."

"Monster? She called you a monster?" Mom reached into the end-table drawer and retrieved a pad and pen. "What's her number?"

"Don't worry, Mom. Put the pen down. She's far away in Boston. Let some other lucky guy have her. Besides, I've just about given up on finding Miss Right." In fact, finding the right woman that would be his all in all so far had met with colossal failure. An elusive dream at best. Maybe it would happen in due time. In due season. But it certainly wouldn't be today. Possibly never, given his current state of health. And was his desire for love so strong that it would even enter his mind at a time like this?

"You just trust God's timing. Any woman would be blessed to have you. Don't you forget that."

Of course, that was what most parents would say. But regardless of Mom's assessment of how much he'd changed in appearance, a fact remained. The reflection in the mirror never once hinted of being handsome, and no woman back in Boston ever convincingly gave him a reason to believe otherwise. And despite the endless opportunities that cell phone technology provided, there was no reason to break his streak of never haven taken a selfie.

In his time-capsule bedroom, Mason slipped a T-shirt on for the night and cupped his hand over the still-sensitive chemo port area in his chest. His room remained a snapshot of the past, all of which bolstered a homey atmosphere. Between growing up in Boone and summer trips to the campground in Fleetwood, it would be unimaginable to have had better years as a teen. It had been a time filled with hopes and dreams for the future and all things possible. But for now, the new hope and dream was simply to *live*.

Mom's and Dad's earlier distressed expressions had lingered, which jabbed stinging regret through Mason, for allowing life's unrelenting busyness to take precedence over things that mattered most—family. Their love and support had been instrumental in launching him into his now-realized dream of being a successful writer. Sadly, it was that same thing that had kept him away.

He viewed the calendar on his laptop. In two days he'd be in Fleetwood Falls. He lifted a framed photo from the dresser and carefully studied the teenage girl, whom he'd never officially met and who'd stolen his heart long ago. She was also the standard by which no woman had ever compared since. Neither would he ever find one like her again, he concluded. But maybe it was time to move on. Let go of the past and open his heart.

Chloe Morgan entered the sanctuary and spotted a man at the altar, holding a cat. She widened her eyes. "No. No. He doesn't like to be held." She held out her palm in the universal stop motion.

The cat darted from his arms and onto an elaborate flower arrangement on the altar. The toppled and shattered glass vase sent the cat scampering under church pews.

"I don't know what happened." The man scooped up the scattered flowers, stepping on several in the process.

"It's okay. You didn't know. He's a stray that hangs around and always gets into trouble. I'll clean this up later." She suppressed a heavy sigh swelling up. The hectic last-minute chores for the spring church fair had begun at sunrise. More work was the last thing she'd needed to add to what already felt like a full day's work. But at least help had arrived to transport boxes of items needed for the fair.

Chloe took the flowers from him and placed them on the altar. "I'm glad Pastor sent someone to give me a hand." She looked down at several boxes filled with items for the fair. "Grab that big box, but you'll have to—"

"Got it. Don't worry." He grabbed the box.

"No. Don't."

He lifted it, and dozens of raffle items swooshed out the bottom. Marbles burst from plastic bags, rolling in all directions. Glitter for crafts spilled onto the freshly cleaned floor. He froze, and his face reddened. His prominent square jawline and curve of his lip stood out. Then in a flash of fur, the cat bolted through the glitter, with sparkly paw prints trailing out the door.

Could the day possibly get any worse? There'd been no help to unload the car or set up the outdoor table when she'd arrived at dawn. Not to mention bagging all the marbles till midnight that were now scattered throughout the sanctuary. She exhaled, with a hand to her forehead. "I was trying to say, hold it from the bottom, because it wasn't taped shut."

He nodded, his attention riveted on Chloe.

"Hello," she said, breaking the trance.

"Sorry. You were saying?"

"Chloe Morgan. I help with office work here, along with my mom." She forced a smile despite her rising stress level.

"Mason. Pleased to meet you." He extended his hand to shake. "So what's going on outside?"

"Fleetwood Assembly's having its spring fair. It's a chance for the community to come together for food, fun, and an auction, with proceeds going to charity. You're here with your family?"

"Uh . . . no. Just me. Looks like a big turnout, for sure. Well, since I'm here, is there anything I can do? Besides make a mess, that is?"

"Actually, yes. How about we each grab a small box and bring them to the craft table for now." She looked over his exquisite attire. Weird. That was a little out of the norm for a church fair. Although that he looked quite handsome was indisputable. Blazer, slacks, and leather Chukkas, topped off with a newsboy cap, gave an air of distinction, and his strong, slender build completed the package. "Not from around here, are ya?"

"Why would you say that?"

"I assumed, given the abundance of flannel and denim around here, and the way you're dressed. You know, nice." The word "studly" nearly escaped her lips. A few accented words gave a clue as well to his outsider status.

They arrived at their destination and placed the boxes on the table.

"Right. Didn't exactly plan to be here. Drove by and saw all this going on. So I decided to stop." He put his hand to his chest.

"Are you all right? You're holding your chest?"

"I'm fine. Just a little pull. That's all." Specks of glitter fell to the ground with a brush of his hand to his jacket and slacks.

She sighed with relief, her first thought being *heart issue. No medical emergencies today Lord, please.* "So why are you here in Fleetwood? If you don't mind me asking." She slid a headband off her wrist and put her hair up in a ponytail.

"Uh . . . just getting away from the city for a while. That's all." He shoved his hands into his pockets, looked down, and gave a nudge with his shoe to a fallen pinecone.

Chloe considered his hesitance to answer. "So . . . you're what? A lawyer?"

"No."

"Insurance salesman?" Maybe car salesman.

"No."

"Scientist?"

His flat look grew into a smile. "So you think I look like a scientist?"

"No. Not really." That ought to flatten the shine on his ego-flavored ChapStick. "You—"

"Is that a cotton candy cart by the parking lot? Haven't seen one of those in a while."

Okay. Master of avoidance, huh? She could play that game. The one thing she prided herself on was her ability to read people, even at first meet. Also questionable was his mystified expression and repeated peek to the back of her. She swatted at her neck. "What's wrong? Is a bug on me?"

"No. I was wondering … is that a style or trend around here?"

Did he always answer a question with a question? "What do you mean?"

"The sales tag on back of the collar."

She reached back for it. "Oh no." She'd intended to try on the new blouse for fit before removing the tag but forgot to in her haste to get out the door this morning. So much for first impressions.

"Don't worry, I've got it." He reached around her neck for the tag, insistent on helping to remove it.

"No! Don't pull it." Uh, personal space.

"I'm not. My jacket button is caught on it."

Chloe twisted in desperation to not damage the shirt, with Mason's arm unintentionally around her neck and the other around her waist, wrapping them up in a tight embrace. The woodsy-musk scent of his cologne gave her pause as she locked her eyes on to his.

"You can let go now." She took an inconspicuous inhale of his cologne again and scrutinized the familiarity of its fragrance, along with its attempt to whisk her away.

There was no response.

"Mason. You're doing it again. Staring." It was impossible to not notice the faint scar just above his brow and the depth of his blue eyes, or the fact that his hand firmly gripping her waist was free to release her at any time, yet remained. A flash of heat blazed up her spine and warmed her cheeks.

"Yeah. Of course."

Chloe pulled away to a ripping sound of a torn collar. No. "Is that what I think I heard?" This couldn't be happening.

"I'm so sorry. I'll pay for a new one. Let me know how much, and I'll—"

"It's okay—just leave it, thank you." If this was his way of meeting women, then it was no wonder he was here alone.

She restrained her frustration and plastered on a forced smile. They were, after all, at a church fair. Patience would be the Christian thing, of course. Only known him for five minutes and already three disasters. Great.

"Hey, Ms. Chloe." Aaron, the youth-group leader, gasped for breath as his sprint came to a halt. "Pastor sent me to help bring a few boxes out here. Sorry I'm late."

She turned to Mason. "Wait. Pastor didn't send you to help me?"

"Uh . . . no. Just wanted to see what the inside of the church looked like. The doors were open, so I went on in."

"Please forgive me. I assumed—"

"It's okay, really. I was glad to help."

Help? And all this could have been avoided if he'd not strayed to inside the church? Just like the other troublemaking stray?

Chloe pulled the ringing phone from her back pocket. "Excuse me a second, Mason." She stepped a short distance away. "Yeah, Mom, what's up?" She listened, then hung her head and put a hand to her forehead. "Okay. I'll be home shortly. Love you." *All right, pull yourself together, Chloe.* People could be watching, and all it would take was an out-of-place expression to send rumors flying. It was just the way things were in small towns, and Fleetwood was no exception.

She turned back to Mason. "Sorry. Had to take that."

"That's okay. Is everything all right? You look a little—"

"No, everything's fine." She looked away to take a calming breath. Not only *could* the day get worse—it just had.

An announcement signifying the start of the auction broke into her jumbled thoughts. Her chance to acquire a pendant she'd wanted since childhood had arrived. Also, creating as much distance from the walking disaster next to her seemed the safe thing to do. If the past fifteen minutes were an indicator of Mason's potential, an extended stay in town would surely result with the mayor declaring a state of emergency. Goodbyes were in order.

"Mason, it's been nice meeting you, but I need to be at the auction and then head out. So thanks for the . . . you know . . . help." Maybe *destruction* would have been a more fitting word. "By the way, if you're still in town tomorrow, church service is at ten."

"Sure. Thanks for the invite. Pleasure meeting you."

Her eyes settled on his before she joined the growing crowd. She positioned herself at the front of the makeshift auction platform and caught a glimpse of Mason at a food table. Repentance was in order for her impatience and the not-so-nice thoughts that ran through her head. Despite the frustration, she had to admit he was trying to help. Never mind that she'd have to return to church later tonight to clean the sanctuary again and salvage what remained of the flowers. Oh, and the blouse. Yes. The special-ordered, now-ripped blouse that had taken only six full weeks and three days to arrive. So yeah. Thanks for the help, Mason.

Chapter 2

*I*n the blink of an eye, a cat zipped under several food service tables, with a golden doodle possessing the speed of a greyhound in hot pursuit. The meager response and sporadic laughter of fairgoers led Mason to believe it wasn't an isolated occurrence between the two opposing species.

Mason set his hotdog on a nearby table and took a sip of soda. Next item up for auction would be an antique heart-shaped pendant, adorned with sapphires and a sprinkling of smaller stones on a sterling-silver chain, as described by the auctioneer. He spotted Chloe in the crowd with the opening bid. Several others countered her, with one woman peering from beneath her straw-brimmed sun hat over to Chloe in a taunting manner, outmatching her every bid. Chloe's occasional glare back to the woman did not go unnoticed by Mason, who suspected the outbidding to be more than about the pendant. Chloe withdrew with visible disappointment, then vanished into the crowd as bidding continued.

He turned for a bite of his hotdog to see a cat, bearing a remarkable resemblance to the one inside the church earlier, scampering off with it. In fact, the same one running for its life a moment before. "You . . ." His attention returned to the auction, with bids still being made on the pendant. Chloe was nowhere in sight.

A half hour later he punched the address of Valley View B&B into his GPS and left the fair. The solemness Chloe exhibited following her phone call lingered, leaving him with hopes that all would be okay.

Mason stepped out of the car and pulled the brochure off the dash. White two-story house with a lower wraparound porch. Four mature flowering dogwood trees bursting with white flowers flanked each side of the home, along with mountain laurels flaunting the pink hue of its buds throughout the property.

Lining the walkway on each side of the B&B's entrance were purple azaleas, with white and pink tulips in between. Half a dozen rocking chairs, along with wooden benches, lined the front porch to either side of the entry. Pots hung from the overhead balcony, with pops of purple and pink flowers and cascading vines.

Upon entering, the hundred-year-old home displayed much of its grandeur with its high ceilings and wooden floors. Mason stood in the lobby and admired several masterfully crafted pottery vases on the entry table. *Captivated* and *intrigued* would be the best way to describe his assessment of the gifting and brilliance of the mind and hands that conceived such beauty.

"A local artist made those. Her work has been featured in magazines, and she has pieces on display at various galleries across the country. Beautiful, aren't they?"

He turned to the voice of a woman coming from a sitting room adjoining the entry. Her age in the fifties, he supposed.

"Yes. Very nice. They're amazing."

"I'm Charlotte. And you must be Mason." She extended her hand, then motioned with her other hand to a man entering the house. "And this is my husband, Bradley."

"Just call me Brad," he said with a hint of a Jersey accent. He removed his gloves and shook hands. "Doing a little gardening. It never ends." His smile conveyed a look that the work brought him joy.

"You have such a beautiful place. I'm sure you hear that often."

Charlotte smiled. "Yes, we do. But never tire from hearing it. We're truly blessed to have continued the family legacy of taking care of such a grand home."

"Mason, I can give you a hand bringing things up to your room if you'd like," Brad said. "You probably brought extras with you since you'll be here for a while."

"That would be great. Thanks."

"So word is you're gonna do one more book in your last series, huh?" Brad winked. "Don't worry, your secret's safe with me."

Charlotte gave an elbow to Brads side. "Would you give him a break. He just got here. Besides, that's none of our business." She shot him a stern look. "Sorry. Your name sounded familiar so, you know, the internet. He's only recently discovered it." She rolled her eyes.

Mason laughed. "That's quite all right. But only a few people know about another book. How do you know?"

He gave a know-it-all look, then whispered, as though not wanting his newfound secret to get out. "Internet."

Mason nodded. "Ah yes. Of course. The internet."

Charlotte sighed. "Stupid internet." She followed with a wide plastered-on smile.

Once settled into his room, Mason pulled up a photo on his phone he'd taken of Chloe in the crowd at the fair, and inwardly admitted to feeling like a private investigator, or worse, a stalker. There was something different and special about the way she handled herself. She emanated a calming of sorts, simply being near her, yet had turned him into a klutz. Something he'd yet to experience around any of his women friends in Boston.

He parted the curtains and opened the window facing the rear of the property. This room would be his home for the next six months. How quickly life had changed. On top of the world one day, and the next wondering how in the world did he get here. The next question being, where was he now going, and where would he end up? The definitive answer being that God alone knew, leaving only time to tell the result of it all. Time. It was something he'd taken for granted but now might be in short supply.

Mason flung open the hood of the Range Rover. "What now? I don't have time for this." He mumbled under his breath while inspecting the engine. "Should have taken out the extended warranty. But no. Had to forget to put it on your reminder list." His Sunday morning run to the market for headache medicine turned out not so quick after all when the SUV hesitated to start. But with the intensity and speed of which the headaches had been coming on, he'd not be caught without it. Thankfully, he'd made it back to the B&B for a closer look. He breathed a sigh of relief at the discovery of a loose battery terminal. A simple fix.

He washed up, then rushed down the stairs and to the dining room. His intent to wake early enough to make it to church on time had been derailed by his restless night, due in large part to stress and anxiety of his many sudden life changes. That combined with being in a town where he knew no one left him wondering exactly where, and how, to fit in.

The lace-vintage curtains waved with the seeping of the cool morning air through the open window. He took a seat at the dining room table, draped with a bright-white cloth, and rubbed his temples to relieve an oncoming headache. The morning rays of the sun partially made their way into the room and warmed his face.

"Morning, Mason. Hope you're hungry." Charlotte entered from the kitchen and added water to the flower arrangement bursting with color in the center of the table.

"Morning, Charlotte. Those are beautiful."

"Brad picked them fresh this morning. It's his way of bragging that he brings me flowers every day. Seems fair to me, since I cook for him every day."

"Good point. And yes, I'm starving. Sorry I'm late. Still exhausted from the trip here from Boston, I guess."

"No problem at all. There's plenty left. Be right back."

A quick bite, then he'd be off to Fleetwood Assembly. It had been far too long since his last visit to any church back in the big city he called home. Apart from his best friend David's wedding and then a funeral, listening to an actual sermon consisted of online teachings and occasional radio programs. All fine, but none of which afforded any real involvement or interaction with a church community, like he'd grown up with.

Church service growing up in Boone was a given and something he'd eagerly attended with Mom and Dad, both of whom had set a fitting example. But now, with Chloe's invitation to attend and given the fact that Fleetwood would be his home for a while, maybe it was time to get back on track.

Charlotte placed an assortment of food on the table and poured Mason a fresh cup of coffee.

"So where ya headed this morning, all dressed up?"

"I was invited to a church, so I thought I'd give it a shot." He savored a quick sip of coffee while placing a napkin on his lap with his other hand.

"What church is that?" Charlotte removed her apron and set it on the back of a chair.

"Fleetwood Assembly."

"Know it well. Brad and I attended there for years. But now with running this place, we're only able to make it when we can." She took a seat and poured herself a cup of coffee.

"Yeah. I can see there'd be a lot to do around this place. Big house and acres of land. Speaking of that, I'd be glad to help with some things around here. I'm pretty good at woodwork and repairs. I could even help Brad with work on the grounds."

"Don't be ridiculous." She gave a light pat to his hand. "We wouldn't think of having a guest working here. But thanks anyway."

"Guess I'm used to being busy—always doing something. Kind of hard to slow down." His mind flashed to David's advice years ago about slowing down and enjoying life's journey. Now he had no choice. But was it too late, and was there anything left to enjoy, given his prognosis?

"I can understand that. But if you're interested in a few odd jobs, I heard Pastor Hank at Fleetwood Assembly is looking for someone to help around there. Maybe talk to him." She rose and placed her cup on a tray.

"I think I may do that. Thanks." Maybe a little work would keep his mind off his problems. And who knew, possibly a chance to see Chloe again. But hopefully, this time he'd not make a bumbling fool out of himself. "Oh, by the way. There's a campground I came to around here when I was young."

Charlotte gave a curious look. "That would have to be Morgan Falls. But it's been closed for years now. Just a bunch of overgrown weeds is all that's left. That place was a big part of this community for so many years. Sad that it's gone."

"Is it close to here?"

"Just stay north on 221 for five miles or so, then a right on Covered Bridge Road. It'll be on the left a few miles down."

"Thanks, Charlotte." He rose and headed to the foyer, stopping in front of the large gold-framed mirror to fix his collar, and jetted out the door to the car. "Please start." With a push of the Start button, he rolled out of the driveway.

A quiver in his stomach now competed with an ache in his head. Was revisiting the past a wise choice? And if so, why the nerves and the overwhelming pull to the old campground? The last thing he needed was more emotional turmoil.

Mason's car came to a stop just off the dry gravel road. He waited for the cloud of dust to clear, then jumped out. Maybe there'd be time for a quick stop before continuing to church. A rusted lock and chain on the gate, along with a faded-weathered sign attached on one side, hung with the name *Morgan Falls Campground*. Charlotte was right.

The desolate property and years of neglect were evident, a stark contrast to the recreation and enjoyment that once abounded there. It was a far cry from his memories of his last visit.

A crisp breeze and the scent of evergreens bathed his face, along with the knocking of a woodpecker and a distant waterfall. Scents and sounds in place of traffic and the hustle and bustle of life in the city.

A glance at his watch revealed he'd be late for the service. He jumped back into his Range Rover.

The crashing of a cymbal greeted Mason as he pulled the church door shut behind him. He took a place to the rear of the sanctuary and joined the worship service already in progress. Guitars, drums, and a keyboard, along with a choir, packed the small platform. The blaring music did little to help his pounding head and wasn't quite the hymnal music he'd expected. His scan found Chloe to the far left, near the front of the church, with her auburn hair catching his attention. The truth was, he'd hoped he'd see her there, along with another chance to talk. But the intensity of his headache made any chat less likely with each passing minute.

"First time visiting?" The elderly gentleman standing next to him shut the lid of his pocket watch and extended his hand to shake. "Name's Tom."

"Mason. Yes, sir. First service." His tumbling stomach returned as he scanned the couple hundred strangers throughout the sanctuary. That was, when he was able to shift his focus away from Chloe.

"You know, you're not here just by chance. You realize that don't you?" Tom cleaned his eyeglass lenses with a cloth, then steadied himself with a grip on the pew in front of him. A raised eyebrow and sideways look at Mason followed.

Mason studied the man's confident expression, which read he believed his words were an absolute certainty. He appeared to be unaffected by the loud music.

"Yeah. Someone invited me."

"That may be true, but I'm talking about the providential will of

God. Today's part two of Pastor Hank's sermon on providence. You may have been invited here, but did you know before you were invited that you'd be here?" Another beaming look of assurance followed. "God knew." He returned his attention to the worship service.

"Never thought of it that way." He also hadn't known he'd be given the news of cancer. The thing that led him to Fleetwood Falls, and then to church. In a way, Tom's mention of providence was a confirmation of sorts, an answer to the night's restlessness. Why had he agreed to come to this town for treatments, and where was his life headed? However much of his life remained, that was. The truth being, he was a dead man walking, as the oncologist had put it. And now all that remained was trust in God.

Mason leaned closer to Tom. "Is the music always this loud?"

"Doesn't bother me." Tom looked straight ahead. "With my hearing aids out, I can only hear as far as you. I put 'em back in when the preachin' starts."

⁓

"Is it over yet?" Abby asked with the skillfulness of a ventriloquist and a gift of wit to rival any paid comedian. Her undiminished Texas twang being permanent and irreversible.

"Not even close." Chloe gave a slight nod.

"I think I forgot something in the car. I'll be right—"

Chloe grabbed her arm. "If I have to suffer through this, then so do you."

They'd seen each other through the many changes in life, and Sunday service was no exception. Somewhere along the way, genuine spirit-filled worship had become more like entertainment, or a ritual of going through the motions. Not that all the music was bad. But the longing to bring back more of the old hymns they'd sung when young would be a pleasant change, to say the least. Songs that lifted the name of Jesus and spoke of the cross.

"Right. Friends till the end." Abby clenched her teeth. "Dumbest thing I ever heard." She smiled wide and gave Chloe a hip bump.

"You're the one who made it up."

"Yeah well, I take it back. And I don't know how much more of this I can take. Just look at her." Her head tilted, and she gaped. "Why on earth would Angel do that?"

"Do what?" Silly question, since Chloe knew the answer.

"Desecrate that Baldwin piano like that in the house of God, with all those contortions and gyrations. Neither your grandpa nor dad would have allowed that when they were the preacher. Would have cast them demons right out."

Chloe eyebrows narrowed. "She keeps looking toward the back. You know what that means. And what is that she's wearing?"

"Looks to me like a cross between Betty Boop and Wonder Woman."

Angel's frequent peering to the rear of the church tipped them off to an obvious male interest, or more accurately, victim. They knew the pattern all too well.

A not-so-casual viewing to the back satisfied Abby's curiosity. "Yep, target identified. Hope he's as smart as he is good looking."

Chloe casually turned her head. Mason. "That's him."

"Who?"

"Mason. The guy I met at the fair yesterday." Her posture straightened, and she patted her hair.

"The walking-disaster guy you were telling me about?"

"Yep. I invited him to the service but didn't really expect him to come."

Abby's eyebrows rose. "I don't know. I think I'd have to overlook those disastrous flaws. 'Cause when it comes to looks, you sure know how to pick 'em."

"I haven't picked anybody," Chloe snapped back, to the shush of eighty-year-old Miss Anderson, with her recently purchased bionic hearing aids with patented stealth technology available to the first one hundred customers to call, and exclusive only to the Last Chance

25

Shopping Network. Her testimony being the miraculous odds of being the final, one hundredth caller.

"Yeah well, Angel looks like a starving wild bull released from the gate, about to chase a rodeo clown," Abby whispered. "You best hope he don't like Betty Boop. Just sayin'."

Chloe turned to find Mason nowhere in sight at the close of the service and wondered why he hadn't stayed to at least say hello. Maybe he didn't care for the service. Conceivably, he could have left for home, wherever that was. No matter the reason, he seemed to be a nice guy. Clumsiness and all.

Chloe exited with Abby at her side. She spotted Mason as he traversed the front lawn of the church and made his way to the parking lot. A faint meow was heard as he reached for the car's door handle. A cat glided around his legs, rendering him unable to slide in.

Mason carried the cat and set him at the base of a nearby tree, then sharply pointed his finger. "Stay! Don't move."

Chloe listened in on the humorous distant ranting. If he stayed around town long enough, he'd see how much havoc the troublemaking furball could dish out. At least they had that in common.

Mason took a few steps back to the car, and the cat followed. Then another command.

"Stop following. Stay."

The cat stopped and meowed. Mason sprinted to the car.

Abby turned to Chloe and poked her. "There goes your man. Betty Boop binge-watcher and cat-lover enthusiast."

Chloe shook her head and looked skyward. "Why me?"

They both stood with arms folded as Mason's car pulled onto Main Street.

"You picked him." Abby chuckled, all the while eyeing Chloe's skirt.

Which she'd thrown on this morning after years of only pants.

"You didn't think you'd get away without me asking about that skirt, did you?"

"Just haven't worn it in a while, that's all." Chloe pressed a few wrinkles out with her hand and tugged it down slightly. What was wrong with wearing something nice to church? It didn't have to always be jeans and a nice T-shirt.

"And don't even get me started on those heels. I don't guess that has anything to do with Mason being here either?"

"What? Of course not. Don't . . . don't be ridiculous. You're talkin' crazy." And the truth.

"Uh, okay. Just checkin'. But I'm not the one stuttering. Or the one still watching his car till out of sight."

"Just for that, you're buying lunch." Chloe gave a nudge to Abby's shoulder.

"Thought I was anyway."

Abby was right about the skirt, dumb heels, and Chloe's gaze, which lingered as he drove off. Chloe had seen numerous guys come and go through the church over the years. But none had made her linger. None that made her question *what if?* Also undeniable was that she couldn't recall a time when Abby was ever wrong when it came to matters of the heart. Until now, that was. She'd break her impeccable winning streak with Mason, for sure. He was just a stranger passing through. Here today, gone tomorrow. Nothing more, nothing less. End of story.

Chapter 3

The crashing of metal rang out with the scattering of tools across the floor of the church nursery. Chloe set a wrench down and exhaled with a heavy sigh. What she thought to be a quick fifteen minutes of work on a shelving unit for the children's classroom had turned out to be half an hour, due mostly to her thoughts on Mason. She felt foolish that she'd dressed up with hopes he'd be at church, only for him to have left without saying hi or goodbye.

But none of it mattered anyway. She had a pottery business to run, land and cabin to save if possible, and occasional volunteer work at church with Mom. It was all she cared to handle. Besides, her motto on relationships over the years had served her well. "Don't get close and you won't get hurt." *Good riddance, stranger.*

Chloe's mom poked her head into the classroom. "What was that loud noise?"

"The toolbox fell off the chair, that's all." She tilted her head up and blew the air out of her ballooned cheeks.

"What are you working on?"

"Just this shelving unit that came in the other day." Chloe shrank down into a child's chair, slouched over, and cradled her forehead in her hands.

"Honey, are you all right?"

All right? Chloe wasn't sure what that even meant anymore. Along with the passage of time and its disappointments also came a redefining of the word. "Have you ever felt like you were forgotten? Like, with all the things going on in the world, do all our little things really matter to God?"

Her mom's fingers combed through her hair a few times. "You know as well as I do, everything we do and experience in life matters to Him. Now where is all this coming from?"

"Just thinking about the land and cabin, that's all. I couldn't believe when you called me at the fair, confirming we could lose it all. Just didn't seem real at the time. Still doesn't. That, combined with Dad gone." She dropped to her knees to pick up the scattered tools.

Despite the years since Dad passing from cancer, she found it difficult to dwell on the many pleasant memories her years with him afforded, keeping them on a short leash and suppressing any recollections as they surfaced. To let them run would cause the dam of tears to break. To make matters worse was the news of Kristen's battle with cancer. Friends since high school, and now Kristen was losing the battle.

"I know it's hard. I miss your dad too. The reason it hurts so much is because these are the people we love most. Family, friends. But we still need to have faith and hope, even if it's by the minute, the hour, or a day at a time. And after that, we trust God for tomorrow."

"Thanks, Mom. Before I forget to ask, are you still meeting Sarah and me at the bookstore tonight?"

"Of course. But I've got even better news. You're in luck. Pastor Hank found someone to help out a little around here, and I'd like you to meet him. He should be here any minute."

"It's about time. We could use the—"

Mason took a step into the room. Chloe drew back. Help? An adrenaline rush brought her out of her moping. His stopping in to say hi, fine. Even visiting for a chat, no harm. But to help?

"Mason. What are you . . ." Chloe stood and slipped her hands into the back pockets of her jeans.

"You two know each other?" Mom said.

"We met at the fair last week. He . . . helped me a little." She swallowed hard, followed by a blink-of-an-eye confirmation of no ring on his wedding finger. A detail she'd neglected to check at the church fair, with the perpetual stream of drama that had unfolded.

"Great. So introductions aren't necessary. I'll leave you two be and get back to some paperwork. Mason, you let me know if you need anything."

"Yes, ma'am." Mason tipped his newsboy cap.

Mom stepped into the hall, then peeked back at the two.

Chloe shot a stern look, sending Mom packing.

"So, Chloe, how've you been?"

"Since yesterday, you mean?" He could have asked her that Sunday after church if he'd stayed long enough. He'd have gotten his answer then, and she wouldn't have had to wear those stupid heels and skirt for nothing. She pushed dangling strands of hair behind her ear.

"Well, yeah. Since yesterday."

"Doing all right, I guess. But I wasn't sure I'd see you again after your disappearing act following the church service."

"Yeah, sorry about that. I really wanted to stay but had to leave right away." He removed his hat and fiddled with it. "I did see you there at the front of the church though. Black skirt, white blouse. Collar intact, of course."

Hmm. So he did notice after all. And a sense of humor. Check. "Glad you came. You know, to visit."

"The truth is, I hadn't been to church in a while and didn't want to put it off. Anyway, about helping around here. I think I've found my first project."

Mason looked down at a disassembled shelving unit. He promptly picked up the wrench on the floor and began to assemble it.

"You don't have to do that." *Really, you don't.*

"Trust me. I'll be finished before you know it. It's all on my résumé. Carpentry, woodworking." He rolled up his sleeves.

"But if you let me explain. I—"

"Excuse me, Ms. Chloe. Professional here." He smiled and continued.

"All right then. Have at it." He didn't listen very well. Wonder if that was on his résumé, or one of the faults Abby would suggest Chloe overlook. She raised an eyebrow, smirked, and motioned with a hand to continue, then stopped in the doorway and spun around. "Oh, and by the way, when you're done, can you come see me in the office? I need you to do one more thing for me, if you don't mind."

"Sure. No problem."

She left him to complete the task and joined her mom in the office to put together flyers for an upcoming event.

"Is there something wrong, sweetheart?" Mom asked. "You haven't said much since you came in here."

"If you must ask, it would have been nice if I was consulted about the help." Chloe straightened several papers on the desk, stapling them together with a vigorous slap.

"What? Mason? I read his résumé. Looks like he can do pretty much anything we need done around here. He's obviously qualified and competent."

"Competent? Is that what we're calling it? Well, we're about to see competence in all its glory. Just hang in there." Another pound to the stapler.

Chloe stepped onto a stool and reached up to hang a clock with fresh batteries. Mason entered the office with a light tap on the open door and rushed over to her.

"Please be careful." He placed a hand on her back. "I've fallen off my share of ladders before. Doesn't end well."

A shared fact she found not so hard to believe, given his track record so far in Fleetwood. Also a fact was the way his hands managed to keep finding their way to her waist. And yep, same flushed-in-the-face feeling she'd sensed at the fair. She readjusted the clock despite its straightness. "Mom, does this look straight to you?"

"Looks fine to me," Mom said, sporting a grin. And not just any grin. Her matchmaking one.

"Are you sure? No one wants to tell time on a crooked clock. Mason, how about you? What do you think? Is it straight?" she said, thinking he really needed to stop it with those baby blues looking back at her. And he was doing it again. Staring. But not at the clock. "Mason. The clock."

"Oh . . . yeah." He checked his watch, then the clock. "Looks like the right time to me. Good job."

Not exactly the answer she was looking for, but flattering nonetheless.

"You mentioned something else for me to do?"

"As a matter of fact, yes." He maintained contact with her waist till she was safely down. A full one step. She took a seat, then placed her elbows on the desk while cradling her chin with both hands. She widened her smile, lifted her brows, and batted her lashes. "You know that shelf you so kindly and competently put together for me?" *Get ready, Mom. Here it comes.*

"What about it?"

"Can you please take it back apart for me?" *Wish I could take a picture right about . . . now.*

Mom spun her chair toward Chloe with a puzzled look.

"Excuse me?" He raked his fingers through his hair and shifted his weight. "But . . . it's together."

"Yes, and no doubt you've done a fabulous job, being a professional and all. Problem is, I had just taken the shelf apart to box it, in order to return it. I tried to tell you." *Oh great. Now his baby blues are puppy dog blues. Sorry, buddy. Not falling for that again.*

"Uh, yeah. I guess you did." He leaned against the doorframe and rubbed his temples. "I'll be taking the shelf apart if you need me. Oh, and Chloe, don't worry. Got it all under control. No problem." He turned and sheepishly retreated from the office with his mumbling carrying into the office. "Great first impression, Mason. Again."

Chloe covered her laugh and gave another exuberant slap to the stapler. "And there you have it, Mom. Competence and professionalism. All under control."

Chloe folded her arms. "What? What was that look?" It wasn't that she didn't know the answer to her own question. It was simply a matter of how it would all play out. This time. She had thought Mom would have given up her matchmaking ideas long ago. Though well meant, in the past it had left Chloe agreeing to a single date, mostly to please Mom, resulting in predictable failure. But that was the past and there was no time, rhyme, or reason to date—simply to date.

Mom took a sip of hot chamomile herbal tea without breaking her grin. She followed up with a peek at Chloe, next to her on the sectional sofa of Holly's Hideaway Bookstore. "What look? I don't know what you're talking about." She placed the tea down on the coffee table and picked up a book.

"That 'I'm gonna burst if I don't say it' look?" Chloe motioned with her thumb and a nod toward her mom as her sister, Sarah, arrived, from Abby's adjoining pastry shop, with an apple fritter in hand.

"She's doing it again, Sarah. Matchmaking. We both know how that turns out." The inside joke being that Sarah's husband, Jeff, was married to sports, leaving her to be the secret girlfriend.

"What are you talking about? She's batting a thousand. Just look how Jeff and I turned out." Sarah locked eyes with Chloe. A pause followed a subtle nod from both. Sarah leaned past Chloe. "She's right, Mom. Don't meddle."

"Who's meddling? Can't your mom just sit here and enjoy her tea with a good book?"

"Not when she's obviously keeping secrets from her favorite daughter." Chloe gave a slap to Sarah's knee.

"Hey." Sarah halfway choked on a mouthful of fritter. "Still here. The other favorite daughter, remember?"

Mom ignored Chloe's obvious stare. "Just thinking about Mason. That's all."

"Mason? Don't even think about it." Chloe preempted any conceivable matchmaking ideas. "Admit it. You have that look." But somehow "this" look was different. Not sure in what way, but different.

"I wasn't gonna say anything."

"But you were thinking it really loud."

"C'mon, you have to admit. He's kind, polite, and that look he gave when you asked him to take that shelf back apart was adorable. Not to mention the way he was protecting you on that tall ladder."

"Yeah, my hero. I was on the one and only step of the stool. One foot off the ground, Mom." Admittedly, it was sweet and showed a thoughtful side. No matter how small the gesture, it felt good to be watched out for and taken care of.

I don't know." Mom shook her head with a sparkle in her eye. "If I were younger—"

"All right. Stop right there. Then you can have him. Oh, and a helpful word of advice—make sure you have health insurance. You're gonna need it. And by the way, my ears are still numb just thinking about what you were about to say."

Chloe held out her hand to Sarah. "So, Mom's withholding secrets from me and you're . . ."

"Just because you're my little sister doesn't mean you get free apple fritters for life. But I did hear something that you might be interested in. You know that pendant you were bidding on at the fair?"

"What about it?" Chloe's curiosity piqued.

"Someone bid over a thousand on it."

"A thousand? That's odd. It probably wasn't worth but a couple hundred. Can't believe Tina paid that much for it. Then again, she'd pay anything to spite me. I knew I didn't stand a chance when she started bidding against me. You'd have thought by now she'd outgrown her teenage drama jealousy days."

Despite the years that had gone by, Chloe could only draw one conclusion when it came to Tina. Some things and some people never changed. The results of all efforts to overlook or find the best in her remained the same. People like her could only be seen for what they really were. Prideful, mean spirited, and devious.

"You'll be happy to know she didn't get it. Someone outbid her."

"They must have wanted it bad to pay that much." She yanked a piece of fritter from Sarah.

"And there's something else you might be interested in knowing." Sarah gave a sideways look. "There seems to be a little rumor going around."

"What rumor?" Chloe's forehead wrinkled and eyes squinched. Rumors historically spread like wildfire in their tight-knit community. By the time the intended target found out, it was already old news.

"Oh, I don't know. Something about you and what's his name, Mason, making goo-goo eyes at each other." She took a loud slurp of her latte, with a tease in her eyes.

Chloe bent the tip of her index finger over Mom's book and lowered it from her face. "Mom, do you know anything about this?"

"Goo-goo eyes? Hold on!" Abby bolted from behind her pastry counter, dashed across the stained concrete floors with a hot-fudge sundae in hand, and with a final slide plopped onto the sofa without spillage. "Why wasn't I first to know about this? Best friends always have dibs on juicy information. Those are the rules. They are not flexible, and neither am I."

"There's nothing to know about. And if anyone's doing the staring, it's him," Chloe said, adding a quirk to her smile. "Besides, either he doesn't listen to me, or he's plain ole clumsy. I don't know which. And what is it with his note-taking? It's like he has a sudden epiphany or something. Caught him a few times stopping in in the middle of what he was doing to write something. Kind of drives me crazy, to tell you the truth."

"Could be he's trying a little too hard. Or maybe he likes you, and that makes him nervous." Sarah waggled her eyebrows.

"*Like* me? I don't think so. Especially after I made him take that bookshelf back apart. Mom might think that look was adorable, but all I saw was revenge in his eyes. Probably plotting to get me back as we speak."

Holly, the ultimate bookworm, and manager of the family-run bookstore adjoined with Abby's shop, found a minute from helping customers and excitedly joined in, bubbling over with her twenty's perkiness.

"Y'all . . . will never guess . . . what I heard . . . today." Her high-pitched, halting speech caught the attention of most in the shop. "Rumor has it that a notable author was spotted here in town at the farmers' market today."

"How notable?" Abby sat up straight.

"Every book . . . a best-seller."

"Wait. Do you really think obviously well-to-do people are flocking to Fleetwood Falls? Think about it," Chloe said. Then again, Holly lived and breathed books and authors. For her to be that excited would mean this author had a fair amount of significance.

"Yeah. You're probably right." Holly took it down a notch. "But it sure would be the highlight of my life to meet 'the' Mason Chadwick in person."

"Wait a minute." Abby turned to Chloe. "What's your Mason's last name?"

"Oh, so now he's *my* Mason?" The words flew out her mouth. But *my Mason* played back in her mind, somehow warming her. She concluded that perhaps she was having a weak moment and snapped herself back to reality.

"Stay put a minute. Be right back." Holly fetched a book and returned, showing the author photo on the back cover. "Is this your Mason?"

Chloe's jaws dropped. As did Abby's, she noted.

"That's him. That's her Mason," Abby said.

Holly squealed and jumped, bouncing on her toes. "Oh . . . my . . . goodness. My friend is dating Mason . . . Chadwick." She fanned her face with the book. "Can you get me his autograph? No, better yet, get him here. This is unbelievable. Have you two kissed? What was it like? Was it as romantic as in his books?" She let out another squeal.

"I am not dating Mason. And no, we haven't kissed. I barely know him." Why would she want him kissing her anyway? Everything he touched fell apart. And that would include her heart if she allowed it.

"Hold all those thoughts. I've got a delivery. Be right back." Holly dashed away with excitement and another squeal.

Abby and Sarah stared at Chloe with grins and heads nodding.

Chloe smothered her face with a throw pillow, yet to recover from the surprise. Things like this just didn't happen in Fleetwood, or her life. And just because he'd stared at her a few times didn't mean he liked her. It wasn't uncommon for a guy to stare at a girl he thought was pretty. Not that he thought Chloe was pretty necessarily. So what was his motive?

"You know as well as I do, Chloe, that there's gonna be no way of stopping this kind of gossip in this town," Sarah said.

"You better stay away from that gossip. You know what Mom says about that. Right, Mom?"

Mom took a long-drawn-out sip of tea.

Sarah laughed. "Spread it while it's still fresh and hot?"

"That's a good one, right, Grace?" Abby chuckled and propped her feet up on the coffee table as she and Sarah high-fived. "Gotta admit, sure is nice of him to step right out the pages of *GQ Magazine* and grace us with his presence right here in our little ole town."

"You two are a terrible influence on me. You know that don't you?" Chloe held the back of her hand to her forehead.

Another Holly-sized squeal reverberated off the interior brick walls of the bookstore. "It's here!" Holly slid a wooden easel across the floor with an ear-piercing nails-across-a-chalkboard cringe effect and placed it in front of Chloe. On the easel sat what appeared to be a four-foot-tall blank posterboard. "Are you ready? Wait for it. Can the day get any better, or what?"

Holly spun the poster around, revealing a mammoth-sized photo of Mason and a shot of his upcoming release. "Well. Was I right, or what?"

Chloe chose Holly's "or what" option. Was all this Mason everywhere an elaborate trick being played on her "or what"? The first prank being their disastrous first meet at the church fair, followed by his momentous first day of work, and now . . . this. So yeah. Was this her fate "or what"?

Abby and Sarah interrupted Chloe's blank stare as another unexpected occurrence took her by surprise. The two celebrated with a musical banter. "Chloe's got a boyfriend. Chloe's got a boyfriend."

Chloe gave Abby a steely look and confiscated her not-yet-eaten sundae. "Best friend, huh? You two backsliders need be the first down to the altar Sunday to repent. Y'all can kneel right on the side of Angel and confess your sins to one another. And you might ought to bring a snack. You'll be there awhile."

She turned back to the poster, with Mom standing next to it, admiring the photo. "Uh, excuse me, Mom. Would you like to see if Holly has an extra one of those posters to take home?"

Mom shrugged. "Well . . . I wasn't gonna ask."

The rapid departure from normal life since Mason's appearance left her reeling at every turn. Even her illustrious career of spontaneity was being challenged. Furthermore, she'd been determined to not even entertain the idea of being swept away by his charm. As quickly as he breezed into town, he could up and leave equally as fast. Her attraction for him was indisputable, but so was inevitable heartbreak if unchecked.

Chapter 4

The wooden ladder creaked as Mason reached to secure the new backdrop curtain on the church platform. He huffed from the weight of it as the curtain settled into place, then made his way down and took a seat on the drummer's stool for a breather.

A check of his pocket calendar reminded him of the many rounds of chemo treatments and doctor appointments beginning the following week. Both Mom and Dad insisted on being there for his first treatment session, with Mom attesting to the fact that it would be unthinkable to not be with their son in his greatest time of need. Given her reaction to a few stiches just above the eyebrow he'd received after falling out of a tree as a teen, he shuddered to think how she'd react to this.

He viewed the rows of pews standing on the platform and thought of how uneasy it would be for a new pastor to give a sermon in front of a congregation for the first time. Equally uneasy was Pastor Hank's last sermon, on forgiveness and the need to let go of past hurts and regrets. The thought of his birth mom had entered his mind during the message. How could he have resentment or unforgiveness concerning her? He never knew her, and for all practical purposes, Aunt Jenny was his real mom. He slid the carpenter's pencil from his pouch and made a quick note.

Mason looked up as Chloe entered the sanctuary. She strolled along the center aisle toward him. As quick as a camera's flash, he envisioned her in a wedding dress. He froze in thought. She had an effortless way of doing that at first sight, it seemed. Like a momentary blank space in time, winding up with her snapping him back to reality.

"Coffee? Mom said you were here working." She removed a cup from the cardboard holder and held it out to him.

"Yeah. That would be great. Thanks." He rose from the drummer's stool to accept it and couldn't recall a time anyone looked so pretty in jeans, V-neck T-shirt, and top siders. His finger brushed hers as he grasped the cup, the sensation comparable only to getting shocked by low voltage when working once on a house with his dad.

"I didn't know you played the drums." She held a hand toward the drum set, then rested it on her hip.

He looked back at the drummer's stool, where he'd been sitting. "No. I don't. I was just resting a bit."

"Oh. Thought for a second that was another one of your many talents, besides being a carpenter. You know, drummer and professional shelf builder."

"No musical talent here, I can assure you." Was she making fun of him with that "shelf builder" comment? He resisted the urge to inform her of the fact he'd helped build an entire house with his dad after graduation, just before moving to Boston.

"Of course, you could have lied to me and said you knew how to play, and I'd have never known. People do that all the time, you know. Some pretend to be someone they're not, while others withhold who they really are. Both are pretty much the same, if you ask me. Guilty and trying to hide something."

"Yeah. I guess so." Now what was she getting at? And there she went again with that amused expression. He grabbed a hammer from his toolbox and slid it into the tool pouch strapped to his waist.

"Well, I need to get this to Mom before it gets cold. Oh, and Mom asked if we could go the cabin and pick up an old desk that's been in the family for generations. She was hoping you could refinish it for her."

"Of course. You mentioned a cabin?"

"It's our family's, though we don't use it anymore. It's just been collecting dust and spider webs over the past few years. Well, more than a few. Just let me know when you're done."

"Sure. And, Chloe, I . . . I just wanted to say you look nice today. Well, every day, but especially today." *Okay. Stop talking. You sound like an idiot, Mason.* And to be more precise, she looked better than nice. In fact, he couldn't imagine her even on her worst day looking anything but nice.

"Thanks, but it's just something I threw on. The T-shirt came from the same place the torn, you know, blouse came from. At the fair, remember? Anyway." She strode back up the aisle.

She had to bring up the blouse incident. "Okay. I'll be here, working on the platform. If you need me."

He thought for sure he saw her smile as she turned to go and watched as she disappeared into the hallway. If it weren't for the fact that he was mesmerized with her beauty and playful sass, he'd take offense to her probing insinuations, regardless of their truth.

No sooner with that thought came Tom, ambling to the platform with a thumb waving in the direction of the office. "They don't come any better than that one."

"Hey, Tom. What one?" Mason stepped off the platform and shook hands.

"That Morgan girl. Been knowing the family my whole life, as well as most families to step foot into this church. But that one, she's a jewel. I have to believe God has a hedge roundabout that girl and has a special someone set aside for her. Only explanation I can see why no man's been able to win her heart."

Mason's curiosity rose. "So she's had boyfriends?" Of course she must have. Every single man in town couldn't possibly be that blind.

"One-date possibilities would be more accurate. At least, that's what I hear. Apparently not one made a good enough first impression. That, combined with the fact she probably could see straight through them all. Ain't pulling nothing over on that girl. Well, I just wanted to drop off a few studs for ya. Heard you'd be doing work on the platform."

"Thanks, but I could have picked them up."

"No problem. Besides, it's where I'm supposed to be just now, right?"

"As in, God's providential will, you mean?"

"Exactly. I learned the hard way a long time ago to . . ." His gazed settled downward and away, then returned with a slight nod. The rise and fall of his Adams apple indicated his hard swallow. "I've learned to not ignore that small, still voice, and just be where I'm meant to be at that moment in time. At least to the best of my ability. That's my prayer for you, Mason. That you never miss the critical decision-making points in life."

"Thanks, Tom. I appreciate it."

"See you in church Sunday." Tom gave a backward wave as he left.

Mason considered Tom's words. Not just his advice on hearing the voice of the Holy Spirit, but also concerning Chloe. If she was the prized jewel of Fleetwood, what chance did he really have anyway? Besides, it wouldn't be fair to Chloe. She had her whole life ahead of her. Which was more than he could say for himself, with his future very much in question. To get her heart tangled up into his immense mess just might qualify him as the "monster" one-date Sherri had labeled him.

The best, and only, thing to do would be to arrest his conflicted heart and mind. He couldn't allow himself to be attracted to her, even though his heart was persuading him that he was.

With a flashlight in hand, he slid into an opening under the stage platform, nailing braces beneath to strengthen its sagging floor.

"'Could you take the shelf back apart please?'" he mumbled, replaying the embarrassing shelf fiasco in imitation of Chloe as he worked. His inability to push his thoughts of her aside left him frustrated.

"'I tried to tell you,'" he muttered. Her words continued to trickle into his mind. The hammering grew louder with each passing thought. Or was it more like the hammering of his heart. "Thinks she can just bat her lashes with those gorgeous eyes, cute dimples, that walk and . . . and why am I talking to myself?" He gave one last hit to a nail, sending its echo throughout the church before coming out from under the platform.

But as wonderful as she was, he'd push his feelings aside. It was time to refocus on the reason for being in Fleetwood in the first place. Get well, not heartbroken. Not only was Boston his home, but there was also the potential movie deal. His career-long dream could finally be within his grasp. But the greater challenge being cancer. Not to mention, the possible side effects chemo could have on his body long term. So there'd be no need for rationalizing, as everything hinged on one simple truth. Most assuredly, beautiful women weren't searching or dreaming of finding a man who was at risk of dying.

Mason rapped on the open office door and stepped inside. "Hey, Chloe. I'm finished for the day, if we still need to get that desk. Oh, and Pastor Hank said if I needed to pick up anything at the hardware store, to give you a list for approval." He pulled a sheet of his small spiral notebook paper from his shirt pocket and handed the list to Chloe, seated at her desk. The faint scent of her perfume hung in the air. He drew near and hoped she wouldn't catch his prolonged stare at the way her hair was in a bun, with a few dangling strands at the side.

"Hmm. Interesting." She nodded and tapped her pen on the desk while scanning the list. Her eyes lifted to him, then shifted back to the note.

"Is something wrong?" He rubbed his five o'clock shadow chin.

"For clarification purposes. Did her auburn hair glimmer, or simply shimmer in the sunlight?"

"Uh . . . what?" Couldn't be. Those were the words he'd written only moments before.

She continued to read. "And, oh my goodness, her beauty was beyond comprehension?"

Mason reached out to retrieve the paper. She jerked it out of his reach and read farther. "I melted as she smiled. Could she be the one to end my searching, longing heart?"

"Could I have that please?"

She released the note as he reached for it again and pursed her lips, unsuccessfully suppressing a smile.

"Sorry. Wrong note. I'll find the right one later." It was the wrong note but all the right details.

"Uh-huh. Okay." She smiled. "I'll grab my keys, and we can go."

Hard. No, impossible would be a more accurate way to describe getting through any amount of time with her without his feelings attempting to seize control. She had a way of simply being *her* that was paralyzing and freeing at the same time. A way of drawing him in, then tripping him up with delight in her eyes. Those beautiful brown eyes.

Grab the desk, load it into the Jeep, and head back to the church. Pronto. Laser focus on the job at hand, not the girl responsible for consistently sending his heart into palpitations. Grab it. Deliver it. Done.

Instead, Mason admired the early-nineteen-hundreds cabin with its rough-cut logs and wraparound porch. He rubbed his hands across the weathered porch railings and stopped at the entry door, next to Chloe.

"My great-grandfather built it," Chloe said. "He passed it on to my grandparents, and afterward my parents. I was born in this house, delivered by a midwife. Guess that's why it means so much to me."

"This place is a big part of your history then."

"Yeah. Wait till you see inside."

The door swung open with the creak of rusty hinges. Vaulted log beams above and wood floors throughout gave the cabin a cozy charm. Chloe parted the sun-bleached curtains to allow natural light in, then slid a finger across the dust-laden antique desk they'd come to retrieve.

"Between Grandpa and Dad, many hours were spent preparing sermons and praying at this desk. Grandpa was the pastor at Fleetwood Assembly till he retired. They couldn't find another pastor after that, so Daddy took over until . . . he passed on."

"What did he—"

"So, I don't know that much about you. Where are you from?"

He gathered she'd rather not talk about her dad. "Boston. But grew up less than an hour away in Boone."

"Hmm. Boone boy, huh? What kind of stuff did you do for fun?" She made her way to the kitchen and parted the curtains over the sink.

"Hung out a lot at the Appalachian Theater as a teen. Also enjoyed what was called the Art Crawl, where you'd go from shop to shop. Galleries, crafts. My friends would tease me and call it the 'Nerd Crawl.' It didn't bother me though. I knew what I was interested in."

"And you're here in Fleetwood now? Why?"

A question he'd rather steer clear of. "Needed to get out the city for a while. Clear my head." Which in a way held some truth. Minus the most important part. The part he'd rather push aside and pretend was just a bad dream. Or more accurately, nightmare.

"Hey. Are you there?" She nudged his elbow. "Seemed like you were far away."

"Sorry. Just thinking. So tell me, was it hard being a preacher's kid?"

"Not really. When Daddy was in the pulpit, he preached nothing but the hard truth. What people needed to hear, not so much what they wanted to hear. Back home, he led his life by example. Everything he did and said spoke volumes of his love for us. My sister, Sarah, and I couldn't have asked for a better dad."

The difficulty to speak of her father was evident. He took hold of her hand to console. She diverted, sliding her hand out of his and was then drawn to the far side of the living room. She gave a wooden baby crib a nudge, sending it swaying.

"And this is what Mom rocked Sarah and me to sleep in." She stopped the motion, pointing out a broken spindle. "Guess I got tired of being in here. Supposedly I threw a tantrum one day and kicked this one out. Mom had to find something else to keep me in." She drew a deep breath and lingered. "Let's check out the stream out back."

The screen door slammed behind him as Chloe stood by one of several wooden barrel planters on the covered porch, with a lone wildflower in bloom in one, amid assorted grass and weeds.

"Mom has pictures from a long time ago with these planters bursting with flowers. She loved anything flowers. Not so much anymore."

He thought it peculiar how vividly he could envision the planters as she described them. In fact, he'd had the same feeling about the cabin when they pulled up. A certain familiarity about the place.

"Speaking of your mom, I overheard her mentioning something about you having a pottery business. There are a few amazing pieces of pottery in the foyer of the Valley View Bed and Breakfast where I'm staying. I was blown away by the talent and skill it must take to create something as incredible as that. It must be a God-given talent, if you ask me."

Chloe smiled as they meandered toward the stream. She plucked off a honeysuckle flower from a vine along the way. "Thanks. I appreciate the compliment."

"Wait a minute. You made that?" He pinched her sleeve and brought her to a stop.

"Yeah. But there's nothing great about it."

"Yes, there is. And you can stop being modest with me, Miss Morgan. I was informed your work is in magazines. That's no little thing, in my book."

"*Was* in magazines. I don't create on that level anymore. Hasn't been in me since Dad passed."

"That's unfortunate." But understandable, as any mention of her dad seemed to draw out heaviness of heart.

They stopped under a large oak tree with towering branches. He viewed the leisurely flowing stream, a good stone's throw wide, then looked back to the cabin. Thoughts and memories flashed in his mind.

"Wait a minute. I think I've been here before. It reminds me of a campground my parents took me to when younger. Only I don't remember getting here this way."

"This was the only campground around back then. Closed over fifteen years ago. It was called Morgan Falls Campground. Morgan is our last name, of course."

"That's it. My parents and I would spend every other weekend here when school was out, and occasional trips in the fall. That was the highlight of my life."

An amazed expression grew on Chloe's face. "Really? You were here? If you remember, the campsites were a little farther down and across the creek. You and I came by way of the rear entrance of the property, leading to the cabin."

"And there was a gazebo in this area, right? Between the cabin and the stream." He swung an arm in a wide arc.

"Yeah, but eventually it had gotten so rotted that it was torn down. I miss it not being here. Spent a lot of time under it, taking in the cool breezes and the sound of the flowing stream."

"And I spent hours sitting on that large rock across the stream." He pointed the boulder out.

Chloe looked across the stream. "That's the rock you used to sit on?"

"Yeah." Mason looked across the stream, then back to the cabin again. It was all coming back to him. Everything as he remembered, including the rock he'd sat on, watching the girl who'd remained in his heart. Regardless of the passage of time, she still had a small hold. Though standing next to Chloe, he found himself letting her drift to the far back of his imagination, to the spot that was a happy memory, and that was enough.

"Are you all right? Maybe we should get going. We still have the desk to load." She shielded her eyes from the sun with her hand.

"Sure." Mason bathed in the ease of which he conversed with her. Other than the delicate subject of her dad, there was no searching for words to say. Maybe it was a good time as any to tell her why he was really in Fleetwood. Someone to talk to who would possibly understand.

They slid the desk into the back of the Jeep and shut the hatch. "Chloe, I have something—"

"Cancer," she said.

"What?" The word twisted the pit of his stomach. Did she already know? How?

She leaned against the Jeep. "You probably wanted to ask earlier how Dad died. Cancer."

"I'm so sorry."

"I never want to live through something like that again. To sit there and watch someone you love suffer that way, then die." She shook her head. "He pretended to be brave. At least best he could. Tried not showing how much he hurt, but of course we knew."

"How long did he have it?"

"About a year. A long, hard year. Sarah and I were there for him as much as possible. Not that there was anything we could really do. I think the hardest part was when we'd hear Mom praying and crying on the front porch in the middle of the night, so Daddy wouldn't hear. For the most part, I try not to remember those things. Does no good anyway. Hurts too much." She swiped the corner of her eye.

"Sounds as though maybe you still are, you know, hurting."

"Yeah. Maybe so." She pulled the keys from her pocket. "I'm sorry. I interrupted you a minute ago, didn't I? You started to say something."

"Oh. Uh. . . nothing that can't wait."

The disheartening revelation caught Mason off guard. Not only about her dad, but how could he possibly tell her about his health situation after what was just said. At some point he'd have to tell her. She would ultimately find out. She'd been through so much over the years, with the wounds still present. He would never want to add more grief or hurt her in any way.

Maybe this was all a mistake. Moving here and meeting someone as wonderful as Chloe and falling in love so quickly. On that thought, he froze, with the realization that he was falling for her. He'd never felt more comfortable or more at peace than when around her. And if the intent with her teasing was to drive him away, well, sorry. She couldn't be more wrong. In fact, it was that captivating attribute that drew him in the most. She was more captivating than anyone he had ever meet. Not back in the big city, or anywhere. Not even close.

On the heel of that thought, he chastised himself for letting his heart be captured so quickly into something that could not possibly end well. His home was in Boston. Not to mention the possible movie deal that he'd dreamed of yet never seriously imagined could happen. In fact, it was as much of a long shot as someone like Chloe falling for him. There was no use getting his hopes up. But at the same time, he couldn't deny what he was feeling for her. Nothing had ever felt more right. Or more complicated.

Chapter 5

Mason twitched at the sting and pressure of the needle pressed into the port in his chest and reminded himself to breathe. All the information and mental preplanning for the dreaded moment did little to nothing to settle his racing heart. Those were books and videos. This was real life.

"Sorry about that. The first time is a little scary for most." Brandy, the treatment nurse, adjusted the flow of the medicine drip, then removed the blood pressure cuff.

"How long will this take?" A flash of heat flooded his face, followed by a coolness in the veins of his arm. He supposed it was the medicine and would be the norm from here on out.

"Unfortunately, five to six hours. We'll have to take it slow for your first day. You may as well make yourself comfortable." She handed him a sheet and pillow. "I'll be right there at the desk, so don't hesitate to let me know if you need anything."

"Thanks, Brandy." But not really. How was it possible to get comfortable with all . . . this. Wires, tubes, drips. His insides knotted with a peek to his chest and the tube going into the port. It wasn't that he was fearful of needles. This was something altogether different. The gravity of the circumstance welled up inside him. But strength to suppress it was what was needed now. Mom and Dad would be coming in soon, and he wouldn't want them to know how overwhelmed he was.

"Don't worry. You'll get used to it." The words came from a voice nearby. A hand pushed a small rolling partition aside, giving Mason a view into the section next to him. A man stared out the large window facing the parking lot. "The needles. Bloodwork, CAT scans, PET scans, biopsies. From this point on, it doesn't end." His weighty, steady monotone voice seeped from his lips.

Mason's assessment could only be equated to an outlook of absolute doom.

"You're here often for treatments?" Mason wasn't certain the man had heard, judging by his lengthy pause and the way he intertwined his fingers and placed his hands on his abdomen.

"Only for years. On and off. But who's counting?" He broke free from his straightforward gaze for a glance at Mason. "Marty's the name. In case you were wondering."

Well, Mason wasn't, since Marty's existence wasn't known till the wall was rolled away. But since he'd introduced himself, maybe there was a nice guy under all that cynicism and negative energy. "Mason. From Boston. Just here for treatments."

"Hmm." Marty gave an ever-so-slight nod. "From here on out, it doesn't really matter where you're from but rather where you're going. And that, my friend, is clearly predictable. At least for people like us." He gave a tap of his finger to his drip bag. "From here on out, your best days are behind you."

Not at all the welcome wagon Mason had expected. But at least he'd called him *friend*. Marty's dismal outlook hung in the air and opposed Mason's much-needed faith to carry him through this most critical time of his life. Faith. Up till now it was something he hadn't thought much about or felt he needed. When everything in life is smooth sailing, what was there to depend on God for?

Mason pulled himself out of Marty's contagious sullen state as Brandy showed Mom and Dad in.

"Hey, Mom. Dad." One look at Mom confirmed why he'd rather her not see him that way.

"Mason." Mom reached out to hug him, then hesitated. Her eyes scanned between the drip, heart-monitor wires, and the tube to the port in his chest.

"It's all right, Mom. I won't break." He reached out for a hug with his free arm.

"Hey, son." Dad took his hand. "We'd have gotten here earlier but were asked to wait till you were set up. So you doing all right? I mean, considering?"

"Yeah. Fine." Mason caught a glimpse of Marty's slight head tilt toward him and could already imagine what Mr. Positivity was thinking.

"You really didn't have to come. There's not much you can do." He pulled the sheet over his chest to conceal the port area, which Mom's eyes were drawn to.

"Don't be silly. We wouldn't think of not being here for you on your first day." Her voice cracked, and her leather purse crunched from her grip.

"Mom." Mason reached out and took her hand. "It's all right. I'm fine. I'll be okay. Really."

Her eyes watered. "If I could take your place, I would. I just . . ." She reached for a tissue in her purse.

Dad put his arm around her.

"Hey. It's just going to take some time." Mason wished he could believe the words he was saying. A sick sinking feeling settled throughout his body, from the chemo. He couldn't imagine another six or more hours of the treatment, much less six months of return visits.

"I know." Mom composed herself. "We'll do what we always do. Put our hope and trust in Jesus. He's still in the miracle-working business. Right, Travis? Tell Mason your little miracle."

"Jenny." Dad shrugged. "Maybe he's not up to this right now."

"What? What miracle, Dad?"

Dad scooted to the edge of his seat. "All right then. You know that truck I told you about at the antique yard? The one I've been eyeing for so long?"

"Yeah. What about it?"

"I got it. And the best part, it was free. Charlie, the owner, said he needed to clear out some inventory that's been there too long. Said he didn't want to see it rusting away out there in the field. Dropped the truck off right there in the driveway."

"That's incredible."

"No," Mom said. "What's incredible is how many trips to that garage I'm gonna have to make bringing him cold drinks and sandwiches till he's finished restoring that old thing. He tells me it's gonna be well worth it when we're cruising the Blue Ridge Parkway."

Mason covered the nausea with a laugh. "I'm happy for you, Dad. Maybe I can give you a hand someday."

"Yeah, sure. That would be great." Dad's eyes cast doubt.

Mason wasn't sure if it was because of the word "someday." Historically, "someday" only came around a few times a year, with his visits being limited to a few days. Or, given his health condition, maybe Dad wondered if there'd ever be another someday. Mason wondered the same.

"So the nurse said you'll be here awhile." Dad laid his hand on Mom's. "Mom and I were thinking of grabbing a bite in the cafeteria, then come right back."

"Of course. Go ahead. I'm not going anywhere." Not anytime soon anyway.

"Travis, can you wait for me in the hall? I'll be right out," Mom said.

Dad left as Mom leaned toward Mason. "You really didn't have to do that, you know."

"Do what?" Mason knew where this was headed.

"You don't think I know my son, or the truth that you bought him that truck?" Her all-knowing look penetrated him.

There was no use pretending he didn't have anything to do with it.

"Look, Mom. It was my chance to do something nice for Dad. I still remember how much he enjoyed working on his first old car when I was in the tenth grade. Working on that thing was like getting a present every day to him."

"Yeah, but the real gift was him working side by side with you."

"I know. But you two have always been there for me." He looked down and away, then back to her. "I just wish I had been there more for you two. There's no excuse good enough—"

"Don't." Mom shook her head. "Don't do that to yourself. We're proud of everything you've accomplished in your life. Sure, the distance apart is hard. But you have to live your life. It's your journey. Not ours. And regardless of how near or far away you are, you're always loved. There's never a moment you're not." She grasped his hand with one of hers. "Now, your dad's waiting for me. Remember, this truck thing is between us. We both know he'd never accept it if he found out it cost you something."

"Right. Our secret. Love you, Mom." He waved as she departed.

Mason reclined back in his seat. He slid a wastebasket closer to him as nausea intensified. He wouldn't be able to pretend anymore that he was fine. What was the use anyway? Mom and Dad knew him better than anyone. He inhaled, then exhaled a slow, calming breath to settle the barrage of thoughts swirling through his mind.

"You're a good actor, Mason." Marty took a sip of bottled water. "Almost had me convinced."

So much for settling his mind. But he was certain Marty had some helpful advice. Maybe would even hook him up with a fatalist cult, of which Marty was likely the president of. Could even possibly waive the initiation fee. "What do you mean?"

"'Don't worry, Mom, I'm doing fine'? 'Everything's gonna be okay'? That's a good one." Marty turned on his side away from Mason. "The sooner you let go of that kind of wishful thinking, the better. It's just the hand you and I were dealt."

What if Marty was right about the wishful thinking? He'd obviously been through all this. He would know. But even if his despairing attitude of life after cancer was accurate and justified, it would mean abandoning all hope and trust in Jesus as a healer, as well as relinquishing all faith in the only One who could provide a needed miracle. Mason determined he'd not give up on hope, faith, or trust in his God. At this point, it was all he had.

A dampened cry carried from the far side of the room. A girl, perhaps twelve, undergoing treatments rested her head on a young woman's shoulder. Presumably it was her mom who wiped the girl's tears and straightened her cap to keep her head warm. It was only moments prior that Mason had assured his mom that everything would be okay. Although he lacked faith to believe it himself, he'd said it. Now it was this mom telling her daughter the same thing. He wondered if she felt the same hopelessness he felt. Or Mom and Dad felt.

To go through something like cancer, or any disease, as an adult would be hard enough. But to watch your child go through it? Mason agonized at the thought as the girl's sniffles emotionally shook him. He inwardly declared that innocent children shouldn't have to suffer like this.

It was evident that up to this point, his life had been truly blessed, and he realized he'd taken so much for granted. Sure, there was hard work and struggles to succeed, but not real suffering. How fleeting life could be for some, shortened by life's tragedies. Even living a full life was considered but a vapor of time, according to God. Maybe he'd had it far too easy. And how did a person go through life and not see the suffering all around? Had he been that wrapped up in his own safe, predictable world?

"Marty, your ride should be here in a minute." Brandy removed everything that tethered him to his chair of doom. "I guess we'll see you next week?"

"Guess so. Got nowhere else to be." He buttoned his shirt and stared out the window as though looking at nothing, possessing an image of life without purpose or meaning.

"Family coming to get you?" Mason awaited his answer as Brandy hung another bag of meds on the stand.

"Now that would be a long wait, my Oscar-winning friend." He slid the cap from his bald head and shoved it into his backpack. "No family. At least, not any that cares. They all got their busy lives to live, you know. More important things to do. But hey, that's their loss, because I'm having the time of my life, right?"

Marty stood and grabbed his belongings to leave. His shoulders, as well as the corners of his eyes, sagged.

"Hey, Marty. I was just wondering. Are you always this cheerful?"

His feet stalled as he bit the side of his mouth and gave a forehead-crinkling expression. "No. Not always. You just caught me on a good day."

Chloe slapped the side of the kiln. "No. Don't do this to me now. There's too much to do." She placed a piece of pottery into the oven and spun the temperature dial to high. "I need coffee. I'm talking to an oven."

She pushed aside several cases of bubble wrap, cleared a path to the couch, and flopped down on her back. Her hand covered her eyes as she thought of the flurry of orders that had come in unexpectantly. A good thing. But with the kiln acting up lately . . . not such a good thing.

A message pinged on her phone. Which would be somewhere amid the wrapping paper, tape, labels, and an assortment of shipping items on the counter. She rose and swiped her hand around in search of it. Another ping. A message from Abby.

> *Don't even think about not coming tonight. Something you should know. This should be interesting. Coffee, danishes, and gossip.*

Another crash onto the couch followed the removal of her apricot-and-orange-colored apron. She brushed a finger across her name on it and placed it on her lap. It's fringe borders showed signs of wear, and an embroidered squash would soon need reattaching. The harvest-themed apron being a gift from Dad when she'd expressed an interest in pottery work as a teen.

He'd snuck off to Boone one day without anyone knowing, and while he'd searched shops for something special, the family had searched for him. Mom's finger had been about to press 911, when Dad had walked into the house and was confronted by Mom and his two girls. No words were needed. His eyes had scanned folded arms, tapping feet, and raised eyebrows. And the best he could come up with was . . . "What?"

She eyed the organized chaos of the shop. Anything needed could be found. Nothing lost. Been working that way for years, so why change now? Admittedly, she could take a page or two from Mason's note-taking organizational almanac. Wouldn't hurt, but not about to get him started on that.

She reflected on the few potential relationships of the past, which had amounted to nothing, ending after only the first date. She didn't need a year or even a month to know what kind of guy he was and would certainly not take a backseat to obsessive hobbies. If she wasn't a priority in the beginning, she surely wouldn't be after marriage. And if he didn't love God, forget it. She wanted a man who knew the importance of prayer and the value of family. A man much like her father. Possibly like . . .

Another ping sounded.

Are you coming or what?

The "or what" options just kept coming. First with Holly, and now Miss Impatient. But Abby was right. Coffee was calling, and dieting was strictly abolished on the Friday night gathering, with it altogether being considered an abomination of the utmost degree. Perhaps shunned even more than wearing heels to church. Except for special occasions of course.

With a toss of her purse onto the passenger's seat, Chloe spotted a small notepad. Mason's, undoubtedly. Must have fallen out of his pocket on their ride from the cabin the day before. Hmm. Wonder what he'd been writing lately. No. It wouldn't be right. There was no time snoop anyway.

It only took the ten-minute ride to Abby's place to justify a quick look. She threw the Jeep into park. Maybe she'd discover more about this auburn-haired babe from Boston he'd written about on that sheet he'd mistakenly handed her the other day. Or anything else her mysterious sojourner friend was conveniently withholding. A quick peek through and she'd give it back to him. No harm, no foul. But what was Mason doing pacing outside his car to the far end of the parking lot? His expression, the way he rubbed his temple with one hand and held the phone to his ear with the other . . . something wasn't right.

A wall of cinnamon baked apples and hazelnut blasted her senses as she pulled open of the pastry shop door. She jumped onto a stool and joined Abby and Sarah at the counter. "How long has he been out there?"

"Not long. And doesn't look all that happy, if you ask me," Abby said as she slid Chloe a latte.

"Don't tell me you two have already gotten into your first fight?" Sarah teased. "But hey, that's okay. You can always kiss and make up. That's the best part. Just admit you was wrong. Say you're sorry—"

"Oh, so you automatically assume I was in the wrong?" Chloe crossed her arms.

Sarah gave a puzzled expression. "So there was a fight then?"

"No. No fight. And why does everyone assume we're together?" It seemed natural that they would, or at least could be. Not that the thought hadn't crossed her mind. Had it even crossed Mason's mind? Didn't matter. She barely knew him. Besides, he had never asked her out.

"Why does everyone see it but you?" Abby shot back, then quickly recoiled with a sip of coffee in response to Chloe's stern look.

"I still don't know all that much about him. And what, some chivalrous knight arrives on his trusty steed right here in Fleetwood and I'm supposed to just swoon as he pulls me up and sweeps me away to his faraway kingdom of Bostonia?"

"Bostonia? Is that a real place?" Abby scrunched her brows.

"I don't know. But he could be secretly married, for all I know. And what, start liking someone, only for him to go right back to his faraway land?" Great. Now she sounded like Sarah going off with one of her sporadic "King James" parodies.

"At least he won't be going back home with Tina," Abby mumbled, and looked away.

Tina? "What about Tina?" Chloe snapped back.

Abby recoiled. "He was in here yesterday when Tina showed up, sashaying over with her wide-brimmed straw hat and sundress, trying to make conversation with him. Kept insisting he looked familiar and all. Sat herself right down at his table, like she belonged there."

"Flirting? She was flirting with him?" Heat engulfed her face.

Abby slid a nearby cake-cutting knife out of Chloe's reach.

"I'll set her hat on fire. I will."

"And how do you expect to get that hat off her overinflated, swollen head?" Abby plopped a hand onto her hip.

"Who said I was planning on taking her hat off?"

"All right, calm down. That sounds like something I would do. Not sweet, adorable Chloe." Abby took Chloe by the hand and sat her down at a nearby table. "Not to worry. He shot her right down. Told her he was already interested in someone. Had a front-row seat right over there at the counter. Not that I was eavesdropping or anything."

"Of course not. Thought never entered my mind." Chloe shook her head.

"Is that jealousy I'm detecting, sis?" Sarah asked with a gentle prod.

"What? Why would I be jealous? Besides, Abby just said she overheard him saying he was interested in someone else. Probably has girls lined up for him back in the city, with his fancy SUV and all his, you know, biceps, triceps, and niceness. Not that I noticed either." She shot a glance to Abby.

"Of course not." Abby's eyes darted to Sarah.

"Oh yeah. She's jealous," Sarah said, with Abby nodding in agreement.

Chloe had to admit, she'd never reacted that way before. Never had a reason to. Maybe it was jealousy. There was no denying the realization of how often her thoughts drifted to him throughout the day or the fact that she did miss not seeing him sometimes.

She watched as Mason took a seat at an outside table, plunked his elbows on the table, and cupped his hands in his face. Maybe he needed someone to talk to. She excused herself and pushed the door open to the outdoor seating area.

"Are you all right?" She slid her hands into her back pockets and hoped she wasn't intruding.

"Chloe, hey. I didn't know you were here." He stood.

"Mind if I join you? Unless you'd rather be alone. I could . . ." She waved a thumb back to the shop.

"No. It's all right. Please, stay." He slid out a chair for her at the black wrought iron table for two.

"Thanks. I'm not trying to pry. Just looks like something's wrong."

"Yeah." His laugh contradicted his undeniable brokenness. "That's an understatement, for sure."

She'd never seen him like that before. Bad news from back home? "Want to talk about it?" she offered, despite his demeanor that indicated he'd rather not.

"My mom just called from Boone. She and Dad were the ones who took me camping here in the summer. The truth is, they're my aunt and uncle. Jenny and Travis. They raised me from a month old." He fidgeted with a straw wrapper left on the table. "My birth mom left me with her sister Jenny. Now after over thirty years she's asking about me. Mentioned wanting to see me." He shook his head and looked away. "Sorry. Didn't mean to dump on you."

63

The heartbreaking revelation floored her. "No. You're not. What about your dad? If you don't mind me asking." The words came out before giving them much thought.

"Mom ran off with him after I got dropped off. He overdosed about a month later. Messed up on drugs and alcohol. Word was that it drove my mom even further into the drug scene. She wasn't heard from for years, according to Mom and Dad. No one knew if she was dead or alive."

No contact for years. Unfathomable. "So she's never come back? You've never met her?"

"Nope." He flashed a quick but unconvincing smile. "Maybe it's best that way."

Without a doubt, he was masking his true emotions. "But if your birth mom is trying to reach out to you, isn't that a good thing?"

"Why, after all these years? What, did she wake up one day and remember? 'Oh, I have a son. I'll explain why I abandoned him and never looked back.'"

As hard as it was for Chloe to hear what was being said, she could only imagine how difficult it was for him to live it out. "Maybe she simply wants a chance to explain. To say she's sorry and be forgiven."

"Yeah. I guess I'm supposed to forget it, just like that. Pretend it never happened. I'm not ready for all that. Not yet. Maybe never."

Lord, help me to be sensitive, she prayed. The last thing she'd want would be to push him away. "It's possible she's made a change in her life. Why else would she be trying to reach out to you? Giving her the benefit of the doubt could be the first step."

He shrugged, with sincerity in his eyes. "But how do you . . . how can you forgive something like this? Something that wasn't even my fault?"

Chloe reached out her hand to his. "We know that God's willing to forgive anyone if they ask for it. But for her to truly be set free, you have to be willing to forgive as well. It's God's way of healing you both. She's not the only one who needs to be set free in this. All I'm saying is, pray about it. Please."

His reddened eyes held to hers. "I will. Thanks for listening, Chloe. Really. I don't what I'd do if . . . if I hadn't met you. It feels good to have a friend."

"Friend?" She attempted to lighten the mood. "Is that written in your little book too? 'Met Chloe, my new best friend'?" She pulled his notepad from her pocket and held it out to him. "Looking for this?"

Concern creased his face. "You didn't read anything, did you?"

She smiled. "You really think I'd stoop that low?" Well, she almost had. But that would be curiosity's fault, not hers.

"No. Of course not," he said with a playful quirk in his smile.

"Well, I'd better get back inside."

He jumped from his seat to pull her chair back for her to stand.

"I'm sorry if I intruded." She laid her hand on his arm.

"No. You didn't. Not at all."

He pulled open the door and held it for her. She stopped in the doorway. "Want to join us? Grab a bite?"

"No thanks. I'm gonna head back now. Chloe, I've never told anyone my entire life about this. About being abandoned. You're the only one."

Hadn't told anyone? No one? She stepped back outside and allowed the door to shut. "Mason. You've been keeping this inside your whole life? You've told no one?"

"No. I figured what was the use. It wouldn't change anything. Besides, until now there's never been anyone I cared about enough to share it."

Humbled? Flattered? Confused? She didn't know what to think or feel. "Thanks for telling me that." She slid a hand into her pocket and with the other pushed strands of hair behind her ear. "Anytime you need to talk, I'll listen."

"Yeah. Thanks. Well, I'd better run now. You don't want to keep your friends waiting." He pulled the door open again.

"They'll just have to understand. I have another friend equally as important. He may think I'm pushy and irritating, but there's one thing I know. If I'm on a ladder or edge of a cliff, he'd never let me fall."

"Right." His smile returned. "You did forget to mention one thing about yourself. Sassy. See you tomorrow."

Chloe watched as he backed out and drove away. Something she'd been doing a lot lately. Watching him leave, but not really wanting him to. And why was she the first he'd chosen to tell something so personal? How difficult it must have been to keep all that suppressed, pushed down, and bottled up inside. There was no way to relate to what he was going through with being abandoned as a baby. She'd always been loved. Never alone or forgotten. But now, only God could heal his wounds. And she could only do what was needed most for now. Be there for him as a friend.

Chapter 6

*P*olitely decline her offer was what he could have done. Or better yet, should have done. *Thank you for offering a pottery lesson, but no thanks.* He'd stick to the plan. Come to Fleetwood Falls to get treatments, not get involved in a relationship. Problem was, how could he say no to her? Not possible, as evidenced by his knocking on her shop door.

Chloe extended an arm wave to usher him in. "I promised I'd show you the shop, so here it is."

He took a step inside, then stopped. "Oh my goodness. What happened here?" He eyed a disarray of boxes, packing paper, and pottery in no particular order. Was her issue with spontaneity also a doorway to hoarding? He'd watched a program once on it and now regretted not paying closer attention. Maybe then he could understand her . . . addiction. Possibly intervene in some way.

Chloe folded her arms and took a step closer to him. "What do you mean, what happened?"

"Is this a high-crime area? Was the place ransacked?" He spun with arms and palms out. "Look at all . . . this."

"Ha-ha funny. What are you trying to say? I'm a—what's the word

I'm looking for?—hoarder?" Another penetrating stare.

"No. Definitely wouldn't say that." He'd maybe think it, but not say it. "To be honest, I don't know how you can find anything in here. A lot going on in this room."

"For your information, I have no problem finding anything in here. Everything's fine just where it is. Bubble wrap is in one of those boxes over there. Tape is somewhere under all that mess on the counter, and . . ." Her hands settled onto her hips and eyes squinched. "Wait. You *are* insinuating that I'm a hoarder, aren't you?"

She closed the gap between them again. Her threatening smile and dimples melted him, somehow offsetting her—ahem—untidiness issue.

"I . . . I just . . ." Mason stammered.

"Yeah, you just what? For your information, I've been very busy lately and haven't had a chance to clean up, that's all. So you can relax, mister. Everything in its place, and a place for everything. Am I right, or what?"

His smile widened as the playful sass he adored returned.

"I was just going to say I'd be glad to help you with organization and developing a system to all this. It would probably help things move along a little easier and faster. Just a thought. You could have a calendar hanging on the wall over here, and—"

"Thank you for your evaluation of my business practices. I promise to take it into consideration. But that's not why we're here, are we? You have your first pottery lesson as soon as I remove my latest creation from the kiln."

Chloe slid her mitts on and removed a piece of pottery from the kiln. "Oh no. Not again."

"What's wrong?"

"The kiln is acting up again. This piece has not fully dried, and it was supposed to be shipped to a buyer in the morning. Served me well for a lot of years, but I'm afraid it's on its way out."

She placed the pottery piece on a nearby table, then pulled up an extra chair for Mason to work on a piece of stoneware clay.

"You ever do this before?" She put on her apron, then handed him one.

"Once in school. Didn't end up good."

"Well, here's your chance to prove you're good at something other than writing in that little notepad you carry around. No pressure, of course." She removed the clay from the bag and handed it to him. "Here's a two-pound piece we'll start with. Now just plop it center of the table so that it'll stick."

Once in place, the clay spun slowly with the table. Chloe wet her hands from the bucket of water. Her hands cupped the clay and began shaping it.

"Now, wet your hands and place them around it, like I did."

He cupped his hands around it. "I don't know about this. It looked easier when you were doing it."

"You're doing fine. Here, let me help." She cupped her hands over his, applying more needed pressure as the clay spun.

His hands warmed. He thought it was from the friction of the clay, but he soon ruled that out, as the warmth traveled to his face and spine. Maybe he should come for more lessons. Yeah. A lifetime plan, to be exact.

Chloe's mom poked her head around the door, then stepped in. "Thought I saw the light on in here. You've got a good teacher, Mason."

"She sure is."

"Don't listen to her. She thinks everything I do is great. Don't you, Mom?"

"The truth is the truth. Well, I'll get out of the way." Grace grinned as she left.

"Now let's begin hollowing out the inside." She guided his hands through the process.

His eyes shifted from the clay to an object covered with a white sheet in the corner of the room. "What are you hiding in the corner? Working on something top secret?"

"Uh . . . that's nothing. Nothing at all."

Hmm . . . he wouldn't pressure her on it, since she was reluctant to talk about it. "I'd imagine it takes considerable time to get as good as you." With her hands on his, he hoped the piece would take at least an hour. Long enough to take in those bursting brown eyes a little longer.

She broke her gaze from his. "It's no different from anything else in life. If it's worth it to you, then you invest the time. Take pottery, for example. You start off with something in mind, but it's not always the way you intend it to end up. Kind of takes on a life of its own."

"Uh . . . yeah. I mean, it's sort of like writing. You may start off with something in mind, but then it changes direction on you in unexpected ways. A lot like life, don't you think?"

Chloe stilled the turning table. "Yeah. You're right. Well, there you have it. Your first piece. Simple and nicely done. Kind of. Despite the fact that it looks more like a soup-ladle holder than a cereal bowl, I think there's hope for you yet."

"It does look pretty sad, doesn't it?"

They laughed, removed their aprons, and washed up.

"Are we ready to put it in the oven?" Mason rubbed his neck, and heat flooded his face. It was time to ask her what had been on his mind all day.

"Not quite. It needs to dry for over a week before it goes in the kiln. Then we'll fire it up."

"So that means I'll have to come back, of course. It wouldn't be right to not finish what I've started."

"Not it wouldn't. You're committed to finish it, I'm afraid. Too late to back down now."

She was right about backing down. And he wouldn't give regret a place for not asking her. "Chloe, I was wondering . . ."

"Yes?"

"Would you allow me to take you to eat out tomorrow night?"

Her eyebrows narrowed. "You mean, like a date?"

"Yes. A date. I heard there's a nice restaurant on the other end of town. The Palace, I think it's called. Valet parking. White tablecloths.

At least that's what the website said."

"I've heard of it all right, and I don't know, Mason. I don't think I'm ready to, you know, date."

"Consider it purely friends getting out then. Please. Besides, I owe you for the pottery lesson."

"Well, good news—first lessons are free. So we're even."

He didn't want to be even. He wanted to treat a special lady out to a special place. "I insist on it. Really. It's either that or drown my sorrows in drum lessons every day at the church. I'll do it while you're there working, of course. You're the one that planted the seed while working on the platform that day, remember?" *Real smart giving her an ultimatum, Mason.* Now he wouldn't know if she was going out of pity or because she genuinely wanted to.

"All right. I'll go. But only because I know you're itching to go someplace nice so you can get back into those city clothes." She dusted a spot of dried clay from his sleeve.

"You seem to forget . . . I was raised just a short way from here. Boone boy at heart. Remember?"

"Yeah. Guess you're not all that bad." She stepped closer, inspected her nails, then plopped her hands onto her hips. "Other than your keeping secrets from me, that is."

Secrets? Did she know about his condition? No. That couldn't be it, judging by her teasing eyes. "Secrets?" He'd never perspired as quickly in his life.

"You don't think I know who you are, Mason Chad*wick*? Big shot romance writer, huh?"

"Excuse me?" He opened his eyes wide. Her eyes held to his. "So you know?" He sighed a heavy relief. It was far better she'd found out that bit of information than the other. Both of which he'd intended to tell her about at the right time.

"Ooh, I know, all right. Is that's what you've been doing here in town? Working on your next story? Writing all that down in your little notebook?"

"Chloe, I was going to tell you." True. He'd simply not found a way of telling her that didn't come across as bragging.

"Really? Got anymore secrets you're not telling me?"

Regrettably, yes. But one that would have to wait. "Well, I do have a surprise for you tomorrow. Pick you up at seven?"

"I'll be ready. So you can relax, now that your secret is out. Unless you have more I don't know about," she said with an animated smile. "About that surprise—"

"See you later," he teased with a grin.

Yes. There was so much more to say. More to explain. And no easy way to do it. He didn't want to say it any more than she'd want to hear it. And he didn't want to live it any more than she'd want to see him suffer through it.

Abandoned, forgotten, and hung out to dry was the way she'd describe the red dress that had been buried for years in the back of her closet. She held it up and tossed it alongside the pants and blouse on the bed. The choice between the two outfits had to be made, and fast. In thirty minutes Mason would be picking her up for their dinner outing. Not date. Her mind was firm about not being ready for a commitment, if that was what he was thinking. But her heart was saying something different. It could possibly turn out good. But then what about when he returned home to Boston? The practical solution to it all would be to remain friends. That was all. No broken heart.

Next decision, heels or flats? It was, after all, a fine-dining restaurant. She wiped the thin layer of dust off the heels and settled on the red dress, which hadn't been worn since agreeing to chaperone Holly's senior prom. Now, four years later and several pounds additional weight, it would certainly result in a snugger fit. Maybe he'd not notice. She'd heard that most men didn't have that much of an eye for detail. She exhaled a lengthy breath. *Relax, Chloe. He's just a friend.*

The doorbell chimed, and Chloe pulled the door open. Mason

gaped. Or was it staring—again. Whatever the case, she was right. Apparently he didn't mind the snug fit. His expression and lack of words said it all. It was more than enough. After all, what girl wouldn't want to be looked at that way? And not in a bad way.

"Please believe me, Chloe, when I say I've never seen a more beautiful woman."

How was a woman who'd never been told that supposed to respond? "And yet another one of your many talents. Bald-faced lying." It was the best she could come up with, but it prompted an amused smile in return. She clutched her purse and patted her hair.

"I've never been more serious. I assure you." Again, more staring.

"Mason. Ready to go?"

"Sure."

She took his arm. Despite it being simply a dinner with a not-so-simple guy, it didn't seem real. Almost like a dream. Maybe one she didn't want to wake up from.

Mason shut the door behind her as she slid into the SUV. Something a man hadn't done for her since, well, forever. She fought back pessimistic thoughts of how long the gentlemanly stage would last. If a census were to be taken, it would end after the altar, according to most women, she presumed. Then again, maybe he wasn't like most men.

After the valet departed to park the car, Mason extended his arm for Chloe to take as they were escorted to a private outdoor dining area, where the deck overhung a small pond with a fountain in the center. Soft music played inside and filtered out through two large French doors. Chloe discerned the ease of which Mason navigated the elegant restaurant. An environment he'd apparently grown accustomed to back in Boston. Had she been there with anyone besides Mason, she'd possibly feel out of place. But not with Mason.

"Thanks for agreeing to tonight. To be honest, I didn't think you'd say yes." He removed his jacket and loosened his tie, held in place by a silver typewriter tie tack.

"Why would you think I wouldn't have?"

"I figured your standards were higher than, you know, me." He raised an eyebrow and smiled. "But when you agreed, a realization hit me."

"And what was that?"

"Either your judgment of character is poor, or your eyesight is failing." He peered at her as he sipped his water.

"And how do you know I'm not sitting here thinking about how special I feel, being with such a kind, considerate man?" Or if she were honest, wondering where was the surprise he'd promised.

"The only kind of man I feel like tonight is a very fortunate one. And in all seriousness, you are an amazingly beautiful woman. Don't ever doubt it."

She had nothing. No come back line. No smart reply. Only a melted heart. Her stomach fluttered. Never had she felt more special. So much so that it brought her back to reality. Boston. *What am I doing?*

"I've been meaning to ask you something. At the church auction, you were bidding on a pendant. It seemed to mean a lot to you."

"So you *were* stalking me?" She stared at him wide eyed.

"Not stalking. Noticing."

"Uh-huh. Right. Okay, so where do I start? The pendant originally belonged to a close friend of my grandma, Mabel. Grandma would take me to visit her. Mabel had a huge collection of jewelry—mostly costume—and she let me play dress-up, with that pendant being my favorite. I remember wanting it so badly as a kid. When she passed recently, I thought maybe that was my chance to get it at the auction. Mostly for memory's sake. Unfortunately, it went for more than I could afford."

"Do you know the woman who was bidding against you?"

"Yeah. Tina. For some reason she's had it out for me ever since high school. Could be insecurity or something. I don't know. Angel, from church, was kind of her sidekick. I don't know though. I think Angel just wanted to fit it, so she went along with Tina's juvenile absurdities."

"Guess it's hard to let go of years of hurt," he said.

"It is. But enough of that. Speaking of Tina. My sources at the pastry shop tell me that you two were sitting together talking. She also overheard you mentioning to Tina that you were already interested in somebody. I assume back in Boston?" Chloe shrugged, hoping to draw out a hint of information.

"First of all, Abby's covert skills are not the best, but I know she means well. You're blessed to have a friend looking out for you like that. And to answer your speculation—no. Nobody special back home, or anywhere. I was being polite by telling her there was someone else."

"Wise man. Because if she was your type, that would mean I've seriously misjudged you."

A chill settled in as the evening grew late. The waiter cleared their table and returned with coffee to conclude the meal. Chloe rubbed her arms briskly to warm them. Mason rose and draped his suit jacket over her shoulders, then sat back down.

"I have something in my jacket pocket for you." The flickering candle reflected in his blue eyes.

"For me?" She reached in and removed a small box. Adrenaline rushed through her. She settled the onset of panic and convinced herself that the shape of the box wasn't one that would contain a ring followed by a life-changing question. Not quite ready for that. She didn't think so anyway.

"Open it."

Her eyes fixated on a pendant. And not just any pendant. Mabel's pendant from the auction.

"Mason, I don't understand. How did you . . ."

"I couldn't bear to see your disappointment when you left the auction. And to see your expression, like right now, was more than worth it."

"Mason, I don't know what to say. So many memories are wrapped up in this. You just don't know." She couldn't have hoped for, or imagined, a better surprise.

"Would you mind if we took a picture together with it on?" He picked up his phone, pulled his chair around, and snapped a picture, then moved his chair back.

Soft music played as the restaurant thinned out of customers. Mason took her hand.

"Would you care to dance before we leave? I've requested a special song for us."

Dance? Her stomach quivered. Dancing was not her thing. But she didn't want to seem unappreciative after all he'd done.

"Only because it's a slow dance. I don't do fast. I'm not a fan of humiliation."

Despite the chill, warmth flooded her. The song "Unforgettable" by Natalie and Nat King Cole filled the room. Hmm. A nostalgic, romantic side? A tingle traveled up her spine and continued with goose bumps on her arms. Soon they were cheek to cheek.

She thought of the day they'd met at the church fair. What a stark contrast, particularly with the torn-collar incident and their entangled embrace. Her inclination then being to push away. Now it was to willingly pull him close. Unforgettable would be the way she'd describe the evening.

The ride back home left her in a state of elation as well as in a daze. On one hand, it was one of the best and most meaningful nights of her life. The fact that he recognized her from the day they'd met and, without being told, knew the pendant meant something special to her was nothing short of impressive. The way he intently listened when she spoke and was alright with her playful razzing gave a sensation of being comfortable and safe. She didn't have to change for him. She could be herself. Who God made her to be.

Then again, she knew little about him. A stranger strolled into town and you were supposed to simply believe any and everything he said? Maybe he told all the girls back in Boston how beautiful they were. With his looks and personality, he could have his pick. He already had two women swooning over him in this town. Both of which would likely take him for every penny he was worth if given the chance.

She took his hand at her front door. The pendant. Going out with such a sweet, handsome man. It was all too much. She wrestled with her conflicted decision to kiss or not. If she did, he'd possibly expect more commitment. One in which she was uncertain she was ready to make.

"Thanks again for tonight. For everything."

He inched closer to her. "No. Thank you. It was the best night of my life."

"Yeah. Me to." *Decide, Chloe.* "See you at church Sunday?"

"Yeah, of course. I'll see you there."

"Good night." She stopped short of opening the door. She took a step back to him and kissed him on the cheek. "Night." She walked up the steps and through the door, resisting the urge to look back.

Sarah sprang from the couch. "All the juicy details. Don't leave anything out."

"What are you doing here this late?" Chloe set her purse down on the kitchen island.

"Mom went to bed. Jeff and Mark are watching a ball game. And I'm curious to see how your date went."

"It was just dinner and a dance." Chloe removed Mason's jacket, which she'd forgotten to return.

Sarah's eyes widened at the sight of the pendant dangling from her neck. "What is that? Is that what I think it is?"

"He gave it to me tonight. He said he had a surprise, but I would have never guessed this."

"Unbelievable. It was Mason who outbid Tina?"

"Yeah." She slid off her heels at the dining room table.

Sarah took a closer look at the pendant. "He paid over a thousand for this. For you. Wait till Abby hears about this."

"I couldn't believe it myself. Still can't." What she also couldn't believe or understand was what made her so special in his eyes. She'd never led him on or pretended to be anything she was not. If anything, she'd have thought her kidding around would have driven him further away, although that would have never been her intent.

"You do realize that no one would do something like this, as thoughtful as this, if they didn't genuinely care. Chloe, I see the way he looks at you. Mom, Abby—we all do. He's an amazing man. I know you see it too. Can't you at least admit it?"

"You're right. He is amazing, but . . ." But what if she got close, only to wake up and it all disappeared.

"But what?"

"I want to take it slow, that's all." Slow enough to not make a mistake she'd regret, but also not talk herself out of what could be God's plan for her life.

"And there's nothing wrong with that. But don't let the fear of commitment stop you from having what could be a wonderful life. And we can't be afraid of getting close to someone because of some foreboding feeling that we may lose them."

"I know, but this is all happening so fast. And why to me? I'm just a plain ole girl from Fleetwood Falls."

"And he's just a plain ole boy from Boone. So why does all that matter?"

"I . . . I don't know." Chloe shook her head and rested her face in her palms. "I can't tell if this is God sending someone into my life or a chance to have my heart broken."

"I think maybe tonight you've taken the first step." Sarah took Chloe's hand. "Admitting you have feelings for him. And why wouldn't you? As far as I'm concerned, it's the beginning of a storybook romance if I've ever seen one. And what would make any other woman more special or deserving than you? Money? Possessions? No. It's what he sees in your heart. You deserve to be happy. You both do."

"Then why is it so hard to let go? To move on? It's been five years since Dad passed, but it feels like yesterday. I wish he were here to help show me the way."

"I know. I can't come into this house without thinking about him. But Dad wouldn't want us to live like this. Moping around and depressed. We know he's in a much better place, and one day we'll see him again. Until then, we need to carry on. It's what he would want."

"Yeah. Thanks for being such a good big sister."

"Please. I'm barely a year older. Then again, I guess the title was thrust upon me."

"Thrust? You're not gonna get all King James on me, are you?" Sarah's *thee and thou* speech had the tendency to last days when she was in the mood. Hopefully, she'd return to her castle tower before the inclination struck.

Sarah rose from the table and gave her a tight hug. "If you force me to, I will. Love you. And you can tell me about that dance later. And that kiss." Sarah blew Chloe a kiss and snickered.

"And how do you know there was a kiss? You were peeking out the window, weren't you?"

"No. That look on your face I've never seen before. That's how I know. Oh, and the heels. Dead giveaway."

"It was a simple kiss on the cheek, that's all." The sensation she felt from that kiss was anything but simple. Maybe it was for the best she didn't find her way to his lips.

"So did he kiss you or you kiss him?"

Chloe put her hands on her hips. "Does it really matter?"

Sarah studied her expression. "I knew it. You kissed him."

"I didn't say that."

"Didn't have to. Call it intuition. Discernment. I don't know. Apparently another thing thrust upon me, I guess. Bye," she said with a smile and a wave.

Chloe dropped her heels onto the bedroom floor and viewed her reflection in the full-length mirror on the wall. She held the pendant to her heart and thought on what it was that Mason saw in her. No guy had ever treated her so special. He was a true gentleman in every way, with his good looks a bonus. At any rate, he was a good friend. No harm in that. But there was something that couldn't be ignored. She'd never lingered in thought about a friend this much before.

She sat on the edge of the bed with her phone and looked at the picture they had taken at the restaurant. She scrolled farther to a picture of Sarah, Jeff, and Mark and wondered if she'd ever have a family of her own. If being single was God's plan for her, then so be it. Nothing wrong with that. No one was a lesser person because of it. God was the one who completed a person and made them whole, whether they were with another or not. But if she were to be honest, her heart did long for *another*. Someone who would treat her like her dad had treated her mom. Or someone like Mason.

Chapter 7

Five miles. Five miles? Chloe wiped the sweat from her forehead and stepped off the elliptical exercise machine in the corner of her bedroom. A recorded hype session along with an unconvincing self-talk and a prayer to Almighty God for strength to make it to one mile, maybe two, was the norm for her morning routine. She rapped the mile meter. Must be acting up. Or maybe she wasn't focused on each grueling minute of exertion for once.

Chloe lifted Mason's suit jacket off the backrest of her vanity chair, lifted it to her face, and inhaled a whiff of his lingering cologne. She flumped onto her back on the bed and snuggled the jacket across her chest. The morning sunlight pierced the blinds of her bedroom window, shooting sparkles of colored light from her pendant onto the ceiling. She rolled over and, with elbows on the bed, cradled her chin in her hands, then lifted the pendant from the nightstand.

The scented jacket. The pendant. Her memory of dancing in his arms. All still fresh in her mind. Despite it all, she couldn't help but wonder where her heart was racing off to. If allowed to do so, would she have the strength or desire to pull back on the reins of desire in full gallop if need be? And what if she were thrown completely off? What then? Too many what-ifs.

She clasped the pendant around her neck and marveled at how it had found its way to her. As though God did care for the small things in life within the grand scheme of things. And was Mason part of the grand plan? However little. However much.

Maybe Sarah was right about not letting fear get in the way of what could be. Perhaps it was time to put down the wall and let someone get close.

A knock on her bedroom door transported Chloe back to her present place and time. Mom poked her head in and took a seat on the bed.

"Hey, sweetheart. How was last night?"

"It was nice." Nice enough to keep her up most of the night, with only a vanilla bean ice cream float and a chocolate candy bar to keep her company.

"Just nice? Sarah told me about the pendant this morning." Mom held it dangling from Chloe's neck.

"Surprised it took her that long to tell you. Thought for sure she'd wake you up in the middle of the night."

"You were barely a teen the last time I saw you wearing this. It was your favorite piece of Mabel's jewelry. And to think, it took Mason to get it to you." Mom eyed the red dress, strewn across the bed, and gave a curious look. "So what did he think about the dress?"

"He said it looked . . . nice on me." All right. Eye-popping, jaw-dropping nice, judging by Mason's reaction. But how embarrassing would that be to tell her mom.

"Oh. Okay. Just *nice* again, huh? We both know there's no question he's quite fond of you. I can't help but think about that list you told me that he gave you in the office that day." Mom giggled. "I had a feeling he was describing you. He liked you from day one. Same thing happened when your dad saw me. At least that's what he said. Of course, I didn't think I was anything special, but you couldn't convince him of that. Not for a minute."

"How did you know he meant it? That he truly loved you?"

"I guess it was the way he looked at me. Like I was his everything. Combine that with the fact that he was kind and gentle and would do anything for me if he could. A lot like your Mason." Mom spun the wedding ring on her finger. "I resisted the feelings I had for your dad for a while, but when I began to miss not being with him on any given day, I surrendered. I knew I was in love."

"He was the best, wasn't he?" Chloe said. "Husband and father."

"That he was." Mom closed her eyes and rubbed her arms in a hug, then exhaled a long-quieted sigh. Chloe had seen Mom that way before many times in the past years. Still missing Dad like it was yesterday. But this was different.

Chloe reached out and took Mom's hand. "What is it, Mom? Is something wrong?"

"You're a grown woman, Chloe, and I know you'll make the right decision about Mason. Just keep your heart open to what God is saying. Listen to the Holy Spirit's small, still voice and you won't go wrong."

"I sense a *but* coming."

"Don't let fear rule your decision-making is all I'm saying. Don't let that stop you from what God may have for you. Regret is . . ."

Mom's lip trembled. Chloe snuggled close and wrapped her arm around her.

"You and Sarah were only a few years old. Your dad came to me full of enthusiasm and asked if we could go to an airshow out of town. He'd never expressed any interest in airplanes before. So I blew it off and laughed, as I remember." A sigh followed. "Then a few weeks before your dad passed, he told me something I'd never known about him."

Chloe hesitated to ask, despite her sureness her dad carried no dark secrets. "What? What did he say?"

"As a teen, your father went to a county fair where they were giving rides in what they call a taildragger airplane. He ran home, broke his piggy bank, and spent it all on that plane ride. Said he never felt freer in his whole life up to that point, or closer to God. So his dream was to get his pilot's license and fly a plane when he grew up."

"I never knew that about him either. But what does this have to do with me and Mason?"

"It was the way your dad's eyes lit up when he told me. Like the dream came alive to him once again." Her smile faded.

"I still don't understand, Mom."

"Regret. It all boils down to regret. It's not always the big things that come back to haunt you. I didn't know at the time how much going to that airshow meant to your dad. It would have been so simple to just agree and let him enjoy his moment to relish his childhood dream."

"But there was no way you could know. He never told you."

"I know. The thing is, regret is like a stray cat. You don't see him for a while, but then there he is, staring through the glass of the back door. Scratching with his paws and meowing. Wanting to come in." Mom patted Chloe's hand and stood. "The point is, don't feed the cat and he won't have a reason to come back. Anyway, breakfast is ready." She took another look at the pendant. "That's strange. I don't remember those stones looking that sparkly. Oh well, biscuits are getting cold."

"Thanks. I'll be right down." Chloe eyed her backpack hanging from the coatrack in the corner of the room, then reached for her phone, scrolled, and dialed. "Mason. You're at the church?"

"Yeah. Why?"

"Think you can meet me in the parking lot in half an hour?"

"Sure. What's up?"

Chloe wandered to the kitchen with the phone to her ear. "Thought we'd go on a short hike if you're up to it. We'll start at the cabin and work our way to the falls. I've got backpacks and supplies." A pause, then a ruffling sound followed. "Is that what I think it is? Are you checking your calendar?"

"Wha—don't be ridiculous."

What a terrible, pathetic liar. Amateur. "Don't worry. I've got water, first-aid kit, and plenty of unhealthy snacks."

"What about bear repellant?"

"Would you lighten up? Geez. See you in a few."

Her phone pinged with a message. Kristen, her friend who'd been fighting ovarian cancer for the past three years. With her husband being out of town for work, she'd like someone there with her for an upcoming chemo treatment.

Mom removed her oven mittens. "Is everything all right?"

"Not really. That was Kristen reminding me to sit with her at her next treatment. Is it wrong to lack the faith to believe for healing when everything in front of you screams out that it's impossible?"

Mom took a seat on the stool beside her. "That's why the Bible says we walk by faith, not by sight. I know it's hard to pray for something for so long and see nothing change, but we can't surrender to hopelessness and despair. That's a dark tunnel that can be hard to get out of once you're in it."

Mom would know. She'd lived it. And thanks to her faith, God had helped her find her way out. But Chloe struggled with the thought of the treatment center. It reminded her too much of her dad being there. Regardless, she wouldn't think of letting her friend down, or as her mom had put it, give place for the stray cat of regret.

Chloe pulled the compact notebook from Mason's hand and stuffed it into his pocket. "You won't be needing that. I know where I'm going. Instead of writing, we can talk."

"Talk, huh? Like telling you how I lost sleep last night thinking of you in that red dress, and wishing you were still in it." A sneak peek confirmed a smile.

"That would be hard to hike in. Especially with the heels. But I did consider sleeping with it on. Although, I am wearing my new pendant. Antique, but new to me." She gave a pat to it, tucked under her T-shirt, and grasped his arm before stepping over a log.

The pendant? On a hike? If she knew the increased value of it since he'd replaced the faux stones with real ones, she would have probably left it at home. Telling her about his trip to the jewelers and what he'd done would hold till another day. But what was becoming increasingly hard to put on hold was his feelings for her.

"I brought a few of Mom's homemade biscuits. Or if you'd prefer, I swung by Abby's shop and picked up a few pastries." She swished up her eyebrows twice. "Only the healthy stuff with extra-cream filling, of course."

"Yes. So healthy. Speaking of Abby, you two been friends for a long time?"

"Since high school. I don't know how I would have made it through some of the hard times without her. She gave balance to my life. If she couldn't make me laugh, no one could."

"And how long have you known Holly?"

"Most of her life. She's such a sweetheart. Her parents owned the bookstore for about ten years but decided to move back to Utah, where they were originally from. When Holly didn't want to go, they left the business to her. So, Abby and I basically adopted her as our little sister."

"She has no lack of enthusiasm, does she?"

Chloe giggled. "Not at all. And we love her for it. It's a shame her business is struggling though. A new bookstore opened across town, and the drop in customers is obvious. Abby and I want to help but don't know how."

"Maybe I can help. I'll talk to her about doing a workshop, book signing, or coming to a book club reading, to possibly draw more people in."

"I guess it's worth a try. I know she'd appreciate that. As well of every other woman in this town, I'm sure." She shot him a sour smirk. "So don't get a swollen head."

Was that a tinge of jealousy or simply her usual poking? "Wouldn't think of it." His breath shortened. They arrived at their destination to observe a ten-foot waterfall, its water sliding down a rock face, then pooling into a whirlpool before continuing its meandering journey downstream.

A glade of several acres with colorful wildflowers lay beside the falls, with a ridge surrounding it creating a majestic backdrop. The remaining morning vapors of dew lifted and dispersed with the warmth of the late-morning sun, with it all being a far cry from the hectic city pace Mason had grown accustomed to.

Chloe climbed onto a large rock. "Beautiful, isn't it?"

He climbed up and scooted next to her. "Sure is."

She looked back to the glade. "I think this would be a great place for a cabin. In the glade, facing the falls. You kind of get the feeling that ridge is giving the glade a big hug. Feels like home. Sounds silly, I know."

"No. Not at all."

"Lay back and close your eyes," she said.

Mason lay back on the inviting coolness of the rock. Despite it being a short hike, he'd tired considerably even before the halfway point. Back in the city, he'd walk several city blocks before tiring. He could only attribute it to the effects of chemo.

"Now relax and listen." Her eyes shut. "Listen for the peaceful, simple things like the sound of water cascading over rocks, birds chirping, and the rustle of the wind through the trees when a gust comes through."

"Can't experience this in the city." He sat up.

She rose as well. "Can't sit still for a minute, can you?"

"Guess it's hard for me to slow down. After all these years. Between deadlines and projects to tackle, it never ends."

"But you're not there right now—back in the city. Look around at where you are and what's right in front of you. As far as I'm concerned, you're looking at the most beautiful scenery in the—"

"That I am," he said with an unflinching stare into her eyes.

"I . . . I was going to say that few people know about this spot, with it being on our land. Well, county land. It's gonna be heartbreaking to give it up."

"What do you mean, give it up?"

"Our lease is up this year. As much as we hate to admit it, Mom, Sarah, and I agree that it doesn't make since to renew it anymore. Although, it may not be our decision. Mom got a letter from the county saying they may want the land for another purpose, so they possibly wouldn't allow another lease."

"That includes the cabin?"

"Land, cabin, all of it." She frowned and shook her head. "It was part of the lease agreement. Any structure built on the land becomes county property upon vacating."

To see the light drain from her eyes when she spoke of losing it all tore at him. "I'm so sorry. Can't imagine how your family must feel. Growing up here and being born in that cabin. Doesn't seem right. Not right at all."

"I know. But things change, and life goes on." She flashed a strained smile and lifted her face toward the sun. "Well, enough about all that. So what do you think about all this?"

"I'd say it feels like home." When around her, he didn't think about the hectic city pace that had carried him along for years. Not that it was all bad. But now he had something, or rather *someone*, to compare it to.

"Speaking of home, what about Boston? Your work and life are there."

"I can write from anywhere. Boston is where I got my start and decided to stay. It was hard in the early years, being away from family. Then I kind of got used to it." Unfortunately, at Mom and Dad's expense, not returning home for visits more than he had.

"I'm sure you've got a lady friend there. Can't imagine you wouldn't."

Was that a comment or a concern? "Not a one my type. They were more interested in the social life and being seen with influential people. None of it felt real. Pretend lives wrapped in materialism. Now, can I ask you something? Is this interrogation session over?"

She nodded. "You're in luck. You'll be happy to know it's confession time. For me, that is."

"Confession?" The way she looked around with her eyes evading his piqued his curiosity. That and a sneaky smile.

"I finished reading one of your books last night."

"What did you think?"

"It was all right, I guess." Another tease of a smile followed.

"You guess just *all right*? Hold on a minute." He gently turned her face toward him by the chin. "Was that the first and only book of mine you've read?"

Her brow furrowed. "Well . . . that's the confession part."

"Unbelievable." He shook his head and smiled. "So in other words, the day you said you knew who I was, you really knew nothing about me. Imagine my shocked . . . shattered world. Chloe Morgan, dabbling in deceit. I don't believe it. Not possible."

She laughed, with a blush to follow. "Possible. And sorry."

He adored her laughs, giggles, and expressions. All of it. "No need to be sorry. It's refreshing to be seen for who I am and not for what I do."

"Guess I blew the chance to get my book signed, didn't I?"

"You could never blow your chances with me." If anyone would blow anything, it would be him.

"Uh . . . you ready to go back?"

Get ahold of yourself, Mason. "Yeah." He slid off the rock, extended his hand, and helped her down.

"So I see you and Tabby are getting along," Chloe said as they started their way back.

"Tabby?"

"The cat from church. That's what I call him. I think he likes you. And that's a compliment, seeing he doesn't want anyone around him."

"Well, I'm deeply touched, but I don't like cats. Never did. Especially that one. Something devious is going on in his twisted mind. I just know it."

"A little dramatic. don't you think?" Chloe laughed. "I think you two need to kiss and make up."

"Sorry. Not gonna happen." The only kissing on his mind, and possibly shouldn't be, was with the most attractive woman he'd ever met. The one walking beside him that sent warmth radiating through him.

"Changing the subject then," she said. "You seem to like that old cabin, don't you?"

"I do. And speaking of that, I was going to ask you something. Would it be okay if I came to the cabin sometimes to do a little work or writing? I understand if you'd prefer that I didn't."

"I don't see why not. I'll get you a key and let Mom know. I'm sure she won't mind. Of course, we'll have to do a background check on you. Could have a criminal record back in the city, for all I know. Multiple counts of breaking and entering women's hearts. Stuff like that." She nudged his shoulder.

A message pinged his phone upon arrival at the cabin. Blake with the latest news on the potential movie deal.

"Everything all right?"

"That was my agent."

Chloe took a seat with him on the step of the porch.

"There's a possibility of a production company making a movie series out of one of my books."

"Wow. That's great." She studied his expression. "Isn't it? You don't look all that enthused."

"No. Yeah, I mean. It's been my hope for a long time. Honestly never expected it to happen, with it being such a long shot. I'll be flying out to California Friday morning to discuss it further. It's a toss-up between a few writers as to who they sign with."

"That's in two days. How long will you be gone?" She picked at the nail polish on her finger and stared away in the distance.

"Not sure. Could be up to a week, I suppose." A week? Away from her? Another week of his stomach in knots for not telling her about his cancer?

"So I'll have no one to pick on for a week?" She bumped her shoulder against his, then wrapped her elbow around his.

"I'm sure you and Abby will get into enough trouble without me."

"Hey, whatever happens, I'm proud of you. Pray for direction and leave the rest to God, right? He knows what's best even when we don't."

Direction. Answers. Mason wished God would come right out and tell him what was best. Following his heart would lead him straight to Chloe. Without question and beyond doubt she was the one he'd give his all to. But given his condition, would there be anything left to offer? Maybe this was where another hope and dream for love should end. To not give heartache another chance or regret to find a resting place.

Chapter 8

Mason snatched Marty's rolling drip-bag stand with one hand before it hit the ground and steadied Marty with the other as he exited the restroom. "I've got you, don't worry." An unsettling ripple coursed through Mason at the sight of Marty's worsened condition. Mason had witnessed the languish and struggle of others since his initial visit, with the relentless assault of both cancer and chemo on their bodies. But until now, he'd not seen it to this extent with Marty.

"Just . . . just get me to my seat." Marty collapsed onto his chair. He grasped his forehead with one hand and stomach with the other. "I got it, Mace. Just give me a second."

To witness Marty's suffering sent a dismal wave of emotion through Mason. The glum atmosphere, with its teary-eyed patients, and his own perception of being an experiment weighed heavy. Suffocating. "Are you all right? What's going on?" Mason helped untangle the lines from two different drip bags and lifted the leg rest for Marty.

"What's going on is the inevitable, my friend. I've run my race, as you Christians put it, right?"

Already? Every sigh. Every word, doom. Not that Mason was

insensitive or didn't care. Or that he'd yet fully understood the difficult journey to recovery either. But how sad and wearing on the mind, not to mention detrimental to the faith, to have an outlook of no hope and all despair. And would he succumb to the same attitude after months and rounds of treatments? Mason hoped and prayed not. "You're just having a bad day. Don't talk like that."

"Talk like what? Say the truth? The truth, that's supposed to set me free? Well, it doesn't look like I'm free, does it? And what about the rest of these people sitting here? Sick and hurting. Those aren't tears of joy, my friend." Marty shook his head and swiped a tear as quickly as it appeared. "No. I'll only be free when my ride gets here and I leave this place. And I don't just mean leave this building, if you know what I mean."

Marty pulled his hand-crocheted cap of brilliant colors and elaborate trim onto his head, then took a swig of water. It was still hard to believe that no one came to sit with him for any of his treatments. No family. No friends. Mason dared not tread on those rough waters in asking Marty why. Why had he seemingly been abandoned by family? Forgotten? And what was the progression or circumstances that had led to this point?

God, please give me the words to say and a chance to influence Marty in a positive way. Or the strength and patience to endure this. "It's too soon to give up. God's not through with you yet."

"Oh. Right. Because he's got more suffering for me to go through? That's the only reason I can see."

Of course. A rebuttal for everything. What else was to be expected. He'd make an excellent lawyer. Or maybe he was one. Whatever the case, the debate class was in session. *Okay, Lord, just a reminder. I'm supposed to influence him. Not the other way around.* "How about I pray with you? Together, for both of us?"

"Nah. Save it for someone who deserves it. Prayers are kinda like a get-out-of-jail-free card, you know. Like Monopoly. You only use it when necessary. Don't blow it on lost causes."

Lost cause? What did he mean by that? No one was a lost cause in God's eyes.

"Ride's here." Brandy unhooked Marty and gave a sideways look to Mason.

He was certain she'd heard it all over the years.

Marty buttoned his shirt, stood, and grabbed his bag. "Getting here a little late today, aren't ya?"

"Had some bloodwork to do. Again." Mason took a seat, unwrapped the stretch bandage and cotton from the bloodwork, and dropped it into the wastebasket.

"Right. Well, this is our home away from home from here on out. For however long that is. We'll always know where to find each other. That's a given. Oh, and about that prayer stuff. If God hears us and answers prayer, then why did he let my wife die? And why doesn't he answer my prayer to let me go so I can be with her? He can do anything, can't he?"

"I . . . I don't—"

"Oh wait. That's right. He's working all things for my good. Well, that's the thanks I get for . . ." He held his words and swallowed hard.

"The thanks you get for what?" He waited for a clue. A possible explanation for Marty's cynicism.

"Doesn't matter. Not anymore." He pushed the straps of the backpack onto his shoulder. "You married, Mace? Girlfriend? Someone you care for?"

"Yeah, a good friend. But hoping there could be more." So much more if it were up to him.

"I see. How is she dealing with you going through all this? Cancer, the treatments and all?"

Was that a smidgen of concern he'd just heard slip pass Marty's lips? Maybe there was hope for him yet.

"Uh . . ." Mason glanced away. And there it was. The hard truth and the reason there'd possibly be no more to his relationship with Chloe, all due to his disclosing his condition from the start.

"Wait a minute. Wait just. a. minute. Isn't this grand?" A happy, almost gleeful smile grew. "You didn't tell her, did you?"

"Not yet." Mason hung his head. "Trying to find the right time. That's all."

"That's all? Hmm."

"What?"

"Nothing. Just interesting, that's all. You know. Our little conversation about truth a minute ago and how it sets you free. And now this?" He shook his head. "Oh what a tangled web we weave." He gave a nod and a tap to his head. "Think about it."

Marty walked out. Mason was left with two established facts. One, he'd now inherited the nickname Mace. And two, "Mace" evidently meant *liar* or *deceiver*. Two words he was certain were interchangeable in God's eyes.

There was also something about the way Marty had said "that's the thanks I get for . . ." and "Doesn't matter. Not anymore." Words that would normally have been laced with sarcasm or cynicism were replaced with hints of hurt or pain. Perhaps even regret.

And the Scripture he'd alluded to. The same verse that hung over Mom's archway to the kitchen about God working things out for our good. Marty appeared to know it well, along with his "truth . . . sets you free" mocking. Or rather than a mocking, a cry for help and for answers and understanding? Answers Mason was also searching for.

A reflection in the window caught Mason's attention. The shiny, protective suit Brandy had donned troubled him. She tore open a packet and pulled out a large syringe containing what could only be described as a bright-red glowing solution.

"What is that?" Concern flooded him.

Brandy's protective hood slid on, completing the head-to-foot medical garment. "This is to protect me from an accidental spill or splashing of the solution."

He was frozen in thought. "So you have to wear that for protection, but that stuff's going inside me?"

"It's one of the six meds for today." She administered the solution.

An experiment. How swiftly the words came. There was no other way to explain the thoughts that swirled through his mind. The bright-red solution solidified the seriousness of it all. Any denial of the severity had been put to rest.

Mason turned on his side to get comfortable. Or was it to hide the tears pooling in his eyes, and with certainty more to follow. *Sorry, Mom. Hate to admit it, but it looks like Marty could be right. Maybe everything isn't going to be all right and my best days are behind.*

Not only was the vial of meds nearly empty, but so was he emotionally. Empty of hope, faith, and the words to pray. *God help me to get through this. I've never needed your help more than now.*

He'd possibly have his answer as to how Chloe would respond to his news of cancer in five minutes, when he'd pull onto her street. That was, if he told her and didn't fear her answer as much as he did. But maybe that would have to wait until he returned from California. He'd need time to think about the right thing to say and the right way to say it without losing the love he'd dreamed, hoped, and prayed for his entire life. Without her he'd have nothing. No Chloe and no assurance of tomorrow as well.

For now, it was to say goodbye before his trip in the morning and to look into the eyes that soothed, warmed, and made his tumultuous thoughts calm. A place where the raging of the seas of doubts and fears ceased. Where the future, however doubtful and uncertain, was pushed aside. At least for that moment in time. With her and beside her.

"Mason. Haven't seen you all week." Chloe's mom's words broke into his thoughts as she stepped out her front door.

"Oh, hey. Chloe said she'd be here, but I don't see her car."

"She should be right back. Made a run to the store for me." She motioned to the porch swing. "Have a seat. I understand you're going out of town for a few days."

"Rather not, to tell you the truth. Hope it goes fast. I'm getting used to not ripping and running across the country so much. I could get used to this slower pace." And being with Chloe, of course.

"I'd imagine so. By the way, that was a real nice thing you did for her. About the pendant. It was a little miracle for her. She's had her eye on that since a child, and now it's come full circle back to her."

He nodded. "I'm glad she liked it."

"She also likes you being around." She gave a corner-of-the-eye look. "Of course, you didn't hear that from me."

"Right. Would you mind if I ask you something?"

"What is it, Mason?"

"I hope you don't mind me saying, but I can't help but notice that Chloe doesn't want to talk much about her dad. Pretty much avoids it."

"Yeah. That's Chloe. When her dad passed away, something inside her died as well. Been five years now, as I'm sure you know, and she still struggles with the loss. Of course, I do too. It's just that she hasn't been able to come to grips with it. Hasn't even been to the gravesite since the funeral. Can't bring herself to go." Chloe's mom spun her wedding ring and sighed.

"I'm sorry you both had to go through that loss."

"We all know he's not in that grave, and visiting it won't change anything. I only hoped by her going and facing it, that it would maybe help with closure in some way. She's always been one to run from pain. Even when she was little."

"I guess it's harder for some to face the tragic things in life." Mason wished he didn't have to face his. He'd rather be speaking out of ignorance and completely unable to relate. "I'd imagine it's easier to try to either ignore it or pretend it never happened."

He'd often considered his abandonment as a baby and questioned if that was what he'd done all his life. Pushed it aside and pretended it never happened. Never truly dealing with it and hoping the recurrent episodes of feeling unwanted and unloved would someday cease.

"You're right," Grace agreed. "But the problem with pushing it aside is, time doesn't slow down or stop, and there's no rewind. Then a funny thing happens as you get older. You realize there's only fast-forward. Years go by, but you're still in the same place. Hiding the pain, still hurting, and a little bit older. These kinds of things only God can heal."

Chloe pulled into the driveway.

Grace gave a pat to his knee and rose from the swing. "I'll let you two be. You have a safe trip."

"Yes, ma'am. Thanks."

Chloe handed a bag of groceries to her mom and took a seat next to Mason. "Here a little early, aren't you? Not that I mind."

"Just couldn't wait to see you, that's all. I'm gonna miss you. Every minute, hour, and day."

"I'll miss you to. Getting kind of used to you being around. Mom says so to. Somehow you've convinced her that you're a nice, sweet guy. Don't know how she fell for that so easy. She can usually see right through those kinds of people." She nudged him with an elbow.

"Go ahead. Have your little fun while you can." He grinned. "This time tomorrow you'll be eating those words."

"What is that supposed to mean?" She shot him a glare. "Is that a threat?"

"You'll see." He took her hand. "I want you to know how special you are to me. You're truly one of a kind. And I don't want you to think I go around telling other women that. You're the only one."

"There you go again. Exaggerations and lies. Expecting me to believe everything you say."

"I wouldn't lie or say anything that wasn't true." Or was withholding the truth of his condition the same as lying? Marty's earlier insinuations dropped in on his conscience. He could visualize Marty's smirk and tap to his head.

"So all my kidding isn't scaring you away?"

He shook his head. "Not a chance. It's what I liked about you to begin with." That, and so many other things. He could say it was also the way she walked, talked, or said his name the way she did. Which would calm his troubled heart . . . or send it racing with just a look. And if she wore a particular red dress and heels? But the truth was, all she needed to do was just be. It was enough.

Her hand slid into his, and their fingers intertwined. He inhaled the scent of her strawberry-flavored lip gloss with hopes that one day he'd taste it as well.

"You'll call me tomorrow to let me know you got there all right?" Her nod required a response of assurance.

"Of course."

Her eyes. Her voice. All said she truly cared. No jesting or poking. An expression he'd only seen when he'd informed her of his departure for California and in this very moment. "Can I call every hour? Every day?"

"Pushing your luck, huh? You're gonna have to sell a lot of books to pay for all those extra minutes on your phone, mister."

Back to classic Chloe, and loving every minute of it. "Fine with me. Whatever the cost."

"You just don't forget to call. Promise me."

"I promise." He lifted her hand and gave it a kiss. "I'll see you soon."

He hadn't even left for LA and was already missing her. In fact, even before he'd finished backing out of her driveway. The contributing factor as to why much of the fifteen-minute drive from Chloe's house resulted in being a blur all the way to the B&B.

He remained in the car to take a call from David, his best friend in Boston. After his wrestling match with his oh-so-optimistic, non-accusing friend Marty earlier in the day, Mason welcomed the kindness and understanding from a true friend. Especially one who was a doctor.

"So did you tell her yet?" David cut to the chase.

"Tell her?"

"Chloe. That's her name, right? The news about cancer. How'd she take it?"

Not again. First Marty and now David. A double portion of conviction. "Well . . . about—"

"You didn't tell her, did you?"

And here we go. You'd think David and Marty had spoken and decided to gang up on Mason. Or maybe God had intervened to set things straight. "Not yet. I tried, but never seemed to be the right time."

"You know this can't possibly go over good with her if she finds out before you tell her."

"I know. I'm so afraid to blow it. I've decided to tell her when I get back from LA. I don't know how she's going to handle this." His elbow rested on center console, and he rubbed his temple. Not another headache.

"You really care for this girl, don't you?"

"I do. She's the most amazing woman I've ever met."

"Then tell her and hope for the best, brother. Give me a call and let me know how it goes."

"Sure. Talk to you when I get back." David was right. Even Marty was right. At least about not withholding the truth.

He was only two steps into the entry of the B&B when Brad nabbed Mason's arm and pulled him into the sitting room.

"I'm glad you're back," Brad said with a hushed voice, followed by a peek into the hallway.

"Is everything all right?"

"Yeah. I mean no. I need some advice." He rubbed the palms of his hands together with enough speed and friction to start a fire.

"What kind of advice?"

"You know, romance. Stuff like that. It's our anniversary coming up, and I want to write something nice. I'm no good at that kind of stuff. So I thought, with you being the master and all, you could help me write something. Whatcha think?"

What Mason really thought was that he was the last person to be asking advice from, given his current lack of success and strategies of romance. "Well, it needs to come from your heart, not mine, but tell me what you want to say. Do you have something to write on?"

"Sure." Brad snagged a sheet of stationery and a pen from an end table and handed it to him.

"Okay. So you'd like to tell her what exactly?"

Brad's hands met together, as if to pray, and then rested on his lips. "I think I'd tell her how much I've loved her from the day we met. And how I've enjoyed every hour and every day of our life together. And that I couldn't possibly image life without her. Oh yeah, and she's the most beautiful woman in the world."

Mason finished writing and handed Brad the paper.

He looked it over. "Wait a minute. This is exactly what I told you."

"That's right. Straight from your heart. You write that in a card and watch her eyes water."

"You sure about this?"

Was his "master" endorsement only a minute prior now at risk of being revoked? "One hundred percent."

Brad patted him on the shoulder. "Thanks, man. You're the best."

"No problem. In fact, I can do better than that. Do you have a dollar?"

"Of course," Brad said with a puzzled look. "Hey, Mason. If you're hurting for money, I can do better than that. I know you're good for it."

"No. That's not it. Meet me at my room in a few minutes."

Five minutes later Brad gave a light tap and slipped into Mason's partially opened door.

"You got the dollar?" Mason held out his hand.

"Yeah."

Mason took it, then handed him a book.

"What's this?"

"An advance copy of my latest novel. Nobody has one yet. This is the first. I signed it to Charlotte, with a message. You give it to her with your note in a card, and I know she'll be happy."

"Wow. Thanks. But what was the dollar for?"

"That's to show you bought it for her. If I gave it to you, it would be like the book was from me to her, right?"

Brad smiled and nodded. "That's why you're the master." He gave a man-hug, then let himself out.

Mason collapsed onto the bed. "If only my problems were that simple to solve."

Chapter 9

Chloe read Abby's text message. Twelve o'clock sharp. Don't be late. She slid the phone into her purse. Suspicion was written all over the text. But whatever Abby was up to would have to be quick. Kristen would be waiting on Chloe at the treatment center. She'd make good on her promise to be there.

And there they were. Mom, Sarah, Abby, and Holly. All sitting at a large round table in Abby's shop. All staring at her with smirks. Evidently, all guilty of . . . kindness and caring as "happy birthday" rang out, followed by cake and ice cream.

I would have never come if I knew this," Chloe said in a loving-scolding way.

"That's exactly why we didn't tell you." Abby scooped up a spoonful of double-fudge ice cream. "And there's one more surprise that arrived for you a while ago."

Sarah ran behind the pastry counter and reappeared. She placed a vase with two dozen red roses on the table in front of Chloe. "Gee. I wonder where these could have come from."

Mom smiled. "Maybe from someone who thought your red dress looked just 'okay' on you?"

Holly joined in. "Could be from the guy in a Range Rover that cruises through the parking lot every day lately, like he's looking for something. Or . . . somebody." She waved her cake-adorned fork in the air before popping the bite into her mouth.

Roses. The last time Chloe had been given roses was for her high school graduation, from Mom and Dad, with one dried-out rose remaining in her keepsake box as a memento. "Guys, ya'll shouldn't have. They're beautiful." She inhaled the fragrance.

"We didn't get them." Sarah took a card from the bouquet and held it out to Chloe.

She opened it, with a rallying cry to read it aloud.

"Think not of yourself as a thief,

For stealing my fragile, yearning heart.

There's but one thing, and one thing alone I ask.

Take all of me, not merely a part.

 Happy birthday, Chloe. Wish I were there. Mason."

Sarah put her arm around her. "Wow. Writer and poet, huh? That terrible, horrible man. You know, I've been thinking. I believe he's all so wrong for you. I'll be glad to take him off your hands if you'd like. Anything to release my baby sis from that burden."

"Excuse me. Get your own man. Or have you forgotten you already have one?"

"Sorry." Sarah inhaled the bouquet with closed eyes. "Got kind of lost in the moment, that's all."

Chloe raised her brows. "Yeah. My moment." Possibly the moment she'd waited for her entire life. The chance to loosen the stronghold surrounding her heart and concede that Mason Chadwick checked off all the boxes on her list. She repented for not trusting God's timing and for failing to remind herself that God works all things out for good to those who love him.

"In all seriousness, sis, I think Abby and I had it all wrong. All that teasing we do about you picking Mason. If you ask me, I'd say he had you picked out from day one. You were on his radar from the beginning. He's a really sweet guy."

"He is." Chloe took another whiff of her roses. The only thing that could have made the surprise any more special would have been for Mason to be there instead of two thousand miles away. She picked up the card and read it again. Abby placed an arm around her.

"Well, this day is starting out full of surprises." Abby twirled her hair around a finger and looked from the corner of her eyes. "Sooo . . . you and Mason huh?"

"Yeah. He's wonderful, thoughtful, terrific, and all that a girl could ask for. But . . ."

"But?" Abby took the card from her hand and set it by the roses. "All right, talk to me. You do realize that no one's asking you to run off and get married tomorrow. What are you afraid of?"

"Over thirty years of saved-up kisses. That's what I'm afraid of." She took a rose from the arrangement and spun it slowly by the stem.

"But you know he's 'the one,' right?"

"I think so. I know it's all me, being afraid. I'm thinking of telling him how I feel when he gets back from LA." Which was why her stomach had been in knots ever since he'd kissed her hand before leaving on his trip. The reason why she'd binge-watched sweet romance movies most of the night, episode after episode. And the justification for more cherry-vanilla ice cream floats and licorice. At that pace, her red-dress-wearing days would be over.

Abby sat back in her chair with folded arms. "Yeah, well, you better tell him before Tina does."

"Or his thousands of followers," Holly chimed.

"Not helping. Neither one of you. And you had to ruin the day by mentioning Tina?" She'd give anything to not hear that name ever again. How often she'd prayed over the years to have that thorn in her flesh removed.

Abby shook her head. "Don't worry. She doesn't have a chance. And in case you haven't noticed, not even Angel at church can catch his attention, with her strategizing and accessorizing. That tight, high-slit skirt and low-cut blouse can't even help her. That man only has eyes for you. But it sure would be nice if he had a twin brother." She drew a deep, audible breath with her eyes closed, then exhaled. "Sorry. I'm back. Now, where were we?"

"First Sarah, now you. Am I gonna have to keep my eye on the both of you?"

"Up to another latte? On me?"

"Bribery and trying to change the subject, huh?"

"Of course."

"No latte for me," Holly said. "I've got a customer at the shop." She headed through the adjoining door to her shop, which she'd left open.

It was undeniable that she felt closer than ever to Mason, and she resolved to possibly commit to sharing her feelings for him when he returned. But the fact remained, how little she really knew about him. What happened when he went back to Boston? He couldn't expect her to up and move practically across the country, if by chance things turned serious. Her family, life, work, and friends were all here.

Besides, how would a small-town girl fare in a big city, knowing no one? It was his world, not hers. If she were there, would it be as though she were hiding in the shadows of the forged-out life, friends, and popularity he'd grown accustomed to? And speaking of hiding, why was Holly lurking behind a rack of books, peering at a customer?

Chloe excused herself from the girls and tiptoed through the door to Holly's bookstore for an answer to her suspicious behavior. She sneaked up behind Holly and tapped her shoulder.

Holly flinched and put a hand to her chest, followed by a finger to her lips. "Shh. He's on aisle five. How do I look?" A quick check with her camera phone followed, then she placed it back in her pocket.

"You look fine. Who's on aisle five, and why are you hiding?"

"The new guy. He's been coming in here close to every day for two weeks. Even came to the last club meeting. Doesn't say much though. Could barely get him to say his name." She gave a brisk run of her fingers through her hair.

"So is there a problem?"

"No. Not at all. He's a sweet guy and all, but we're so total opposites, with him being an introvert, it seems, and me—well, you know, slightly perky."

"Yeah. Slightly." More like over the top. Possibly exceeding industry standards for perkiness. "Does this sweet guy have a name?" Chloe had never seen Holly act that way before over a guy.

"Wesley. I think m-maybe he likes me," she stammered, leaving little room to breathe. "He asked me to call him Wes. Of course, I'd call him whatever he wants me to. But that's beside the point. I mean, how do you know when you meet the right guy? What do you look for?"

Chloe took her by both shoulders. "Okay, slow down. I get the impression you like him, and maybe he likes you. Isn't that a good thing?"

"No. Not a good thing. He's the competition. I found out that it's his family who opened the new bookstore in town. He's the enemy."

"Okay, but even enemies sometimes become friends. And as for what to look for in a guy, I'd say kindness and thoughtfulness would be at the top of my list. And—"

"You mean, like Mason? The way he treats you?" Holly smirked.

"Well, yeah. Kind of like that." No. It was exactly like that. It exemplified the way Mason was, and nothing since their meeting indicated anything other than kind, gentle, and thoughtful. "Another biggie in my book would be that he possess godly morals and values."

Holly folded her arms and nodded. "Again, like Mason, huh? So that would make it easy to decide what to do next, right?"

Wait a minute. Who was the one supposed to be giving wise counsel here? Holly might not have a psychology degree, but it wasn't a far stretch to believe that she'd read more than a few self-help or psychology-related books over the years. She evidently knew how to effectively apply what she'd learned as well. Case study in point—Chloe.

"Hold on. We're talking about you right now."

"Are we really?" A curious look and a pause followed. "Ooh. Gotta go. He's going to the counter to purchase a book." She straightened her shirt and name tag.

"I think he's coming here to check you out," Chloe said with a giggle.

"Uh, do I look like I really care?" Holly took her dark-rimmed glasses off and hooked them onto her shirt collar, followed by a quick pass of lip gloss.

"Looks like you care to me."

Holly bumped into the corner of the bookshelf with her shoulder when she stepped out.

"I think you might want to put those glasses back on." Chloe removed the glasses from Holly's shirt and handed them to her.

"Yeah. Thanks. You're probably right."

But Chloe wasn't the only one who was right. So was Holly, with her bookstore, in-house reverse-psychology degree. If Mason checked all the boxes, then what was the cloud of uncertainty hovering above? Regardless of the questions and reasoning, faith would have to arise and overtake her fear.

~

Chloe's hand froze on the handle of the door to the treatment center. It was the last place she wanted to be. Despite the queasiness in her stomach, she resolved to not disappoint Kristen. She needed a friend now more than ever. After three years of battling cancer, her condition was none the better. In fact, barring a miracle, there seemed to be no hope.

The treatment had already begun as Chloe took a seat next to her friend, reading Bible verses at Kristen's request. A part of her felt hypocritical, offering hope when she lacked the faith to believe it herself. Too many memories were there, and none of them good. First with Dad, and now her friend since high school. She couldn't help but wonder why God would put her in this position not once but twice. For what purpose? What could be learned from all this other than to experience pain and sorrow?

Brandy checked on Kristen and greeted Chloe. She'd known Brandy since her dad's treatments.

"Hey, Chloe. How are you and Grace and Sarah doing?" Brandy handed a bottle of water to Kristen.

"We're okay. Mom helps a little with the pottery and church duties. Just enough to keep her mind off things and from being bored."

"She didn't look all that bored when I saw her at the diner with Pastor Hank." Brandy's grin widened.

Chloe sat up straight. "Mom with Pastor Hank? When was this?"

"Last month, about. And she looked pretty happy to me."

"Wow. That's a shocker. I had no idea. I mean, I'm sure they're just friends. They've known each other for some time now."

Kristen forced a smile and patted Chloe's arm. "Looks to me like she's not the only one with a man interest. Saw you going into The Palace restaurant with someone last week as I drove past. Red dress, huh? Must be serious."

Chloe scrunched her brows. "I had no idea red signified 'seriously involved' in a relationship, Kristen. Someone should have clued me in on that detail," Chloe teased. "But I think maybe I am ready to give us a chance. He's more than I could have asked for, to tell you the truth. Like God knew what I needed."

"Got any pictures of the lucky guy?" Kristen's voice struggled for strength, her eyes tired and red. "All I saw was the back of him. What's his name?"

"Mason." Chloe scrolled the pics on her phone while Brandy took Kristen's blood pressure. "We took this one at the restaurant." She handed the phone to Kristen.

Kristen stared at the picture, then Chloe, and the picture again. "Chloe how . . ." Her expressionless gaze fell on Chloe.

"What? What's that look?"

"This is . . ." She turned to Brandy, in the process of removing the pressure cuff. "This is Mason, right?"

Brandy leaned over to see the photo. Another curious look at Chloe. "Ya'll have to excuse me. I . . . I need to check on someone. Be right back."

What were those looks? "Kristen, what's going on? How do you know Mason? I didn't think he knew very many people here yet. He's new here, from Boston."

"Yeah. That's him. Mason Chadwick, the writer. Met him doing chemo here once."

She leaned forward in her chair. Something wasn't making sense. Couldn't be the same Mason. Not the one she knew and was falling for. "You mean while *you* were having treatments, right?"

Her hesitation to answer troubled Chloe.

"Both of us were getting treatments."

Chloe bolted to her feet and held out both palms to Kristen. "No. Wait. There's some kind of mistake here. Cancer? Mason? My Mason has cancer?"

"Chloe. You don't know? I assumed with you two being together he'd have—"

"No. I wasn't aware. He . . ." Her breathing stuttered, as if oxygen were being sucked out of the room. "He never told me." The blood fled from her face, leaving her lightheaded, and she slumped onto her seat. *No. None of this is real or happening. It can't be.*

"I'm sorry, Chloe. I feel terrible. I shouldn't have—"

"No, Kristen. You didn't know." She covered her face with both hands, and her heart raced. "Oh God, what's happening here?" Her hands trembled. A tear slid down in defiance of her will to suppress it, and her chest tightened, squeezing out what little oxygen remained.

"Why? Why didn't he tell me? He's had all this time. Why? Why would he lead me on like that, telling me how much he cares for me and making me care for him. Only to find out . . . this?"

"I don't know why either, but one thing's for certain. He's going to need you. And you're gonna have to be strong because . . ." Kristen shook her head.

"What? There's more?" She couldn't handle more. Didn't want to. Not able to. First Dad. Now Mason?

"I'm so sorry, Chloe, but it's not good. I overheard one of the nurses mention stage four."

Chloe rose from the chair again and faced the window with a hand pressed over her mouth. She'd gone from the mountaintop to the lowest of valleys within the hour. If it was all a dream, she prayed to God she'd awaken. Then she'd be able to validate her reasons for guarding her heart like a fortress, as well as justifying her reasons for not allowing anyone in.

Kristen's ride arrived, releasing Chloe to leave. She entered the hallway and leaned against the nearest wall to gather her thoughts before driving home. How could something that seemed so right quickly become so wrong? And now all this just after she'd decided to tell him how she felt about him. Perhaps even commit to saying she loved him. Yesterday, she was certain he was the one. Today, the only thing certain was her shattered heart.

The walk down the hall never seemed so long, with the doors open to several rooms. Loved ones visiting patients offering encouragement, simultaneous with marked despair. Then came a shrill from a nearby room. Family members grieving the loss of a loved one who had passed away. Chloe gasped and searched for oxygen to fill her surging lungs. Her walk became a jog, unable to get out soon enough.

Once in the car, the swell of tears and emotion could no longer be contained. The dam burst, followed by mourning she hadn't experienced since her dad had passed. It was something she'd prayed she'd never have go through again. But here it was. "God, help me get through this." The words barely made it out with a whisper. "I don't know if I can do this again. I just don't know if I can."

Chloe wiped the trail of mascara from her face. She'd have to talk with him when he returned. There was no avoiding it. Whatever reason he had for not telling her about it no longer mattered. The fact was, he might be dying. There was no use going any further in their relationship, no matter her deepening feelings for him.

Sure, he was everything she could have asked for in a man. Perhaps even the one she could see spending the rest of her life with. With him she felt loved, safe, and that she could be herself in every way. But had she known the day Mason strolled into town at the church fair that it would wind up like this, she'd have run. Pushed away from their entangled embrace, with his arms wrapped around her, which had initially sent her heart racing.

No. If her heart was already breaking, she could only imagine it shattered into a million pieces if it ended up like Dad. To remain friends, but no more, was the right thing. He'd do what she now presumed he'd come to Fleetwood Falls for—to get well. That was the priority and all that mattered now.

As far as their growing relationship was concerned, him falling for a small-town girl couldn't possibly have been on his calendar anyway. It just happened. And she certainly never expected a guy to come into town and steal her heart. But that was exactly what had happened. Why else would it hurt so much? Why else would it feel like her life and entire world had fallen apart? Again.

Chapter 10

The scent of cinnamon-cider potpourri double downed on her already tangled insides. She prevented her mind from racing off when a customer took a seat at a nearby table, pulled out a bag of potpourri, and took a whiff. She'd sworn to never mentally visit that place in time again if at all possible. That, combined with her recent discovery of Mason's condition, pummeled her insides.

"Hey. Are you all right?" Abby set a cup of hot coco and an apple fritter in front of Chloe, then took a seat on the stool beside her.

"Guess I'll have to be." But no amount of hot coco could fix this. For most things, maybe. But not this. Any given day an apple fritter would have never made it past a few minutes. That, combined with Abby's natural ability to cheer her up, would have resulted in at least a partial smile. This morning would be the exception.

Chloe slid the fritter aside. "I don't understand why he didn't or couldn't tell me. We opened up to things with each other. I was beginning to think we could talk about anything. Maybe we weren't as close as I thought."

"No," Abby said. "It's only my opinion, but I believe the reason he didn't say anything was because he does, in fact, care deeply for you.

Look—guys don't always think the way girls do. We may not understand it, but that's the way it is. Give him a chance to explain. You owe him that much." Abby yanked a napkin from the counter dispenser and wiped the eyeliner smudge from the corner of Chloe's cheek. The smudge she was aware was there. But what was the use? There'd soon be another to replace it.

"He sent a text when he landed last night. Wanted me to know he was all right and driving home. Said he wanted to talk to me about something today. Maybe this was what he wanted to talk to me about. I don't know. Maybe he tried or wanted to tell me." Her stomach quivered, thinking about the upcoming conversation. "I don't know what I'm gonna say. What I'm gonna do." She pushed the coco next to the fritter and laid her head into her folded arms on the counter.

"Hey, take a breath, and remember, God's your peace in the middle of the storm. You hold on to him. And know that I'm praying for you two, and for a miracle you'll get to keep your land and cabin."

"About that. I stopped in at the county office before coming here." She shook her head. "It's not gonna happen. Nothing I can do or say about it anymore. I sent numerous emails over the weeks and even went all the way to the top and spoke to Mr. Stone today. If anyone could have helped, it would have been him. He said their plans for the property were almost finalized."

"Wow. Sorry." Abby jumped off the stool and made her way around the counter to her register. "I thought maybe there was at least a chance."

"It's just the way it is. And Tina's just the way she is and will always be."

"Tina? What's she got to do with anything?"

"Ran into her coming out the courthouse. She wanted to give her condolences for us having to turn the land back over to the county. Of course, she looked so sincere and concerned." Chloe rolled her eyes and shook her head. "Thankfully, a gust of wind came along and blew her straw hat across the parking lot, sending her chasing after it. I couldn't take a minute more of her fake self."

"How does she know anything about the land?" Abby slid the cup of hot cocoa with marshmallows back to her.

"You know Tina. Connections everywhere." Connections infected with contention, manipulation, and self-seeking motives.

"That's her all right. But hey, don't give up all hope. Remember what the pastor says. Don't think of your world as falling apart. Think of it as falling into place."

"That might be easy for him to say." Chloe sipped her cocoa.

"Yeah, I know. Seemed like the right thing to say. You know I'm not used to all this serious stuff." Abby slid Chloe's half-bitten apple fritter back to her.

"You think pastries are the answer to everything, don't you?"

"No, not everything. Just most things."

Chloe forced a smile and looked down at the fritter. "You got a truckload of these?"

Chloe slid off the stool and wandered to the bookshelves at Holly's place. Something, anything to get her mind off her discouragement. Even if only for a moment. Six—no, eight books written by Mason. She suspected he'd written even more. The cover of one held an uncanny resemblance to her family's cabin and its gazebo beside a stream. He did mention his fondest memories were from there. Could be that was where the inspiration for the picture came from.

"Hey, Chloe." Holly hugged Chloe's neck. "Abby told me about Mason. I'm so sorry. I'm still in shock. I know you must be."

"Thanks, Holly. I'm just glad to have friends like you. If you don't mind, I'm gonna just go read in the corner."

"Of course. Let me know if you need anything."

She cradled a few of Mason's novels in her arms and retired to a sofa chair snuggled in the corner of the reading area. The same corner where she'd sat on her dad's lap many years ago, when Holly's parents ran the shop. A cherished spot where Dad had taken the time to read stories to her and Sarah.

Time. Dad always took the time to create memories. Only after growing up did she realize that it wasn't so much the fact that he *had* time but that he *made* time for the things and people that mattered most. But now for Chloe, the things and people that mattered most were slipping away.

Confusion. Heartbreak. Sadness. She couldn't pick one over the other. Feelings, emotions she'd thought were drifting away little by little since Dad's passing. But now with Mason, all of it had returned with a vengeance. Her initial fear of falling for him when they'd met was that he'd head back home to Boston, leaving her heartbroken. But she'd chosen to take a chance with opening her heart and now felt foolish thinking that maybe he was initially hanging around town because of her.

And as for Mason, it was worse for him than her wounded heart and spirit. He didn't choose cancer but did have a chance to tell her and didn't. It wasn't fair. Neither was it right. But it would be selfish to think only of her pain, no matter how much it hurt.

She turned to the dedication page of Mason's book and wiped away the track of a tear that had fallen onto the page. Maybe it would shed light on what he was thinking, or possibly who he was thinking of, in the process of writing. Not that it mattered anymore. Not that it would ease her pain. Nothing could.

The fragments of her memory I dare not release,
Though the assault of time would try.
She is my all in all—my everything.
My all-encompassing reason why.

His all in all? His everything? She set the book down and pulled a napkin from her purse. She never should have opened the book. No. Never took it from the shelf. Never sat down in her special corner nook where she harbored all her special memories with Dad. All happy memories. Each one of them. But now this?

She exhaled a breath of refusal. Refusal to break down at the very thought of Mason and all the time they'd spent together. Refusal to realize what she thought was meant to be was no more. But even still, refusal mocked her, and she knew the stray cat would soon be scratching at the door, coming back time and time again.

Then again, maybe it was for the best. She should know . . . needed to know that there was someone special in his life, if she was still around perhaps. Someone he loved dearly. At least in his memory. How could she possibly compete with that? With . . . *her*. To take a backseat to another, never knowing if he'd be harboring feelings for the other woman. Being compared to her. No. Maybe it was all for the best that she'd found out now. Just another lesson learned for not guarding her foolish heart.

Mason's teeth brushing came to a halt upon noting hair strands in the sink. A light brush of the hand on his head sent more falling. It was going to happen at some point, but so soon was a shock. Thankfully, he was back in Fleetwood. A return to his pillow revealed it covered with more shards of hair. It would all have to be shaved off. No more withholding the truth from Chloe. She would know soon.

He sat on the edge of his bed, attempting to resist weeping, but to no avail. Conceivably, it was chemo brain, or so some called it. At least that was what he'd read on his return flight, in a book on chemo, which explained there could be occasional outbursts of emotions and lack of concentration.

Another chapter in the book described the reactions of friends and family when discovering someone they knew had cancer. Some would withdraw and not contact the person simply because they didn't know what to say, often leaving the one suffering feeling even more lonely and isolated.

The breakfast table was already set as Mason made his way down the stairs and into the dining room.

"Good morning, Mason." Charlotte set a pan of steaming rolls in the middle of the table. "Hope you're hungry. You're the last to eat, and we have all this left." Her hand motioned to the expansive variety of food.

"I am starving. Delays, and late getting in. Haven't eaten since yesterday afternoon for the layover in Dallas."

As he plated his food, he noticed her eyeing the newsboy cap he was wearing.

"Mason, may I sit for a chat?" She'd already slid her chair out.

"Of course. Is everything okay?"

"About our conversation over the phone before you arrived to stay here. I'm so sorry about your condition. I know it must be devastating. But I want you to know that Brad and I will do whatever it takes to make your stay comfortable. Whatever it is, please don't hesitate to ask."

"Thanks. I do appreciate everything." He removed his hat. "Woke up to most of my hair falling out, so I shaved off the rest. Don't have to worry about washing or brushing my hair anymore, right?" He forced a laugh, then withdrew to the darkened reality of his new norm.

Her hand cupped his, and her eyes revealed the tenderness and sincerity of his own mom. "If it's any comfort, please know that we're praying for you. You're family here, so if you ever need to talk . . ."

"Thanks. That means a lot to me. By the way, I wanted to mention that I've had the pleasure of meeting the talented pottery artist who created those pieces in the foyer." The same talented artist who'd molded and painted a picture in his heart of what he'd prayed for most of his life. A picture of what could be. A final resting place where he would find his heart a home. A place he'd found with Chloe.

She gave a curious look. "You know Chloe Morgan?"

"Yes. But only since getting into town. We met at the church fair, then I began doing a little volunteer work at the church. So I guess you can say we've been hanging out a little."

"She's a wonderful girl. I've known the Morgan family for some time. In fact, my family spent time at their campground way back when I was young. Can't for the life of me figure out how some man hasn't yet swept that girl her off her feet. She really is special." An inquisitive glance followed.

"Yes, she is." The very thought of her was as fresh as the mountain breeze seeping through the open kitchen window.

"I can still remember when she was about seven or eight. Her dad rescued a baby dove that had fallen out the tree at the campground. Chloe fed it every day for a week. Of course, she was brokenhearted when it got strong enough to fly away. So her mom bought her a little stuffed dove. She carried it around everywhere. Till that got lost somehow. The result being, she never wanted another bird, or anything else, to get close to, to have it fly away and break her heart." She looked toward the window with eyes that held a puzzled look. "I honestly don't know how or why that came into my mind. Anyway, I'll let you eat."

"Thanks, Charlotte. I'm glad you shared that with me."

"We'll, I've got some cleaning to do. Oh, and thank you for the book. Couldn't put it down. I'm looking forward to your next one. Again, let me know if you need anything."

Anything? A new lease on life would do. Or the immediacy of the moment would be courage to face and confess to Chloe what he should have done from the start. That, followed by an apology that he'd not blame her for not accepting.

He couldn't help but think that maybe the breeze seeping inside were really the trade winds of change. How could he expect anything to remain the same between them once all was revealed. Guilty. Guilty for withholding the truth and not protecting her delicate heart. For not putting her feelings above his fears. Fears of missing out on a love he'd hoped and prayed his whole life for, and fears of continuing life in an endless search, resulting only in disappointment. And he couldn't . . . shouldn't expect her forgiveness, when it didn't seem possible to forgive himself.

Mason stepped onto the front porch of the B&B. The scent of night jasmines climbing one of the columns constrained him. Not because its powerful scent greeted him each day, but rather its lack thereof. Loss of hair. Changes in smell and taste. The results of chemo. The winds of change.

"Where you off to, Mason?" Tom called out, rocking in a chair at the far side of the porch. "Looks like it's gonna be a good day to just sit, enjoy this nice breeze, and think."

Why was Tom here? The old wooden chair crackled as Mason took a seat next to him. "I'm all out of thinking." Yep. That was what had gotten him in the mess he was in with Chloe to begin with. "Too much thinking and not enough doing what I should have done."

"Hmm. I see." Tom gave a casual nod. "Wouldn't have anything to do with that Morgan girl, would it?"

"Is it that obvious?" Of course it was. Especially to Tom and his mysterious prophet-like insights, which Mason suspected came with closeness to God and years of accumulated wisdom. "And why are you here anyway, if you don't mind me asking?"

"Oh, I come for breakfast or lunch once a week. Good food. Beautiful setting. Oddly enough, today's not a usual day I'd come. No. Just was compelled to be here for some reason."

As usual for Tom. Always being where he felt he was supposed to be. Was it a goal? A calling? A divine assignment? "Been sitting out here long this morning?"

Tom nodded. "Long enough to hear your and Charlotte's discussion through that open window. Sorry about that. Didn't mean to listen in."

Mason removed his hat. Frankly, it was a relief to know that a praying man was now aware of his condition. Not to mention having someone to talk to freely instead of suppressing and hiding what should have been known by the praying community.

"Yeah. I should have opened up about it from the start. Didn't really make sense keeping it from the church. Or Chloe. Who doesn't need others praying for their needs?"

"Chloe doesn't know then?"

He rubbed his shaven head for warmth and tugged his hat back on.

"She will by the end of the day. That's why I hadn't told anyone yet. I was trying to find the right way . . . the right time to tell her before she heard it from someone else."

Tom nodded. "Guess I can see your dilemma. But that's where trust comes in. Don't you think? Trust in her. Trust that if something is meant to be, then it will be."

"Trust in what? That Chloe won't be affected by the news? That I'd even remotely have a chance with her when she finds out? I don't want to lose her."

"What about trusting in a God who knows where you've been, where you're at now, and where you're headed to? When you come to an understanding of that, then you can already see the Father waiting for you at the finish line. He's the one that walks before you and prepares the way. No one removes the pen from his hand for the promises he's written concerning his children. No one. Rest in that Mason. Rest."

Tom pointed to the chess game on the small table between them. "You play chess much?"

"Can't remember the last time. Single and alone, remember?" Alone. The word hung in his throat as though a precursor of things to come.

"Guess I can relate. Alone in life with our thoughts and only God to hear us. I get it." Tom pointed across the meticulously landscaped lawn and pointed out a young couple sitting on a picnic blanket. "At least they're not alone."

"Yeah. Hopefully, they'll have a happily-ever-after storybook ending." All his books had them. Pages of the ups and downs of life. From triumph to tragedy. All culminating in an ending that brought everything together in the final pages, wrapped nicely with a bow. At least in that moment, the reader could escape the realities of a broken world. A chance at the what-if moment—what if that could really happen for me? To me?

Tom pulled out his pocket watch, on a chain attached to his belt loop, flipped open the cover, then closed it. "Interesting you'd say that. Kind of like life, don't you think? It plays out like a story, like one of those novels like you write. Without even realizing or thinking about it, we're all writing a story of our lives each day. The way we live. The decisions we make. They all add a page to the story with each passing day."

Mason slid a chess piece across the board to nowhere in particular. "The exception being, in a book we choose the ending. Real life doesn't always give us that option, does it? Some things we can control. Others we can't. Then it's checkmate."

"True. So true." Tom took his Stetson hat from the porch deck beside him and pushed himself up from the rocker. "But most can accept or learn to live with the things out of their control, I reckon. For me, it's the one thing I could have controlled but didn't. That's a twist in the story that's hard to live with. Well, I'll see you around Mason. Maybe we'll finish our game another day. And of course, I'll be praying for you."

"Thanks." Mason stood as Tom made his way down the porch steps. There was no denying the solemnness in his friend's voice. But what did he mean by not controlling something he could have? "Hey, Tom. Hope you don't mind me asking. About your story. Is there any chance for a happy ending? Any at all?"

Tom stopped and dusted the rim of his hat with a brush of his hand, then dipped his head and carefully placed the hat on his head. "For me, only when I get to the other side. Not till then."

"And for me? My story doesn't look all that promising, does it?"

"It all boils down to a page a day, right? Just make each page count. Day by day to the best of your ability. That choice is yours."

"And what if I fail? What if my days are numbered?"

"Everyone's days are numbered. No one's guaranteed tomorrow. But there's one thing we can be certain of." Toms countenance brightened with assurance. "He'll still be waiting for you at the finish line with arms wide open. Finish strong and with no regrets. Remember, truth conquers the lie, and light overtakes darkness. And the beginning of that new chapter of the story begins today."

Chapters. How many he'd carefully crafted over the years. Fine-tuning and manipulating each word with absolute intent and control in an attempt to convey clarity to the reader. But in his real-life chapter now, there'd be no manipulating or withholding of truth. As well as no control. Only acceptance of Chloe's response. As for clarity concerning the outcome, there was none. As though a fog bank had rolled in, obscuring the radiant beam of even the grandest lighthouse. Only faith remained. However much or little.

Chapter 11

Mason had crossed the mile-high swing bridge of Grandfather Mountain just outside Boone many times as a teen. But always with either friends or family. This day would be different. Same views, only a different day, with an unfamiliar perspective, and alone.

He snapped a picture with his 35 mm camera he hadn't used in years, with the incorrect setting making for a blurred photo. The view hadn't changed over the decades, but the lens wasn't focused correctly. Which was pretty much the way he'd viewed the world since his diagnosis. How distorted and different things were when viewed through his broken, fogged-up, and out-of-focus emotional lens. A world viewed from lens of hurt, pain, loss, and regret, which was now attempting to render him unable to see the expanse of beauty before him.

Options and choices. He'd always had them in his life. Some good. Others not so good. But it was clear when standing midway on the bridge that there was only one choice now. Of course, there was no going down or up from that point. Even moving ahead onto the other side would be a dead end. There was only going back. Back the way he'd come. Turn around and head back to Chloe to make things right and lay his cards on the table. No more putting it off. The time was now.

The pounding of Mason's heart drowned out his knocking on Chloe's shop door. There'd be no more excuses. It was past time to bring what was in darkness into the light. He shut his eyes and prayed. *Lord, help me. Then again, not me.* This was about Chloe, not himself. It was about how she'd be affected and how her life could be turned upside down. He'd invaded her life and unintentionally led her on. She didn't deserve any of this.

Chloe opened the door. "Hey. Come in." She removed an empty packing box and roll of bubble wrap from the couch, tossing it aside. "So how was the trip?"

Palatable tension hung in the air with her avoidance of prolonged eye contact. Uh-oh. "Good, but wish I could have gotten back sooner." He stuffed his hands into his pockets, then pulled them back out again, followed by a press down on his cap. He was certain she'd noticed the lack of sideburns. Maybe even his thinning brows.

"You want to sit?" She motioned with her hand toward the couch and took a seat, curling her legs under her.

"Sure." He took a seat next to her in hopes of capturing a whiff of her favorite perfume, but there was only the faintest scent. He inched closer for a touch of his shoulder on hers. His trip away from her was harder than he'd expected it to be. He'd missed everything about being with her. "Is everything all right? You look a little tired." That combined with something not right. Not like Chloe at all.

"Just a little. Had to get out some back orders today. Been falling behind, with the kiln still acting up." She brushed a spot of dry clay from her pants.

"Yeah, I remember you telling me about that." He adjusted his newsboy cap she'd been eyeing since his arrival. Her project remained covered with a sheet in the corner of the shop, just as it had been for his pottery lesson. "Been working on your secret project lately?"

"Not really." She stared down at her hands in her lap.

"Not feeling all that inspired?"

"It's not that. Sometimes you start things and don't finish. Or maybe shouldn't have started to begin with." Her eyes seldom held to his for more than a second, and she pulled strands of threads unraveling at the hem of her jeans. "So is it good news? About the movie deal?"

"It's a toss-up. They'll let me know when it's decided." He rubbed the back of his neck. *Just say it.* "Chloe—"

"Nice cap. One of the first things I noticed about you when we met at the church fair. I don't see too many people wearing that kind. So your text said you wanted to talk to me about something?"

He looked down and swallowed hard from his dry throat. It was the moment he'd been dreading. "About that. I have something to tell you. I've been trying, but it never seemed to be the right time. Chloe, I have . . ." The words failed to come. He hung his head and looked away. His eyes misted over. *Hold it together, Mason.*

"I know, Mason." This time her eyes held to his. "I know."

"Know what?"

"I know about the cancer." Her voice shook.

"How?" So she'd known all along this morning. It was the reason she'd been acting out of sorts and why she'd possibly not responded to several of his texts or his calls. "When did you find out?"

"When I visited my friend Kristen at the hospital. She saw us going into The Palace together and assumed I knew about your condition. That's when it accidently came out. I didn't want to believe it. And of course, Brandy couldn't tell me and avoided it when I asked if it was true."

"Chloe, I'm sorry I didn't tell you sooner. Please believe me. I wanted to but didn't want to ruin everything. You know . . . with us. I was going to tell you on our ride back from the cabin when we picked up the desk, but then you mentioned your dad, and I didn't want to make you feel worse. Then when I had the chance to tell you again, I didn't have the heart or courage to."

"But you could have just told me. Instead of me finding out like I did." She brushed her wet cheek with her sleeve.

She was right. How could she trust him after this? Trust. The foundation on which relationships were built. Now that was possibly shattered beyond repair.

"Is it true? About it being stage four?"

"Yeah." He removed his hat. "Knew I'd have to tell you when this would happen. Didn't expect it to start falling out so fast." Sympathy wasn't what he was looking for. If anything, his heart ached for Chloe and what she must have been going through. She didn't deserve to find out from someone other than him.

"I was wondering why you were hanging around this town for as long as you did. Now I know. I'm so sorry you're going through all this, but please understand how hard this is for me too. I know that sounds selfish, but I don't know how I can do this . . . a relationship."

"What are you saying?" It was the point where hope and the likely outcome collided. He was certain his heart skipped a few beats.

"Maybe we need to simply be friends. Focus on you getting well. That's all. That's what's most important, right?"

A numbness overtook him, regardless of his expected prediction and inevitability of how it would all end. The one thing going right in his life was now falling apart, and there was no one else to blame. He'd sabotaged himself at every turn and was reaping what he'd sown. It wasn't fair to her, and she had every right to feel the way she did. This was her town and her life. She didn't need someone complicating things.

"Mason. Say something. Please."

Say something? Like, *Why does it feel like I'm going to die twice?* First, by losing a love he'd prayed for all his life. Then by disease? A poster on the far wall displayed the 1 Corinthians 13 love chapter. His eyes settled on verse 5: "Love does not seek its own." *God, give me the strength to move on. Because I love her, I have to let her go and honor her wishes.*

"You're right, about just being friends. Why would anyone want to get close to someone who could be dying, right? Guess my heart was doing the thinking, not my head. I simply couldn't stop myself from falling for you."

It wasn't so much that he couldn't stop himself. But more like not wanting to. Why would he stop what had lifted him from a lifetime in the valley of loneliness? And who would not want to be brought unto a wellspring on a mountaintop of his heart's desire?

"Mason, I didn't mean to make this worse for you." She rose from the couch and paced with a hand to her forehead. "Believe me when I say how much I care, but I just can't—"

"It's okay. I understand. I may not like it, but I do get it." He walked to the door and settled his hat back on his head. "By the way, you were wrong in saying you were selfish. I'm the selfish one, wanting all of you, and in return you'd only get what's left of me. I have to be honest enough to admit it. It isn't fair to you."

"Mason, please don't go like this." She took him by the arm.

"It's all right. Really. Guess it wasn't meant to be." Mason reached down for a gift bag he'd left outside the door and handed it to her. "Just a little something I thought you'd like. I'll see you."

The same beautiful brown eyes that had once sparkled with life now cast shadows of pain. *Sorry* would not be sufficient to erase it. But maybe allowing her to move on—both of them to move on—was where the healing could begin.

He pushed down his emotions and walked away to the arrival of raindrops dancing off his car. His confession of what she'd already known, and the anxiety of the secret he'd held since his arrival in Fleetwood, was all behind now. Also in the rearview mirror was his greatest regret. Not being with Chloe. Now, all that remained was to press on and face the storm that raged within him. Maybe he could go on acting and pretending that everything would be okay, as Marty aptly implied. But healing would never come with denial. And if brokenness and humility were what the Lord was seeking, then he'd found it.

Chloe sprinted through the downpour and into the house.

Sarah pulled a kitchen towel from the drawer and handed it to her sister. "Storming out there, huh?"

Chloe slid off her wet shoes at the door. "Yeah. It's storming in here too."

Sarah hugged Chloe tight as her tears welled up. "You gonna be all right?"

Chloe gave a mixed laugh and cry at the sight of her sister's pout, then grabbed a tissue from the counter. "Don't you start crying to. I have enough tears for the both of us. Trust me." She didn't know there were any more to shed since finding out about Mason's condition. And now after seeing and confronting him, it was as though it would all begin again.

Chloe pulled open the fridge door and took out lettuce, tomatoes, and dressing. Sit and sulk was the last thing she wanted to do. She'd already spent days doing that. "Why are you here anyway?" She grabbed a bowl from the cabinet.

"Thought maybe you'd need someone to talk to after you and Mason had your confrontation."

"I'll be all right. Go be with Jeff and Mark. You don't have to stay here." She cut the lettuce and tomatoes, then placed them in a bowl.

"Hey, when family hurts, we all do, right? Just like when I miscarried my first pregnancy. You were there for me. To the point that Jeff suggested we start charging you rent." She giggled and put a hand on each of Chloe's shoulders. "The point is, you're gonna make it. We're going to make it together. Mom has you and Mason on the prayer list at church. That's where she is tonight."

"Thanks. But it doesn't change the fact that your sister's a cruel, hateful person." She placed the box of tissues in the fridge.

Sarah opened the fridge and removed the tissues. "First, tissues don't go in the fridge. Second, what are you talking about, being a cruel person?"

Chloe took a seat next to Sarah on the barstool. "He's crushed. I told him we should just be friends. It was the way he looked at me. Never seen him like that before. It was like everything in him gave up. I can only guess what he's thinking of me right now. How terribly lonely he must be." Why would God put her in such an impossible situation? To have to choose between her broken heart and his. A decision where both would lose and suffer the consequence.

"I can't even imagine. Being here in a strange town. Not knowing anyone. Battling cancer. But what I do know is that you're his best friend. Maybe his only friend. The fact that he may be giving up is more the reason why you can't. Not only for him, but you too."

"But what am I supposed to do about any of this? I can't not have feelings for him. What if just being friends starts to be more—again?" She pushed her salad aside and laid her head in her arms, folded on the counter.

"I don't know. But for starters, be there for him. Even if it's to simply listen. And maybe you haven't quite thought about it yet, but I have a feeling he may be even more crushed than you are. And if it's meant to be between you two, that man's not going anywhere."

If it's meant to be. To go out in blind faith and trust that God had all things under control for those who love him. How many times had her dad encouraged her with those words? Stepping out when everything looked impossible pleased God, he'd say. Never once did he claim it was easy. But he did say it was necessary. "You know, at times you sound like Mom and Dad."

"Speaking of Mom. She's believing for a miracle. We both are. So you can mope around or join us in believing. It's up to you."

A flash of lightning pierced the kitchen blinds, followed by a thunderous boom, leaving the house dark.

"Great." Chloe turned on her phone's flashlight and grabbed an LED lantern from beneath the counter. "I wonder how long the power's going to be out?"

"I just hope Mom isn't trying to drive home in this." Sarah flicked the lantern switch on. "Hey, you know what this reminds me of?"

"Let me guess. Camping in the glade by the falls?" A dreamy place where her earliest memories of her childhood originated. Where she and Sarah caught fireflies by night and an assortment of dragonflies of many colors by day. Once the collection of insects was gathered into jars, they'd be admired and then released to return to their families. Chloe insisted on it. Sarah, not so much.

Before settling into their tent for the night, they'd spread out a blanket with Mom and Dad, with hopes of catching a glimpse of a shooting star. Mom had said it was all about creating memories, which she'd equated to shooting stars. In a second they were there, and the next gone. Most saw the flash in the sky merely by chance, she'd say. But the flash of memories concerning rapidly growing children and families were meant to be savored. Those opportunities would have to be looked for and anticipated before they'd escape. Dad would say memories caught with the heart would last longer than those caught in thought. He was right. His passing was proof.

"Hey." Sarah took her hand. "Are you all right? Looked like you were dreaming there."

"Speaking of dreams. I had the craziest one I've had in a long time. I was at the cabin with Mason, and the stream was moving fast as rapids from days of rain. He fell in and was swept away. I ran along the bank trying to keep up and eventually dove in for him, grabbed on to a fallen branch, and pulled us onto the bank."

"So you saved him."

"Exactly. But the crazy part was that word around town and all over social media was that I was the one who needed saving and Mason got all the credit. Can you believe it?"

Sarah giggled as the lights flickered back on. "Thank goodness. Hope my lights are on when I get home so I'm not trying to read Mason's book by candlelight." She slid her purse onto her shoulder.

"Exactly how many of his books have you read?"

"Let's see . . . after tonight, all of them. Except for his latest release, which hasn't hit the shelves yet. Holly promised me first dibs when they come in. And speaking of Holly, she wanted to ask you to thank Mason for all he's done, but when she found out about his condition, she didn't want to bother you. Sales are up and more customers than ever are stopping in. His book signings and book club visits have been a real success."

Chloe nodded. "Uh-huh. Just an observation, but Holly doesn't sound like the only one enthusiastic about Mason Chadwick's charisma and charm. You wouldn't happen to be crushing on my guy through his books, would you?"

"Oh, so *now* he's your guy? You do realize there's a possibility his readers know him better than you?" She crossed her arms and gave a smart look.

"What do you mean?"

"The men in his books are much the same as the way he treats you. It's as though he was thinking of someone like you in every book." Sarah poked a finger to her shoulder. "The way he looks at you . . . I don't know. It's like you're everything to him."

"Jeff never looked at you that way?"

"Are you serious? Let's just say he comes close on Saturdays, when I tell him I'm ordering pizza before the game." She shook her head. "So romantic."

"You're not planning on living vicariously through me now, are you? Because that would be a little weird."

"Hey, I've got bragging rights. I am your sister." Sarah gave a playful backhanded slap to her shoulder.

"Don't be thinking of my man when you're reading that book. You might have dibs on his book, but I have dibs on him."

Sarah nodded with a curious look and a pause.

"What?" Chloe looked with suspicion.

"About that dream. What if it wasn't all that crazy after all? What if everyone else was right? About him saving you. Or . . . maybe you saved each other. Think about it."

Chloe wondered if there was, in fact, a deeper meaning behind what Sarah had said, but she was too tired to process it. She could only think of her unsettling meeting with Mason and how she *could* have handled things differently. What she *should* have said instead. Mom always said coulda, woulda, and shoulda were a trap of the devil that captured everyone at some point in their lives and only led to regret. Chloe could already feel its undercurrent threatening to pull her under. Mom was right again. As always.

Chloe opened Masons gift bag. Inside lay a nest of hay in a small wicker basket, with a porcelain dove in the center. Her thoughts traveled back to when she was young and had her pet dove. Her nurturing of it, then its quick departure, never to see it again. She pulled a card from the bag.

Not all things fly away,
For true love has a broken wing.
It has no need to wander,
True love always stays.

How could he know that had meaning to her? Maybe he had no idea. And what did he mean by true love always stays? Did he mean his love for her? Whatever the reason, the gift was special and unique. Much like Mason.

Chapter 12

Mason pulled the respirator from his face and tossed it aside. The final sanding of a replaced oak plank on the cabin floor was complete and the old board thrown out, due to a weak spot he'd stepped through on his last visit. A hole in the floor, easy to fix. The Grand Canyon–sized hole in his heart, not so much. He'd been coming to the cabin one or two days a week since Grace had given the okay. For that he was grateful. But the realization that he'd need to pace himself was obvious with each visit.

With a plop down onto a rickety wicker chair and a pull of his notebook from his back pocket, he reviewed the grocery list he'd made the night before. All items listed were healthy foods for a natural cancer diet, and all necessary if he was to take getting better seriously.

Between a few books he'd picked up from the bookstore and online research, the wealth of information was staggering. But at least it was a start, with one commonality of all suggested diets being the elimination of sugars that cancer cells thrived on. Of which would be easier said than done given his love for frozen coffees and late-night ice cream.

He retreated to the porch through the screen door propped open with fireplace wood and stripped off his flannel to his T-shirt. A robust patting of his jeans sent a cloud of sanding dust floating, then rising with the midmorning breeze. The weather-beaten porch railing bowed as he leaned against it. He could say the tear streaming down his face was the result of dust in his eyes but knew that would be a lie. Just like the delusional, convincing lie he'd told himself about him and Chloe. The one where miracles happened and somehow, someway, everything fell into place, and they meandered off together, living happily ever after. Yeah, right. That one. And the title of that story? *A Fool's Dream.*

The large rock across the stream, which Mason had sat on as a teen, drew his attention as he cupped his hands and splashed cool river water onto his face. He'd only braved crossing it once back then, when the stream's height and strength during heavy rain seasons prevented the younger, less strong from doing so.

On "that day," the potential reward far outweighed the risk. It was worth the chance. She was worth it. Conquering the swift stream—the easy part. At least by comparison to conquering his fear of meeting her. He'd only seen and heard her voice from afar, across the stream. But to see her face to face? He recalled his hand stopping short, within inches of knocking on the cabin door. Stomach in knots and heart pounding. Instead of knocking, he'd slunk away, along with what would be his last chance to ever meet her. He'd conquered the stream but not the fear within himself, and in the process had allowed timidity and a lack of self-esteem to continue its rule and rein.

It was now long past time to set aside the foolish dreams and visions of the past. He mentally wrote them down, rolled them up into a scroll, and slid the regrets into an imaginary bottle, corking it tight. With a toss, it was sent floating down the stream. He wouldn't chase it or try to find it again. The burdens and heartache of the present were more than sufficient for the day. Even for a lifetime. It was all far too heavy to carry. His mom's timeless advice to lift all life's troubles to the Lord, then lay them down at the cross, invaded his thoughts. Today was that day.

As for the heaviest decision of all, that bottle of regrets would have to be dropped into the depths of the ocean, where there'd be no chance of retrieving it. No way of finding it again and reliving the pain of losing Chloe. But it was what had to be done. Her intentions were clear that they could be no more than friends, and he'd respect that. What other choice was there?

Now he needed to move on with his life. However much was left. He'd continue his dream of writing, with the pursuit and hopes of seeing his work on the screen. A chance of seeing and experiencing true love colliding and intertwining. Never releasing. Always embracing. At least on the page. Maybe the big screen. But more than likely, only in his dreams.

Mason's sweeping of the remaining dust came to a stop, with Chloe at the door. What was she doing here? Especially after their talk only the night before. He never thought he'd hear himself thinking that he wasn't ready to see her. Still trying to process it all. Whether it was nerves or awkwardness, he couldn't determine. Maybe both.

"Hey, mind if I come in?" She took a step inside.

"Of course not. It is your house." He forced a smile, determined to not let an indication of his wounded spirit seep through, adding to an already awkward meeting.

"Didn't see you at church this morning, so I thought maybe you'd be here." She placed her keys atop the fireplace mantel. "I changed into some work clothes in case you needed a hand with something."

As usual, her soothing voice was as a balm washing over him. An inexplicable amalgamation of all things good and all things right. But he'd restrain his heart and mind, which were prone to morph into mush at the sight of her. Couldn't go there. Not anymore. "Well . . . I appreciate the offer, but I think I'm about to call it a day. Been here all morning, and I am a little tired."

Chloe rubbed her shoe across the new floor plank and looked around the room. He hoped she wouldn't notice his pillow and rolled-up sleeping bag in the corner by the fireplace but was certain she did.

It was where he'd been drawn to be last night, to sort out the barrage of thoughts, feelings, and decisions that engulfed him following his meeting with her. As nice as the B&B was with all its luxuries, the old cabin felt like home. It was a place where he could think clearer. See things in a different way.

"I see you've been busy. And as much as it's appreciated, I feel terrible that's it's all for nothing. I've done all I can to keep this home and land. It's just not going to happen."

"It's not for nothing. Really." He swept a pile of wood dust into the dustpan and dumped it into the wastebasket.

She leaned against the kitchen counter, with her hands in the pockets of her cargo shorts. "Is this the real reason you wanted to come here to the cabin? To keep your mind off things? The cancer and all?"

Mason joined her at the counter and stared out the window above the sink. "Yeah. At first, that was the reason. Come here. Busy myself so I wouldn't have to think so much about everything. About living . . . dying. But now, I don't know. It feels like . . ." He wanted to say how much it felt like a place he belonged. Even more so, with the person it all belonged to. The land. The cabin. Its mysterious draw within his spirit.

Chloe grabbed his hand and gave him a hug. "Mason, I'm so sorry you're going through this. About last night . . ."

He held on tight, as though it would be their last embrace, then slowly pulled away. "I know." He took her hand, then released it. "I understand the need to be just friends. I do." He broke his eyes from hers. He'd have to be strong. "You've got your life to live, and I've got mine. Right? This is your home. You belong here. And as for me, back in Boston." The place he thought less and less about.

"Yeah. I guess." She nodded and motioned with her head. "Want to sit out back for a minute? Won't be many more chances to do so."

"Sure." She wouldn't believe or understand how much he'd hate to see her lose the cabin. He'd memorialized his fondness with the young girl who had captured his heart, carrying bits and pieces with him throughout his life. And it all started with her under the gazebo, wearing a sundress and straw hat. But he'd let that go today. A good decision.

Sitting next to her on the porch steps would normally have sent a tingle up his spine. This time a shiver of emotion ran through him, resembling more of an ache. A tug of war between what he desperately longed for and what wouldn't be. He cursed the cancer standing between him and Chloe. How terribly ironic. On one side was the cancer within him that threatened to take his life. And on the other, sitting next to him, was the woman who took all his heart's yearnings and brought them back to life.

"Any thoughts for your next book?"

"I think so. I've been tossing a few things around in my mind." A peek at her revealed a burgeoning smile along her pressed-together lips. It was a look he'd quickly grown to adore. He anticipated whatever it was that she had to say from that wonderful, beautiful mind of hers.

"Hey. Gotta do something with all that empty space up there, right?" She cracked her adorable smile and tapped her shoe against his.

Mason's returned smile soon faded with the thought of how much he'd miss her once he finished his treatment. Her smile, laugh, teasing. Every bit of it. But it was time to move on. "I can only imagine the hundreds of people who sat under the old gazebo over the years before it rotted away."

Chloe nodded. "Quite a few people, for sure. So since you're making your trip down memory lane, do you mind me asking what your happiest moment was here?"

He figured what did he have to lose by mentioning it. That bottle of regret and missed opportunities was downstream and far away by now. And the other bottle, he didn't want to think about. "I'd have to say seeing a certain somebody."

"A little vague, don't you think? Are we talking about a girl? Maybe a girlfriend?" Her brows arched along with an amused smile.

"No, not a girlfriend." To have a girlfriend you'd have to have met,

139

talked, and gotten to know her. None of which had happened.

"I see. So what's her name?"

It was clear that she wasn't going to let it go. *Bring on more humiliation, why don't you.* "Don't know."

"Hold on." Her arched brows now curved down as she drew back her head. "Your happiest moment was because of a girl, and you don't even know her name?"

"That's right. Too shy to even talk to her. Don't even know the color of her eyes looking from across the stream. Didn't know where she lived, went to school, or anything about her. But I could tell there was something different about her, something worthwhile. The way she smiled. Laughed. Just looking at her made me feel . . . that life had possibilities. There you have it. Happy?" His face burned from embarrassment. Not only from what he'd revealed to Chloe but how more and more ridiculous his confession sounded once spoken aloud. To hold on to something based on nothing but a feeling for someone he never knew.

"Wow." Her smirk disappeared.

"Yeah. Wow is right. Ridiculous, huh?" Pathetic or laughable would fit just as well.

"No. Not really." Her voice and eyes softened. "She must have been . . . extraordinarily special, that's all. Not ridiculous. Not at all. But I hope you don't mind me asking … Do you still think of her sometimes?"

What was he supposed to say? It was all too complicated and impossible to fully explain. And would any of it make a difference or matter anyway? He'd simply tell the truth. "Yeah. I thought about her quite a bit. Most of my life, in fact. That is, till I met you. Then I had no reason to."

To guess her thoughts and feelings would only be speculation. But something in her eyes and tone of voice held questions, he was sure. Whether she wanted to share them or not was up to her. Then again, maybe it was best not to know. He was only a friend to her. No more than that. It wasn't what he wanted it to be, but it was the right thing. At least for her.

Screeching tires followed by blaring horns sounded as Chloe and Abby took swigs of water, pausing from a brisk walk around the park trail. A cat dashed between cars, crossed a grassy area, and scampered up a nearby red maple tree.

"Isn't that . . . Yep, it is." Abby shook her head and took a seat with Chloe on a park bench.

Chloe nodded. It was Tabby, the stray that hung around the church. "I think it's true about cats having nine lives. At least for that one."

"Personally, I think that cats in cahoots with the body and fender place down the road." Abby poured water onto her rag and patted her face. "Running around town. Causing all those little fender-benders. Drumming up business, you know."

Chloe gave a blank stare. "Are you serious? Is that your new conspiracy theory? Cats in cahoots, bolstering the free-enterprise system?" Granted, most conspiracy theories did contain some elements of truth. But this was not one of them. At least, she didn't think so.

Abby capped her water bottle and spun toward Chloe. "All right. Talk to me. You didn't pick up after I called twice this morning, and you're not laughing at any of my jokes. What's up? Is this about your talk with Mason?"

Unquestionably, the thing that was up would have to be the striking, stifling similarity between her reaction to Mason and her dad. The feeling of helplessness. Hopelessness. A replay of events in which there was no escape from. Neither could she escape the unmistakable deep-seated feelings she had for Mason in that she'd even compared the sense of potential loss of him with Dad.

"I'm just worried about Mason. I don't like seeing him this way, and I feel partially responsible with the way I handled things. I can't do this commitment thing with everything I know about cancer and what it's gonna take for him to get through this. Then I keep thinking about Dad and Kristen. I—"

"Whoa. Hold up. Slow down." Abby put an arm around her and took her hand with the other. "Breathe. You're gonna get through this. This is all new to you. You just found out that the only man you've ever loved is facing a life-changing event. Who wouldn't be devastated?"

"I know. But I can't stop replaying the moment I found out about his condition and how I felt. It's like I'm living that moment every minute all over again." She could still remember the exact moment and time she'd found out about her dad's diagnosis and the abrupt sinking feeling of despair. Then to have the revelation of Mason's condition reinforce her worst fears.

Even more vividly, she could remember the day Dad's battle with the disease ended—while she was making a delivery in Boone. Ever since then, she could still smell the aroma of cinnamon-cider potpourri inside of the candle shop—when Mom had called. The way her voice trembled and broke. *Chloe, it's your dad.* The way she'd raced out of the shop and how she'd pounded her fists on the steering wheel when the traffic lights took far too long to change. And when the ambulance passed her going the opposite way on the highway, somehow, someway she knew. It was Dad.

Abby rubbed her friend's shoulder. "I know it's all still a shock, but I want you to think about something. You just explained how you felt when you found out. Now imagine what Mason must have felt like when he did. I know I can't fathom it. And if your heart is broken, can you imagine his? He needs a friend, Chloe. He needs you."

"Yeah. I know. But tell me I'm doing the right thing. I mean, what if I had already deeply committed to him and then I'd have found out? Then what? I'd really be considered a horrible person to bail out on him. On the other hand, what if I'm blowing it and passing up something that's meant to be?" She put both hands on the top of her head and shut her eyes.

"Is that what you feel like you're doing? Bailing out? Because that's not the way I see it."

"I don't . . . I don't know what I'm thinking or doing anymore. I really don't." Chloe slouched on the bench and rested her head on Abby's shoulder.

"Must have been really hard talking with him at the cabin."

Chloe sniffled. "Awkward was more like it. For both of us, I'm sure. But I have my suspicions now as to who the mystery woman is he'd dedicated his book to. You know, the one I'd told you about. He said his best memory was of a girl at the campground. And get this—a girl he'd never actually met."

"What? That sounds crazy."

"There was nothing crazy about the way he spoke or the way he just stared off when he talked about her."

Abby nodded. "Chloe . . ." Abby looked away.

Chloe sat up. "What? What is it?"

"I think you should know about a rumor going around. Mind you, I personally don't believe it. Not for a minute."

"Rumor? What rumor?" When would the deluge of problems end?

Abby drew in a steady breath, then exhaled. "Word has it that Mason has something to do with you losing the property and cabin."

Chloe jumped to her feet and placed her hands on her hips. "What? That's insane. Mason may have had his reasons for not telling me about the cancer, but I don't believe for a second that he came to Fleetwood Falls to buy a piece of property. And on top of that, not tell me about it. No. I refuse to believe it."

Abby took her shoulders and steadied her. "Listen. I don't believe it either. Especially when Tina's name was traced back as the possible source."

Chloe sat back down. "I don't get it. Why . . . how is all this happening to me? Where is God in all this?" *Lord, help me get through all this.*

"Don't worry. He knows exactly where you are. But for now, you need to breathe, and we'll talk more about this later. So how about we bolt across the street like Tabby does and grab something to eat? Pizza or burgers?" Abby's rationale being, to walk a mile in advance of consuming not-so-nutritious choices so that it would all equal out in the end.

Today Chloe wouldn't argue the point. Just as she rose from the bench, Abby grasped her arm and yanked her back down.

"What? What's wrong?" Chloe asked.

"It's Bill. He's taking a seat on the bench outside his office."

"Bill the lawyer?"

"Yeah. He's been coming into the pastry shop almost every day now. Think he's tried everything on the menu. Said he likes my Texas accent. Especially when I say, 'Will that be all?' I think it's the way I drag out the *all*. Keeps adding things after he's already ordered just so he can hear me say it again. His way of flirting, I guess."

"Hold on. What's that glassy-eyed look? You like Bill?"

"Psst. Not a chance. Of course, he probably thinks I'd burn down every barn in Texas for him if he asked me to, with his swept-back red hair, freckles, and fancy suits."

Maybe it was for the best that she didn't like Bill. Or at least she said she didn't. Chloe recalled the last guy Abby thought might be the one. He'd crashed and burned when he'd slipped up by saying horses were a freak of nature and should have gone extinct with the dinosaurs. And with that, her longtime curiosity of what it would feel like to smash a pie in someone's face was finally realized. His broken nose exposing her novice level of the activity, as well as being an indicator of how passionate of a horse lover she was.

She'd later confessed and repented sorely at the altar for her actions with much sorrow and tears after several sleepless nights of conviction, hanging her head in shame and admitting it to be such a waste of a perfectly good pie.

"So you're ready to grab a bite?" Chloe asked.

"But we're gonna have to walk right past Bill."

"Why does that matter? You said you didn't like him anyway."

Chloe grinned. "We're just gonna casually walk past him on the way to get a slice of pizza, and see what happens, all right?"

"Yeah. I think I can do that." Abby stood and adjusted her jogging pants and patted her hair.

This time Chloe pulled Abby back down.

"What?"

"It's Mason," Chloe said. "And he's talking to Bill. They're going into his business." She couldn't recall Mason mentioning any problem or issue that would require legal advice and hoped it was nothing serious. Or maybe . . . Chloe didn't even want to think about it. "Abby, how does he know Bill? You don't think this has anything to do with the . . ."

"The cabin? No. No way. There must be a reasonable explanation. Maybe he just needs legal advice." Abby nodded unconvincingly and stared in the direction of Bill's office.

"It does seem a little odd though. Why would someone so new in town need to see an attorney?" Chloe didn't want to even remotely consider the possibility of Mason not admitting if he did have anything to do with her losing the land. Then again, he did show an interest in everything about the land and cabin from his first visit there. And why was he insistent on working on a cabin he knew she would lose? None of it was making any sense. Or . . . was it?

Abby patted Chloe's hand. "Could be he just needs something notarized. Or maybe he's getting a divorce. Yeah. That's probably it."

Chloe gave a sideways grin. "He'd better not be. Married or getting a divorce." Of course, she suspected there were many more things she didn't know about Mason's life. Same as he didn't know about hers as well. All things she'd been anxious to discover until . . . But did it even matter now?

"What do you say we skip the pizza and go back to the car," Abby suggested. "Might be awkward running into them."

"Yeah, for both of us."

Once again Tabby darted across the road, setting off screeching tires followed by eruptions of crunching bumpers. Chloe and Abby cringed.

Chloe shook her head. "Drumming up business again?"

"Yep. Keepin it real and keepin it local. Can't question his loyalty."

The thing Chloe often questioned was whether Abby had a single serious bone in her body. Truth was, she hoped Abbey would never change or lay aside her gift of balancing out the scales of heartbreak by bringing humor into Chloe's life. What she needed now more than anything was God to bring understanding, wisdom, and healing. And the sooner the better.

Chapter 13

"Hope for the best . . ." The middle-aged woman said as she grabbed on to the hand of the man sitting next to her in the waiting room of suite 333. "But prepare for the worst. That's the hope they give? Is that the best they can do?" The man wrapped his arm around her. "How many times do you have to go through this? How many years?" She covered her mouth to suppress her sobbing.

How many times? The woman's words singed Mason like a branding iron. They were the same words he'd overheard his mom say while on the phone with her sister—the woman who had abandoned him. "How many times have you passed through this town and down this street without as much as even stopping to meet your son? Do you even think about him?" Sure, he'd seen Mom cry tears before, but those were usually tears of joy. That was not one of those times. He could also remember the phone slipping from her hand and onto the floor when she saw him standing there, listening to it all. It was when he'd found out. Ten. Ten years old. Old enough to believe he wasn't wanted, yet not old enough to process it all.

Much like a guarded secret, he'd stuffed the hurt, along with the convoluted hodgepodge of feelings, into a vessel, burying it deep into the soil of his heart, never to be found. He'd never want to see Mom break down like that again. He wouldn't let her see the wound the news had inflicted on him. As a result, he'd told no one. Not a friend growing up or an adult ever since. Until Chloe. She was the only one. The one he'd shared his treasured secrets with. The one from whom he'd had nothing to hide. Yet he had. He'd hid his condition from her to not cause her pain. Similarly, it was what he'd done with Mom. As a result, no one was for the better. No one's burden lightened. Only delayed healing.

Mason squelched his swelling emotions from erupting. He'd save it for his potential "prepare for the worst" moment, when he'd get the results of the latest PET scan. He reached out, took a travel magazine from a nearby bookrack, and flipped through the pages. Hawaii, Switzerland, Breckenridge. Page after page of exotic destinations. Oddly enough, Pastor Hank had spoken of destinations for last week's midweek teaching. Eternal destinations. Of which there were only two choices. A subject most people wouldn't give much thought to, Mason presumed. That was, until faced with its inevitability and the tremendous importance of making one's salvation sure.

"Mr. Chadwick." The nurse flipped through pages on a clipboard. "We'll get you weighed in, then get you into the exam room."

Five pounds less than the last weigh-in. Pounds shedding off his already thinning frame each time. Loss of appetite. Painful mouth ulcers. Headaches. Cramping and nausea from chemo. A host of other associated issues. All factors recorded by the nurse before she left the exam room.

Waiting. Always waiting. Waiting for the next doctor's appointment. The next time bloodwork would be needed, then the results. The next chemo session followed by another scan and its results. The strain of anticipation for something, anything to indicate even the faintest existence of a flicker of light at the end of the tunnel.

"Mason." The doctor entered and took a seat at the counter, looking through his chart. "How are you holding up?" He scrolled pages on the computer.

"Could be better. Guess you hear that a lot." It didn't look like he heard it this time, judging by his attention to the screen and delay in answering.

"Oh. Yeah, right." His intent stare at a frame on the computer held Mason in suspense.

"So those are the results?" Another pause.

The doctor removed his glasses and placed them on the counter. Never a good sign. Not in real life. Not even in movies. Always precursors to bad news. He was certain this would be no exception. That, combined with the insufferable defining silence. Again, waiting.

"So what's the verdict? Any improvement?" A cold tremor ran through his body as he prepared for the news. *Please, God, let it be good news.* Anything to offer hope. If even just a glimpse.

"I'm afraid not. None. The tumor in your lower abdomen hasn't shrunk in size, and the cancer is still spread throughout the entire abdominal area, along with several organs affected. It's spread throughout the spinal area as well."

None. No change. None the better. What was all this for if nothing was working? Vials of chemo and meds coursing through his body for hours. Test after test. Life in perpetual limbo and suffering the repercussions of it all. "What are my options? Continue what's not working?"

"These things take time. In this case, a different course of action is needed. I recommend a more radical approach, including bone marrow transplant. I'll set it all up with—"

"No." It didn't matter what else the doctor had to say. He'd already made up his mind what he'd do if treatment got more intense.

"What do you mean *no*?" the doctor said with a surprised expression, as though he'd never heard the word uttered from a patient. He wiped his glasses on the breast of his lab coat and placed them on his face. "We've had success in the past with what I'm recommending."

"What percent? How much success?" Mason leaned back in his chair and folded his arms.

"Well . . ." He cleared his throat and fidgeted with the stethoscope dangling from neck. "I don't have those figures in front of me now."

"I'm not going along with treatments that are more radical than I'm already doing. I'll do my final treatment coming up, and I'm done. I'll go with natural cancer cures from then on out."

"Natural cures?" A smug expression replaced his former solemn one. "Mason, you don't understand the severity of this all. The medical protocol—"

"Isn't working, is it? One more treatment and I'm done." He placed his hat on his head and stood. "Are we done here?" They were. Same routine. Same results. Only a different day.

"Are you sure about this? You're serious?" He straightened the pages of printed documents with a few taps on the counter and placed them in the file.

"I am."

The doctor nodded. "I hope you have enough faith for miracle. You're gonna need one."

A miracle. He'd take his chances with something that at least offered hope. Unlike the results he'd gotten so far. Belief for a miracle along with a natural cancer diet was settled. Maybe he would have done it from the very beginning had he not been so blindsided with the sudden revelation of his condition and it being in its advanced stages. "You don't know what you don't know," as the saying went. But whatever he didn't know, God certainly knew beforehand. He had no choice other than trust, and rest in that.

Mason stepped into the hallway and took a seat on a bench nearby. He stilled his jumbled thoughts and considered the Scripture he'd read earlier that morning about the woman who touched the hem of Jesus's garment and was healed. Jesus's response was that her faith had made her whole. Her faith in the healer. Not faith in herself or her own ability. If the Bible taught complete dependency on God in every aspect of life, why would the burden of being healed be the exception? Within himself, Mason knew he didn't possess the faith to be healed. But he did have the faith to believe in the One who could. *Lord, let your will be done. My life is in your hands.*

Mason checked his watch. It was story time for children in the recreation room. He was honored to agree to read to them when asked to do so, with several children undergoing treatment for various issues and diseases. He could now relate to their struggles and empathize to an extent for the brokenness of the parents' hearts.

He took a deep, cleansing breath. For the children's sake he'd put on a smile and pretend like all would be all right. Whether he believed it or not, he'd do it for them.

Stories that came to life. What child under ten didn't want to immerse themselves into a make-believe world? Such was the expression of eight-year-old Hannah sitting next to her mom. With cute dimples adorning her pale face and a dangling pink pom-pom from her cotton hat, she anticipated the turning of each page. Her beaming smile gave little indication of the storm raging within her, threatening to launch her into her eternal destiny. The weightiness of that astronomical prospect would be reflected in the eyes of her mom. It was unimaginable the grief she was holding. Mason struggled to hold himself together as he turned the last page of the book.

Chloe. She'd sneaked in, taking a seat to the rear of the room during his reading. The edges of her lips tilted with a smile. He'd never mentioned to her about his volunteering to read to the children a few times a week.

Hannah raised her hand. "Mr. Mason, when I go to heaven, will you be there? Maybe you could tell us stories there to." Her mom shrugged with watery eyes.

Mason hadn't a clue as to how that question could come from a story about a fish wanting a shiny new blue bike. "Uh . . . well—"

"I just noticed you didn't have any hair. My friend Janci said people without hair might be dying. But Mom said that's not always true."

Chloe's mouth gaped open.

"Your mom is right, Hannah. And if your friend tells you that again, just let her know you're believing God for a miracle."

Eternal destinations and the need for miracles seemed to be the theme of the day. Chloe took a seat next to Mason as the activities director escorted everyone out.

"It's nice what you're doing here. Kids can come up with tough questions, can't they?"

The tenderness of Chloe's voice settled him. Admittedly, it was what he'd needed to pacify his tumultuous spirit. Between the troublesome test report and looking into helpless little eyes, he'd had enough for the day.

"So I'm finding out." He fumbled with the book still in his hands, then tossed it aside, along with the gloom of the day. At least for Chloe's sake. "What I'd also like to find out is how you found me here." He cast her a questioning smile.

"Brandy mentioned it when I was visiting with Kristen." A muffled announcement of the loudspeaker in the hallway sounded, followed by workers in lab coats rushing down the hall.

"How's Kristen holding up?"

"She's not. That's what I'm afraid of. I don't think she has much longer." She shut her eyes and looked down.

"Sorry." It was no wonder Chloe feared commitment. To see her dad, and now Kristen, slipping away.

She stood. "Well, it's almost lunch. Want to grab a bite? I'm thinking maybe soup and salad."

"Hmm. I'm thinking hot dogs, a hayride, and a walk through the corn maze. I've never been there. What do you say? As friends, of course." He didn't want to chase her away any more than he already had. He simply wanted—no, needed—to be with her.

"Corn maze? You're up to that? That's a lot of walking. Especially if you get lost trying to find your way out of that thing."

"I don't know. I can't think of a better person I'd want to get lost with." If only she knew how much he'd meant that. Even if the world was falling apart—of which his was—he'd spend whatever time that remained with her. The same auburn-haired beauty he'd met at the altar. The same touch of sass that captured his heart, ignited a spark, and with just "that look" set his heart ablaze. The same girl before him now.

Chloe's eyes met his and stayed. He was certain that in the silence, there was much being said between their torn hearts. She shook herself out of the moment and suggested a new pecking order of events. "I think the hayride should come before the hotdog, don't you think?"

The corn maze. Of all places, he'd pick that. He could have picked a historical site tour. Maybe even antiquing a few shops. Or better yet, a leisurely tour of the alpaca farm in Banner Elk. But no. The corn maze.

Chloe extended her hand to Mason for him to help her off the hay wagon. He picked a blade of straw from her hair, then brushed himself off. There was never a time he didn't put her first. She didn't think men like him existed anymore, and certainly didn't believe she'd done anything to deserve one.

Her concern for Mason's emotional well-being since their talk about remaining friends had been partially put to rest. Sure, things were different, but at least they were talking with no known resentments. She'd have felt horrible if something had happened to him while they were at odds.

Mason reached down and picked up a corn husk on the way to the food truck. "I want the old Chloe back."

"Okay. You'll have to explain that one. The old Chloe?" And where was this headed? Though the hayride was enjoyable, he did come across as more reserved.

"You know. The Chloe that poked and prodded, and never without a smart remark. The Chloe who didn't feel sorry for me before she found out."

"Mason I . . ." She wanted to say she didn't feel sorry for him, but she did. It was the only way she knew how to feel, given the circumstance. But he was right. He was the same person with the same feelings, only going through the toughest battle of his life. She needed to be true, not only him but herself. The truth was that no matter how much she tried to distance herself and gently push away, she found her heart drifting right back to him.

Memories of how they'd met, the pendant, and dance they'd shared. She couldn't simply forget all those sweet, thoughtful, and meaningful things that had grafted their hearts together. All leaving her wonder if God had a plan and part in it all. Still, she'd take it slow.

"You were saying?" He edged her on.

"I promise to try harder to be myself. But in all fairness, I don't think you can handle what I can dish out." She raised her brows with a tease, then inwardly pulled back. She could see herself plummeting right back into his arms if not careful. Most any woman would have latched on to him if given the chance, yet he chose her. She wasn't sure why. He just did.

"Oh, you don't worry about me. We'll grab a hot dog and then I'll have plenty of time to pick on you when we get lost in that maze. And speaking of hot dogs, the last one I had was at the church fair. Ate half of it until that troublemaking cat stole the rest."

"Yep. Sounds like Tabby. Running around town. Getting into trouble." Too bad Mason wasn't a cat lover. Tabby sure took a liking to him. Maybe he could have tamed that wild spirit.

Chloe and Mason stood at the entrance of the corn maze, under an increasingly overcast sky. If he knew the embarrassment she'd experienced on her last visit there while in high school, he'd never have suggested it.

She looked up as a gust of wind blew her hair across her face. "I think we'd better get through this fast. Looks like rain setting in soon. We wouldn't want to be stuck in the middle of this thing."

"Exactly how does this work?" Mason asked. "We have to correctly answer the questions on these signs to get out the other side?"

"What did you think you had to do?" Been in the city too long, she guessed. Or maybe he was toying with her. He was obviously brilliant.

"I don't know. Wander around till you find your way out, I guess." He cracked a smile.

"Ah yeah. Good way to be lost in here for a million years." She grabbed his hand and started to walk.

"Wait." He pulled her back to him. "Before we start, we each have to share our most embarrassing moment."

Had he talked to Abby? She knew well that her most embarrassing moment was right there in the maze. "Okay then, but talk and walk please." She pulled him along. "My most embarrassing moment was . . ."

"You really don't want to tell me, do you?"

"No, I don't," she said without hesitation. "But I'm willing to bare my soul. And only to you. I was a junior in high school when Abby and I came to the maze with a few classmates after school one day. Regrettably, Bud and Thor happened to be there to."

"Thor?" His steps stalled, and she pulled him along again.

"Yeah. A little delusional. But a nice guy. That is, until he and Bud would start pulling pranks. They caught me so many times at school that day. But I'd had enough and was determined to not fall for anything they said anymore."

"They tried again, didn't they?"

"So I thought. We were halfway through the maze when I saw this big rubber snake on the side of the path, so I picked it up. Everyone jumped back, including Abby. I couldn't believe she was in on it too. My best friend, right? But then I realized why the snake looked so real. When its tongue came out his mouth, I threw it. Of course, everyone scattered, leaving me alone and lost in this godforsaken maze."

Mason laughed as the patter of rain hit the corn.

"Oh great," she said. "Rain. And we're stuck in this maze. We must have been getting the answers wrong. Isn't this the same question we've had before?"

Mason placed his hat on her head. "Don't worry, I know the way out." He took her hand and led her out to the car just as the drizzle became a downpour. Once inside the car, he pulled a towel from a duffel bag and handed it to her.

She dried her face and handed it back to him. "You may be as much of a prankster as Thor. You knew the answers all along, didn't you?"

"We wouldn't have had much time to talk if we'd gotten them all right to begin with."

"So you want to talk, do you? Then maybe you know something about a brand-new kiln delivered to my house yesterday evening. Well?" She'd guessed he was the only one who would have given her one. He'd known that her old kiln was acting up when he took his pottery lesson. The anonymous gift had all the earmarks of his kind generosity.

"Kiln? You mean one of those oven thingies?"

As suspected, he'd play dumb.

"Yes. An oven thing. I'd like to thank him or her, if I knew who it was." He remained silent and looked out his side window. "If you won't answer that, then you owe me your most embarrassing moment. And you're not weaseling out of it." She rubbed her arms and shivered. "Or else that'll be your next embarrassing moment. When I go around calling you weasel. That's right. Think hard about it." Finally, a chance to know something new about him.

"Okay. I'll tell you." He sighed and cleared his throat. "At the cabin the other day when you asked me about my happiest moment at the campground. I told you about that certain someone I never spoke to or even met."

"I remember." Maybe it was his pause or the way he stared out the window without expression. A knot twisted in her stomach. She pushed the joking aside. Whatever it was could keep. She put her hand on his forearm gripping the steering wheel. "It's all right. You don't have to tell me. We can just—"

"No. It's all right. It'll sound silly to you, I'm sure. But that's the one thing that's haunted me most of my life. I mean, where would my life have ended up if I'd met her? A simple 'Hi, my name is Mason' would have done." He wiped his fogged-up window with the towel. "It was embarrassing because I didn't have the nerve to simply introduce myself. I've carried that regret around ever since. Or at least till lately. It didn't matter that anyone else knew about it. I knew. So I swore I wouldn't ever let that happen again if, or when, I met that special someone."

He sighed, as though he'd shed a heavy burden, and continued his stare out the window as the tapping of rain on the roof subsided.

"Thanks. For telling me that." Despite the fact that she'd found out about his cancer from another, there was no reason to doubt the way he trusted her with his most guarded secrets. First about his real mom, and now this. There was no reason to believe that he'd ever intentionally hurt or misled her. In that she found comfort and security. If only she could be so free to share her concerns, anxieties, and fears.

"Mason, how do you do it? Face cancer without falling apart? Without losing all hope and just giving up? And earlier today with those children . . ."

"Only by God's grace I haven't seriously shut down. Wanted to. Believe me. And I don't have a choice, do I? I'd imagine it's easy to walk away from things when we have a choice. When times get tough. Run from the hard things. I don't have that privilege. Neither do those children."

"I think you're incredibly brave having to go through this." She wondered if her dad had similar thoughts and fears before passing.

"Not really. There's one thing I keep in mind when I feel like having a pity party. It's the realization that there's always someone worse off than I am. I think the brave ones are the parents hanging on to every ounce of hope for their children. Praying for even the smallest miracle for them to live."

In a single day, he'd opened up with so much of himself. His thoughts, feelings. The things he'd buried deep inside. Maybe it was her silence, or the fact that he'd begun to know her so well that he'd noticed her in thought.

He put a finger under her chin and turned her face to him. "Whatever it is you want to ask me . . ."

She didn't know if she was more afraid to ask it or not to. "Are you afraid to die?"

Mason looked down, then away for a moment. "To be truthful, no. You would think so. But dying's not the thing I'm afraid of."

"Then what is?"

"To live, only to die without finding true love. And being deeply loved in return." He shrugged. "It's the only thing on my list."

She wondered if he'd come to this conclusion as a result of facing death or if he'd always felt that way. Could love be so powerful that it would be the overarching desire of a person before departing the land of the living? Her suspicion was that it had always been in him. It had been reflected in his writing long before his diagnosis. She didn't need to confront death either to realize the same God-given yearning. To love and to be loved. It was all she needed as well.

He reached into his pocket, pulled out his keys, and dangled them before her.

"What?"

"How about you drive." He feigned a smile. "I know you've been wanting to." He twirled the keys, then dropped them into her hands.

Sure. If seeing her happy delighted him, she'd play along. As though her chance to drive Mason Chadwick's fancy, fully equipped Range Rover, with every available feature known to man, was the biggest thing to hit Fleetwood Falls, or to happen to her . . . It was. But it wasn't the flash of the car's interior. It was the fully equipped Mason, with all the right features built in. Polite. Thoughtful. Tender. Kind. The way his world would revolve around hers if she'd allow it, and a true love for God. Sure, maybe there was a little fender bender on the outside of his exterior now. A few scratches and dents due to the toll of disease. But she loved him just the same. So yeah. It was the biggest thing to ever happen to her. And now all she needed was a little body and fender work on her heart. Or more truthfully, a major overhaul.

Chapter 14

Survey of land and proposed demolition of the cabin? Mason pulled the taped notice off the cabin door and read farther. Chloe had mentioned the lease was about up and a notice would be sent simply as a legal formality. Despite its certainty, she would be heartsick to see things moving forward so quickly. Once the deal was done, all she'd have were old photos and memories of her childhood there. And the way she'd shared with him her love for the glade by the falls was dreamlike. He'd never seen her mind drift off that way. It was as though it were her special place of solace. Freed from the burdens of life and a resting place for her soul. How he'd wished he could have been a part of that resting place for her.

He collapsed onto a sheet-covered recliner and set the notice on the aged end table that had seen better days. Despite her persuasion for him to not invest much time and energy on the cabin, given its impending loss, it had only bolstered his resolve to bring it back to at least a resemblance of the passing decade. With the clock ticking on work to be done, as well as his departure from Fleetwood, he'd do whatever he could within his power, resources, and energy. It wasn't about money. It was about softening the blow. However much that was in his control.

The broken spindle of Chloe's baby crib, sitting in the corner of the living room, drew his attention. One of the next things on the list to repair. Brokenness. Not only was he experiencing it for himself but witnessing its effects on others around him. Hurting people with real battles and struggles affecting them each day. A perspective not afforded him from his ritzy condo in the city. *God, if my time is possibly up, then let my life count for something. Lord, your Word says that in my weakness you are made strong. I need strength that only you can give. I need . . .*

A desk and a typewriter? Mason pushed himself up from the recliner. Was that . . . It was the same desk he and Chloe had retrieved from the cabin that he'd refinished at Chloe's mom's request. What was it doing back here? He'd not been there in several days—it must have come then. And a typewriter setting on it with a typed note in it. He spun the roller knob to release the sheet of paper and sat in the antique desk chair for a closer look.

> *A typewriter to match your tie tack and nostalgic side. And a desk awaiting that moment of inspiration. Just a small way to thank you for the pendant and the dance. A memory we'll always share.*
> *Chloe*

How? How was he supposed to move on with his life without her when a simple note threatened to bring him to tears? And the way she caught that small detail of the tie tack. Maybe she was paying attention a little more than he'd realized. Knew him more than she'd led on to. Possibly even loved him to the point of the words escaping her lips but withheld out of fear of his condition. Fear of loss.

His fingers slid across the desk's satin finish. He had no idea the desk would return to him. The sanding, staining, and finish. Every brush stroke was for her. Pleasing her was his source of inspiration and motivation, as though built into him. All done out of love for someone who was so much more than a friend.

Mason moved outside, grabbed the sickle, and cut away the knee-high weeds and brush. He then removed the gloves and sank his blistered hands into the cool stream. Swinging a sickle was not what he was accustomed to, nor needed in the city. An unobstructed view of the stream from the cabin could now be had, with knee-high weeds and brush cleared. The old foundational corner blocks remained where the gazebo once stood. They'd remain, as he'd lined up a carpentry crew to erect a new one, giving Chloe the chance to sit under it before all would be gone.

Next would be a much-needed pressure washing to the cabin and porch areas, along with repairs to the porch railings. All of which would have to wait till another day, as the sun ducked behind the canopy of trees.

He removed his notebook from his pocket. Book club night at Holly's. He'd make good on his commitment to attend. Besides, Chloe would be there. Her interest in his writing warmed his heart. A new sense of pride arose that he'd never felt before. It made him feel like he mattered and, in part, was more complete. It was amazing the effect a woman could have on a man when she believed in him. If only they could have been more than friends.

Mason paused at the foot of the porch steps. A silver compact car pulled up to the cabin. Only Chloe had ever come onto the property since he'd been coming there, and he wasn't expecting anyone.

A man slid out the car. Blake? What was his agent doing at the cabin?

"Hey, Mason." Blake hesitantly reached out his hand to shake, all the while studying Mason's appearance.

"Blake. Not quite what you were expecting to see, right?" It was clear that his thinner frame, rather gaunt facial features, and paleness caught Blake off guard.

"No. Not at all man. I mean, I knew you were going through a rough time but . . ."

"Yeah. That would be an understatement." Mason pulled a rag from his back pocket and wiped the sweat from his forehead. "What are you doing here? How did you find me?"

"Hopped on a flight to Charlotte to visit family for a few days and thought I'd stop in on you for a quick visit. Brad from the bed and breakfast gave me directions to get here when I told him I was your agent." He scanned the surroundings and swatted a mosquito on his forearm. "Out in the sticks, huh?"

"A lot quieter than the city. And better scenery for sure." Still no answer to why Blake was there. "So what's going on?"

"Just stopping in to make sure you're still in on the possible movie deal. I don't know, man. I just have a feeling you're gonna finally cash in on your big dream. I can only imagine how stoked you must be."

Mason looked away then back again. "Yeah. That would be . . . great." His voice lacked enthusiasm and his smile wavered.

Blake tilted his head, crossed his arms, and shifted his weight. "You are still interested in this, aren't you? You don't look all that—"

"Yeah. Of course I'm interested. Just tired, that's all." His chest tightened at the thought of so many things now racing toward their conclusions. His soon departure from Fleetwood and Chloe. Her losing the land and the cabin she'd been born in. But with her decision to be only friends, there was only one option that remained. To move forward.

Blake looked around and held out his palms. "What are you doing here anyway? Brad said something about working on the cabin. You got a job?"

"Not a job. Just helping out a friend." He kicked the dirt with the tip of his boot.

"Uh-huh. Just a friend?" Blake smiled with another folding of his arms. "All right. How pretty is she?"

"Well . . . very pretty, to tell you the truth. But that's beside the point. I needed something to keep my mind off things. Staying busy seemed to be the right thing to do."

"I hope you've been busy writing. You know your followers are always looking for your next one."

Yep. That was Blake, all right. Always pushing for the next book.

The next deal. It was his job after all. "Yeah. Think I might just be on to something."

"Great. That's what I like to hear." Blake swatted another mosquito. "By the way, the pot could be getting a lot sweeter. The production company would need the writer they select to be a little more hands on, like being on the set for script-change approvals on the spot. And with it developing into a series, you could be in LA for a year at least. Even more if there's another season to shoot."

"Wait. What?" He rubbed the back of his neck. Move to California? A year or more? "Hold on. There was no mention of this when I went to LA. Where's all this coming from?"

"New developments. The executive producer is investing heavily in the show and has moved up the production timeline. Which means, if you're selected, you're gonna have to hit the ground running."

"You're sure about all this?"

"That's the word." Blake opened his car door. "Gotta run, but I'll talk to you later." He put one leg in the car then stopped. "Oh, and Mason. You know what they say about long-distance relationships. Pretty just makes it harder." The car started, and he pulled off.

Mason clasped his fingers together behind his head and looked up with a heavy exhale. *God, what's happening here?* It was bad enough knowing he'd be returning to Boston. But California? He took a seat on the porch step. If there were any chance at all of Chloe loving him and wanting him to stay, he would in a heartbeat. He'd back out of the running for the deal and simply continue to write. But it remained clear that he had only one choice. And that was to move on.

The cooing of a dove settling in for the night sounded above one of the porch beams. It reminded him of the porcelain dove he'd given Chloe and the poem he'd written, with the last line standing out to him. *True love always stays.* He'd meant every word. But in this case, maybe true love would have to let go in order to free another.

If she didn't take her eyes off Mason . . . Chloe shifted positions in her seat and crossed both her legs and arms. Maybe holding a cup of iced coffee to her face would cool the heat building. No less than two dozen seats were taken at Holly's Hideaway book club night. Oddly, all but four were guys—the rest were women. Not too happy about that. And the most scantily dressed was the one with eyes more on Mason than her book.

All this woman knew of him was from his book bio and picture, presumably. Sure, maybe a longtime fan of his writing. But if she knew of his condition, she'd certainly not be interested. She'd see no long-term guarantee, turn, and walk away as fast . . .

Was that what she was doing as well? Keeping a distance from him and committing to only a friendship out fear of the uncertain future? The feet of Chloe's chair squeaked as she shuffled her chair closer, shutting the two-inch gap between her and Mason. She rubbed her arms to warm.

"Hey." Mason removed his sport coat and placed it around her shoulders. Not at all a surprise. "This ought to warm you. And don't worry about her." He gave a reassuring smile and squeezed her shoulder in a hug before releasing.

"Thanks." What an amazing man. He knew her fears and insecurities more than she'd realized. Chloe spotted Abby at her pastry counter, who'd obviously been observing miss floozy face with her ill intent. Abby grinned and shook her head.

And was her jealousy so evident that even Mason noticed? She held her finger under her nose to avert a sneeze. Aha. That was it. That was what the bookstore reminded her of. The perfume department at the mall. The amalgamation of inundating scents hung in the air, triggering sneezes, mostly from the guys.

Thankfully, the meeting concluded after snippets of lines were read from Mason's last novel. The way he held his hand to his stomach left her questioning whether he should have come at all.

Mason rubbed his stomach and took shallow breaths. "Chloe, I'm not feeling so well."

She took his hand. "Let's get you home."

"Yeah. That would be best."

Chloe held on to his arm to cross the parking lot. "I'll take you in my car, if that's all right. We can come back for your car in the morning." He eased himself into the passenger seat of Chloe's Jeep.

Mason reclined back and held one hand on his forehead and the other on his stomach. "I'm going to see Mom and Dad tomorrow. They couldn't make the last treatment, so I told them I'd go see them."

"You sure you're feeling up to that? Aren't you sick?" Chloe pushed down the remembrance of what her dad had been through, to get rid of the twist in the pit of her stomach. She steered around turning cars.

"No. I'll be fine by morning. It should pass by then."

He shouldn't drive to Boone in that condition, even if he felt better. "I'll drive you there." The words came out without much thought. She did want to meet his parents at some point. It would be a good chance to get to know more about Mason and possibly uncover the vaguer parts of his life.

Mason sat up, as though energized. "You . . . you want to come? To my parents?"

Was he faking being sick? By the way he perked up, she would think so. But she knew him better. Wait, what was she doing? She hoped she wasn't leading him on. Friends was what they were. One friend supporting another, as friends should do.

"Yeah. I'd like to meet them, if that's all right with you. But if you'd rather me not, I—"

"No. I mean, that would be great if you could. Just didn't think you'd want to. That's all."

"First things first. Getting you into your room."

Mason raced up the stairs of the B&B, pushed his door open, and headed straight to the bathroom. Chloe sat in his desk chair with her elbows on her knees and covered her face. She'd yet to be with Mason when he was sick with nausea and vomiting. On one hand, she wanted to desperately help him, but knew there was nothing she could do. In another way, she wanted to run. Run from feeling so helpless and, at the same time, run from the memories of her dad's worst days.

She paced the floor, then tapped on the bathroom door. "Mason, is there anything I can do? Anything I can get you?"

"It's all right. Be out in a minute."

Chloe looked over Mason's wall calendar strewn with doctor appointments, tests, and follow-ups. She hadn't realized he had so many. Scan results? Only a few days ago? In fact, the day he'd read to the children at the hospital. He never mentioned the follow-up or shared the results with her. He could have told her there or at the corn maze. She couldn't imagine him not sharing the results if it were good news. Now *she* was getting nauseous.

Mason came out and lay on the bed. "I'm sorry. I don't want to keep you. You can go if—"

"It's all right. Let me get you a cool rag." She wet a towel in the bathroom and placed it on his forehead. "How often do you feel this bad?"

"Uh, well . . ."

Not so reassuring. "Every day?"

He nodded, then sat up. "Just about. That's to be expected with the chemo. At least the kind and dosage I have to take." His eyes drooped, as though pleading for her to not run away. To understand.

"The test results from your scan the other day. I saw it on the calendar. You didn't tell me how it went." She sat next to him on the bed and rubbed her sweaty palms on her jeans.

"It's the same. No improvement." He wiped his face with the towel. "All this time—nothing working. They want to do even more radical treatments when the last treatment is up." He shook his head. "Not doing it. I'll do a natural cancer diet from there on out and pray to Jesus for a healing. And whatever happens . . . happens. Mom said she'd get me started with juicing while I'm . . . still in town."

Still in town. The words hit her with a thud. Thankfully, his mom was willing to help as far as the cancer diet was concerned. And she especially agreed with Mason's faith-in-God comment. She'd heard of others having success with natural cancer cures, as opposed to failing results with chemo, like for Dad, Kristen, and now Mason. "I'll keep praying for you. You know that."

"I do."

A brush against Chloe's ankle launched her feet onto the bed. "What was that?"

A cat jumped onto the bed. "It's okay." He pulled the cat to him. "It's Tabby."

"What are you doing with him?" Was there no place in town that cat hadn't been? The last time she and Abby had seen him, he was sprinting for his life and about to check into cat eternity.

Tabby purred with a stroke of his back. "He kept following me everywhere. It was only a matter of time before he was going to get hit by a car. Couldn't have that on my conscience, could I? Mom offered to keep Tabby until I finish up everything here. I told her I may keep him for another week. I'm already getting used to him being around."

Finish up? Then what? Go back to Boston, leaving her with the extreme of memories? Some wonderful, others heartbreaking. And with them being so far apart, how would she handle always wondering how he was doing? Would they talk on the phone? Text back and forth? More importantly, would it be enough? Would friendship be enough?

"Thanks for coming tonight. And I also I want to thank you for the desk and typewriter. I love them both, but you shouldn't have."

"It's the least I can do for all you've done for me. The pendant, the kiln, the dance. Mason, I don't deserve any of it. It's all too much. But I do appreciate it." She scratched Tabby's neck and slid off the bed. "Just let me know what time you want to pick up your car and leave in the morning."

"Yeah. I'll let you know." He stood at the door with her. "Chloe, you said you didn't deserve anything and that it was all too much. Is there really such a thing as giving too much for someone you care for? Or . . . love?"

Love. He hadn't said that word to her. The way he looked at her, treated her, and everything he'd done for her said it. In all fairness, she'd made it clear she only wanted them to be friends. Maybe he did want to say he loved her but was afraid to cross the boundary she'd placed. But how she longed to one day hear those words. "No, I guess not. Maybe there is no such thing." *He's leaving soon, Chloe.* He was never here to stay. Never meant to fall in love. And only by chance had their paths crossed. "See you tomorrow."

Chapter 15

Mason skipped a stone across the water of the roadside pull-off. Chloe clasped her fingers together behind her head and took in a splash of warmth from the sun. It wasn't that he was stalling with hopes of spending more time with Chloe before arriving at Mom and Dad's. Or attempting to capture mementos of each minute, seeing it could be one of the few remaining things they'd do together. No . . . wasn't that at all.

"So tell me again why we're here. Aren't your mom and dad expecting us?"

He skipped another stone, then took a seat next to her on a bench made of thick wooden planks cradled by large stones on each end. He'd have thought that after close to a half year of knowing and being with her that his breath wouldn't still shorten when near her. But it did. Or the way she looked into his eyes and obliterated all his deepest worries and fears, casting them into the depths of the ocean. If at least for that space of time. So yeah. He'd harness whatever time there was.

"They can wait. Although, they are anxious to meet you." He cracked a smile. His mom had pried enough information from him to know that Chloe was the most beautiful and wonderful woman he'd ever met. She'd probably began cleaning, dusting, and polishing furniture within minutes of ending the call of her coerced-info dump. Oh no. He'd failed to place one final demand on Mom. Under no circumstance was she to break out the photo albums. Not that.

"What?" She sat up straight and slapped his shoulder. "What did you tell them? That I'm a pushy smarty-pants who drives you nuts?" She folded her arms in her characteristic smarty-pants way and shot a glare. "This is my waiting-for-an-answer face. In case you didn't know."

"Oh, I know." There wasn't a curve of her face he didn't know. He'd deciphered the arch of her brows, the gleam in her eyes, and the twist of her lips, all in record time. Unlike fleeting dates in the past, where he'd not had a clue of the real motives or sincerity. With Chloe, he knew her intentions intuitively. She was real. Kind, loving, and beautiful in every way. "Just thought we'd stop here for a minute. Spent a lot of time in this spot as a teen."

"You and your friends?" She folded loose strands of hair, picked up by the wind, behind her ear.

"No. Just me. It was all a little too boring for them. But for me, I could never get tired of this. So peaceful, tranquil. When I needed time to think, this was the place." His smile faded.

"What is it?"

"It was the year I got my driver's license and Dad gave me my first car. An old Chevy Camaro. We worked on it for months. Custom rims. New paint job. Thought I was helping to fix it up for him, but turns out he'd planned on giving it to me all along." He could sum up Mom and Dad's raising of him in a single word. Sacrifice. Working on a construction site all day left little to no energy for Dad. Something Mason wouldn't fully understand till later in life. But there Dad was every evening and into the night working on the car.

"Sounds like he was a great dad to you."

"Yeah. He was. That's when I started coming here. I'd park right here and just sit and think." He paused to collect his thoughts. Dragging up the past was the thing he'd always tried to avoid. Push it aside and move on. But today was different. He was with his best friend. "Years had gone by after finding out about my real mom and dad. I thought it didn't bother me anymore. But it did. The older I got, the more I understood being tossed aside like I didn't matter." He leaned over, picked up a rock, and tossed it into the stream along with the hidden things he'd suppressed in his heart. Talking to Chloe came easy. Even for the difficult things.

"I can't imagine how hard that must have been for you. Trying to process all that alone. I've always had Sarah, Mom, or Abby to talk to. Funny how we can take things or people for granted. As though they'll always be there for us."

He nodded. "In my mind, I thought that if I moved farther away to Boston, I'd leave all that hurt behind. Of course, I didn't. So I'd busy myself with as many things I could handle, just to keep from thinking too much. Worked for a while. But deep down I knew I was just fooling myself. I was running from painful memories. More importantly, running from forgiveness for my birth mom." Maybe even forgiveness for himself for a lifetime of resentment that should have been dealt with long ago. He had no excuse, having been brought up in church and raised by godly parents. He knew what the Bible said about roots of bitterness taking hold and the trappings of the Enemy. It was past time to confront the lie.

"I hope you don't mind me asking, but any more news about your mom wanting to see you?"

"I'm supposed to be meeting with her in a few weeks. We'll see how it goes. Supposedly she's been drug-free and alcohol-free for a year now. Even volunteers at a recovery center a few hours away from here."

"Mason, that's terrific. I mean, you sounded dead set against it when you told me about her. What changed your mind?"

"Oh, I don't know. Some auburn-haired smarty-pants beauty convinced me, I guess. The best part is, she doesn't realize that there's nothing I wouldn't do to make her happy." His eyes met hers. If she only knew how true his words were, maybe then she'd see him in a different light. Then again, there was nothing screaming more truth than that of his condition. He stood and held out his hand to her. "We should get going, I guess."

He started the car, turned the air conditioner on high, then steered onto the roadway.

Chloe reached over and straightened the collar of his polo shirt. "Tell me, do you ever miss that old car?"

"Still have it. Stays covered in a barn at my friend David's vacation home in the country, about an hour outside the city. I go there every now and then, but not nearly as much as I'd like to. Drive it around a little just to keep it running. Gives me time to think."

"What color is it? Typical woman question, I know."

"Red. Same color as the dress you wore when you asked me out on our first date. And about the same color as your cheeks when you hugged me at the fair when we met." He shot her a grin.

"For being a writer, you sure don't have an eye for detail or reality. For the record, you asked me out, and you hugged me. Get the story straight." She nudged him with her finger.

He shrugged. "But you liked it. It's as simple as admitting it." His smile gave way to a laugh.

A warning flashed in her eyes. "Just drive. Eyes on the road, not me." She reached over and turned the volume up on the radio. "Oh, remind me to ask your mom if she has any old photos of you. This ought to be good."

Why did he feel like a teenager bringing a girl home to meet Mom and Dad for the first time? And if he felt that way, what was Chloe thinking? His prayer the entire drive was that Mom wouldn't get into his childhood stories and thoroughly embarrass him. Of course, he suspected this would be quite amusing to Chloe, seeing it was right up her alley of poking and prodding. Hmm. Mom and Chloe in league together. Maybe this wasn't such a great idea after all.

The screen door to Mom's sun porch barely had time to shut before Mom wrapped her arms around Mason.

"Oh, I missed you." Mom kissed his cheek and, just as quickly, took Chloe's hands. "And of course, you're Chloe." She pulled Chloe into a hug. "It's so nice to finally meet you. Mason did say you were pretty but . . ."

"Oh, he did, did he?" Chloe gave Mason a smirk. "What else did he say?"

Yes. Things were already going predictably awry. Mason shook his head. These two women were already out the gate and in full gallop. It was time to pull back on the reins.

"Mom, is Dad—"

"Mason." Dad came into the sunroom and gave him a hug. "Glad you could come. And, Chloe, nice to meet you." Another hug. "Mason said you were pretty—"

"Uh, Dad." Mason took note of Chloe's blush and wondered if Mom and Dad were trying to make up for lost years of embarrassment. "You been doing a little bodywork on that dream truck, I hear." Something. Anything, to derail this fast-moving humiliation train from its tracks.

Dad put an arm around Mason's shoulder. "Want to check it out? Maybe Mom will run us out soft drinks and a few sandwiches." He winked at Mom.

Mom threw her hands in the air. "Didn't I say this would happen? Who needs a treadmill with as many trips a day I make out there." She laughed and shook her head.

It warmed Mason to see Chloe laugh with Mom and Dad. He could already see that she fit right in with the family. There was no doubt that both Mom and Dad adored her. Besides, what was there not to like?

Mason ran his hand alongside the truck's fender that Dad had patched and sanded. "Nice work, Dad. She's gonna be something else when you're done."

Dad beamed a smile. "Yeah. She will be." Then the smile was gone. "Just wish you could stay around once your treatments are done. We could take a ride on the Parkway. See how she handles the road."

"Yeah. Wish I could to." *Wish I could?* The words sounded hollow. Like they were an excuse. Why wouldn't he be able to choose what to do with his life? That was, if he wanted to. More importantly, what would God want him to do.? What were his plans for Mason's life? *Lord, help me to make the right decision. Help me to . . . not worry about what those two women are talking about.* He was certain that by the time that information-interrogation swap was over, Chloe would see him in a different way. Not good.

"Good. Now we can have our girl talk," Jenny said after Mason and his dad disappeared into the workshop. They took seats on floral-print-cushioned wicker chairs in the sunroom.

Chloe squirmed. What kind of girl talk? Skirts or pants? Heels or flats? Tea or coffee? It didn't matter. She liked Mason's mom. She was warm and inviting. The kind of person most would instantly take a liking to. Mason was truly blessed to have such a loving and caring parent.

"So Mason tells me you two met in church at the altar?" She readjusted the wildflower arraignment on the end table beside her.

Wow. Okay. Jumping right in there and starting from the beginning. Chloe decluttered all the disastrous mishaps that took place at her and Mason's first meeting. The broken vase and spilled flowers. Marbles all over the floor and glitter everywhere. Torn collar and tangled embrace. Scratch the embrace. That wasn't so bad. "Right. Yeah, I guess we did." Somehow that realization hadn't crossed her mind. The altar part.

She doubted Mason had overlooked that detail like she had. He was all about details, all scribbled into his pocket notebook. But what he could have missed then, he probably didn't miss the day he worked on the platform at church, when she'd walked up the aisle and to the altar to bring him coffee. She thought she'd have to wave smelling salts under his nose to bring that statue back to life. It was then that she'd realized he possibly had feelings for her. At least more than he was leading on. Whether it was his fear of telling her because of the cancer or him still thinking of the past love of his life was uncertain. What she was sure of was his love for her.

"He's lucky to have found a friend like you, Chloe. I was worried about him moving where he didn't know anyone. I know he's a grown man, but still. Moms worry." She gave a heavy sigh.

"I can understand that, I guess. But isn't he used to being away, way out in Boston? Probably has lots of friends there." She could picture mobs of woman fighting for his attention at his book signings or book clubs, like at Holly's. How could he not have lady friends?

"Not really. From what I can tell anyway. He has one good friend, David. His doctor. Other than that, no one I know of. And never a serious girlfriend either. They always had other motives, he'd tell me. Hate to say it, but maybe they were in it for the money. I don't know."

"Never a girlfriend? Even in school? As nice and handsome as he is, I can't imagine not having at least a few."

She giggled. "He looked quite different back then. Thin as everything with dark-rimmed glasses. Of course, they're in style now. Had braces and acne. A far cry from how he looks now. Had the girls known how he'd turn out, they would have been fighting over him for sure."

"I can relate. I went through quite a change myself. Had a chubby face and wore fake eyeglasses for a while, thinking it would detract from my acne stage."

Jenny looked back toward the shop. "How about a cup of coffee inside?" They took their seats at the kitchen table as she poured them each a cup. "I wouldn't want Mason to know I told you this. But I find it interesting that the only girl he ever liked was one that he never actually met. And it happened on your family's campground. He told me recently that your family owned it."

"Yeah. We did. But tell me, how old was he when he met this girl?"

"Well, we started taking him there every summer starting at about ten. Loved every minute of it. Active, like most boys. Playing in the stream, riding bikes. Then something changed the summer he was thirteen. He wasn't so active anymore. We'd find him sitting on a big rock looking across the stream at the cabin on the other side. Sometimes for hours." Mom shook her head.

"Looking at what?"

"We didn't know at first. He came back home from that trip depressed. Spent most of his time in his room after that. Started writing a lot for some reason. Before the next summer even arrived, he kept asking if we were going back camping when school let out. Anxious as everything."

"Then what?"

"Travis and I never saw him pitch a tent so fast when we arrived at the campground that summer. Then off he went to the stream. I decided to follow, and there he was sitting on that rock again. Had a journal in his hand. Spent more time looking across toward the cabin than writing. So I took a picture of him sitting there.

"He came back to the camp later to eat, then said he'd be right back. Well, it had been a while since he left, and it started to get dark. Just as we decided to go look for him, he came back soaking wet, limping, and a cut above his eye. Said he fell in the stream."

"I don't understand. I'm a little lost here. What about the girl?" Chloe asked.

"Trust me. I was lost about it too. But I didn't know why and what happened until years later. In fact, it was the day before he left for Boston after graduation that he told me. I'd imagine boys typically wouldn't talk about girl things to their moms, but for some reason he did. Come to find out he was watching a young girl the whole time, by the cabin."

"Yeah. He did mention something about that to me, but not much detail."

"Don't know how he fell in love with someone he never met or spoke to, but he insisted he did. Said he'd watch her playing volleyball with a friend or just sitting under that gazebo by the cabin. Said she was always smiling and laughing and carefree. Couldn't help himself, he said."

It all made sense. His interest in the cabin. The gazebo. All part of his memories with the girl. "But never once talked to her? Why?"

"Too shy. Low self-image. But he almost did. He saw her on our last day at the campground, playing volleyball with a friend. The ball got stuck in that big tree by the cabin, and she couldn't get it down. So that evening he went back. He crossed the stream and climbed the tree, trying to hold a flashlight at the same time. Got the ball—and a cut above his eye from a branch—then fell in the process."

"That's why he was limping?"

"Yep. Told me he'd mustered the courage to go to the cabin door to give it to her but didn't have the nerve to knock. So he just left the ball right there on the porch. Lost his girl and his favorite cap all at the same time."

He had the courage to cross the stream, climb a tall tree, then fall out. But not the courage to meet her? "You mentioned a favorite cap?"

"Yeah. One of those . . . I think they call them newsboy caps. The kind like he still wears sometimes."

"Wow. Can't believe he told you all that. Do you think he still regrets not meeting her?" She suspected he did.

"I know he does. Till this day, he says every story he writes is with her in mind. She's been his inspiration all these years. She's why he started writing in the first place. It's just my assumption, but sometimes I think he's never settled down with a girl because no one's matched how he felt back then when he watched her." Jenny got up from the table and brought their empty cups to the sink.

"You mentioned taking a picture of Mason sitting on the rock. Do you still have it?"

"Are you kidding? He had it blown up and framed. It's been on the dresser in his old room all these years. He tells me if the house catches fire, grab the picture first, then worry about everything else." Jenny laughed.

"Can I see the photo?"

"Sure, but let's hurry before they come back in." She led the way to Mason's childhood bedroom.

Chloe lifted the gold-framed eight-by-ten photo from off the dresser and studied it.

Jenny tapped the glass. "That's the girl under the gazebo, with the straw hat and sundress. Her head is down, with her face covered by the wide brim of the hat, so you can't make her out. Wish we could."

Chloe drew air into her lungs at the realization that she'd stopped breathing. Maybe her heart even slowed. She didn't need to see the girl's face. She knew precisely who it was and who'd wore that hat. She tried to convince herself that it could not possibly be. This was who he'd been emotionally hanging on to all these years? Who'd inspired all his writing? The one he was possibly still in love with? Though she did have the impression he'd let her go and had moved on with Chloe. Except . . . Her heart raced and ached at the same time.

The picture frame rattled on the dresser as she set it down. She'd heard of pivotal points in life where time stood still. For just that moment, there was no outside world, no sound—only stillness. This was one of those times.

Jenny placed a hand on Chloe's shoulder. "Are you all right, dear?"

Was her changed expression that noticeable? "Yeah. Fine." She pressed her lips together to prevent her jaw from trembling.

"We'd better go before they get back," Jenny said.

Chloe snapped a picture of the framed photo with her phone on the way out, then settled back into the dining room as Mason and his dad returned. She strained out an at-ease expression, then realized the futility of it all when Mason's eyes caught hers. He knew her well.

"Would you like more coffee, Chloe?" Jenny asked.

Chloe sat motionless, her head still spinning. Still in disbelief.

"Chloe?"

"I'm sorry ... you were saying?" She noticed all eyes on her.

"More coffee?"

"No thanks. I think I'm done." She forced a quick smile.

Mason stood next to Chloe's chair and gave a soft rub to her back. She looked up at him in a way she hadn't before. *Breathe.* This couldn't be happening. But it was, and she needed time to think.

"Mom, I'm wiped out, and I think Chloe and I will head for home," Mason said.

They exchanged hugs at the door and then walked down the steps together.

Chloe took Mason's hand and pulled him to a stop before reaching the car. "Wait."

Secrets. Sure, Mason had kept quiet about his condition. He should have told her from the beginning. As a result, she had felt hurt, confused, and deceived. She understood why he'd done so afterward, but it would have been easier to deal with if he'd confessed it from the start.

Now it was her turn. Would she be the next keeper of a secret that should be brought to light? No one would know if she remained silent. But she would.

"Is something wrong, Chloe?"

"Mason . . ." She placed a hand to his face, drew near, and gently pressed her lips to his. Another fleeting moment when time stood still, followed by a flood of warmth and prickles of goose bumps on her skin. Mason's perplexed look when he opened his eyes mirrored what was going on inside her. The secret would have to wait. Far too much to think about. Too much to consider. And now that she'd kissed him, possibly no way out.

Chapter 16

Sarah's jaw hung when Chloe unfolded the events Mason's mom had revealed. They dipped their tea bags one last time, standing at Sarah's kitchen island, then moved to the living room couch.

Chloe set her cup down on the coffee table. "I didn't mean to come here this late, but there was no way I could keep this in till morning."

Sarah half choked on her sip of tea. "Are you kidding me? I can assure you there's not a hotter topic being talked about in all of Fleetwood tonight. My sister is seeing the most desired romance writer in the country. Sorry. Just a fact. And he was in love with a childhood sweetheart he never really met. Or maybe still thinking of? And it all happened at our campground. You have to admit, that does sound romantic. It's like he's held off being committed his whole life because of her. Come to think of it, sounds a little sad too."

"That's not all." Chloe rose from the couch and ran her fingers through her hair. She'd burst if she didn't tell someone. "I haven't told you the most important part. And this has to stay between us for now."

"There's more?"

"So much more. I know who the girl is."

"No way?" Sarah sat straight and slapped the arm of the couch. "Who is it?"

"His mom showed me a framed photo of her, and I took a picture of it with my phone." Chloe paced the floor and pulled the phone from her back pocket.

"All right, you're killing me here. Picture please." Sarah snapped her fingers and jabbed out her hand. She grabbed the phone. Her eyes widened, and she jumped from the sofa. She stared briefly at the picture, then back to Chloe. "No. Way." Sarah shook her head, then fell back down on the sofa. "This is you. Beyond a doubt. And that's me in the background. Does he even suspect it?"

"No. I think he would have told me if he did." He would have, wouldn't he? He'd already had the courage to tell her about the girl. What better time to come out with it then. Just spill it all and leave everything on the table. No more secrets. Nothing to hide.

"More importantly, are you going to tell him? I mean, what did you do? What did you say to him when you found out? My goodness, Chloe. This man has carried you around in his heart most of his life." She handed the phone back.

"I don't know. It was like I froze when I found out. My head was still spinning when we walked out of the house, and all I could think to do was kiss him." What in the world was she thinking? More importantly, what was *he* now thinking? She'd insisted they be only friends. And even though it was a one-second kiss, friends didn't kiss like that. Why would she send such mixed signals? How could she still say she only wanted to be friends?

"Kiss him? You kissed? Like on the lips, kissed?" Sarah folded her legs onto the couch and under her, with bulging eyes. "Girl, you better spill the rest."

"That was all. Just the kiss, then we left. And yes, it was great and wonderful. But I don't know what I was thinking." She put a hand to her forehead and shook her head. "He's gonna want to know what that was all about. He must be thinking more commitment." ·

"And this is bad for some reason? How is it bad? You have to tell him, Chloe." Sarah crossed her arms and gave a stern look.

"I don't know. If I tell him, he'd never agree to take it slow on my terms, and I can't say that I wouldn't blame him. I know he loves me."

Sarah picked up a fingernail file from off the end table and gave her nail a few swipes. "Think about it. How incredibly improbable this is. I mean, after all these years. This is not an accident, Chloe. It can't be. It's not a fluke. Not a coincidence. What if it's a God thing?"

"That's what part of me keeps saying, but—"

"But what? There is no *but*."

"How can I be sure he's the one?" She'd been waiting her entire life for *the one*. Hoped and prayed for the right guy. Even had her name on the prayer list at church several times. Anonymously, of course. She'd envisioned exactly how it would all play out and what it would be like. And how everything would effortlessly fall into place. Although not a single detail had fit into that template with her and Mason from the day they'd met.

"This is just like you. Always looking for a sign. A voice."

"And what's wrong with making sure of something so important?"

"I'm just saying, we don't hear booming voices from heaven telling us what to do, but this comes close. Think about it. A stranger shows up in town. You meet in the church—at the altar, of all places. He falls in love with you. In fact, never stopped loving you and is spending time at the cabin where he first saw you. Well, from afar, sitting on a rock anyway. Buys you a pendant the first day you meet, because somehow he knew how much it meant to you. On top of all that, it's obvious to everyone he adores you. And you still need a sign?"

Sarah was right. How many times would she question herself? Question God? But there were legitimate issues to consider. "I know I'm being ridiculous, but it's not that simple."

"It's about the cancer, isn't it?" Sarah slid closer and put an arm around her. "I think you need to leave that up to God. Pray for him. He needs it. You both need each other."

"You're right." Prayer. If she'd spend more time praying, less time worrying, and stop second-guessing, then maybe she could hear God's direction.

"Let me ask you one question." Sarah pressed the issue. "Do you love him?"

"Well, I . . ."

"No no no. You're not getting out of this. It's a simple question."

"Okay." She didn't need time to think about it. No need to rationalize or explain all the reasons why. All that remained was to simply admit it. "Yes, I do."

"You do what? Go on, say it. Say the words."

"All right. I love Mason. I do." The words gushed from deep within for the first time. She'd held them in her heart, guarding them carefully, as well she should. They weren't reckless words to throw around without meaning, but a solemn declaration to bind two hearts.

"So he loves you, and you love him. There's your sign." Sarah grabbed her and Chloe's teacups. "How about a refill?"

Chloe followed her to the island as Sarah freshened their cups. "How did you and Jeff know you were meant to be? Did you two get a sign?"

"Of course. You really want to know how Jeff and I knew we were meant to be before getting married?" She rubbed her bloodshot eyes.

"I'm warning you. I'll plug my ears if this gets weirdly uncomfortable."

"I said he could watch sports on the weekend if he promised he'd do the dishes and laundry at least once a week. Of course he said yes. Why, you ask? Because that's what men do before you tie the knot, right? With the exception of Mason, of course," she said with assurance. "They make promises they don't intend to keep. And in this case, you know what? Big fat liar. Anyway, back to getting a sign. I get a sign every weekend that assures me we were meant to be. It's written on a piece of torn cardboard that Jeff waves in the air while watching the game, which reads 'More chips please.'"

Chloe giggled. "At least it says *please*."

Sarah's brows narrowed. "Yippie!"

Yippie wasn't exactly how she'd define the way she'd have to explain to Mason what she'd meant by the kiss. Had she gotten his hopes up only to have him crushed if she didn't follow through? What else was a man to think if a woman had kissed him that way? No. Hearts were too delicate. And the words "I love you" were not intended to be thrown around unless they had real meaning. She'd have to explain to Mason if he asked her to. And she would. As soon as she settled her heart on the matter.

Maybe a farewell hike to the falls in the midday heat wasn't such a great idea. Mason hunched forward with his hands on his knees and gasped for breath. He was nowhere near the physical condition that he'd been back in the city, where walking city blocks were effortless. But now he'd gladly trade heavily traveled concrete sidewalks for tranquil nature trails, and city lights for starlit nights. If only . . .

The winding path following the stream called to mind one of his mom's favorite words of advice he'd drawn upon in his high school years. A wise reminder that oftentimes God uses the winding road to get us to where he wants us to be. God's detours, she would say, were his way of providing opportunities for growth so that a person would be able to stand and accomplish his will for our lives. All of which would allow Mason to ultimately reach and fulfill his destiny.

Detours. Weren't they also designed to go around and avoid problem areas? If so, what was God doing? The detour of life through Fleetwood Falls had only brought heartache and defeat. How could the departure from health to cancer lead to accomplishing God's will? Or to finding the love he'd searched for, only to lose it? Rather than being equipped, it was more like being stripped. If God was looking for an empty vessel, he'd found one.

Could it be that Tom's mantra of always being where you're

supposed to be, especially in the critical decisions of life, were playing out? Only this time not in a good way. Maybe he didn't belong here to begin with. But then again, what if God had brought him here to be released from his lovestruck childhood that had held him for so long? A detour to shed the baggage of lingering regret.

And now as impossible and daunting as it would be, he'd have to do the same with Chloe. The difference being, he'd gotten to know how wonderful she was. Not one of lustful desires but rather a deeper, unexplainable spiritual way. (Not that he didn't desire her, of course.) He'd held her in his arms in their dance and experienced sensations that he'd prayed would never end. Looked into eyes that immersed him in a culmination of all his longings. Held her hand and brushed her skin. And then, the unexpected kiss, followed by the sleepless night. This time, cancer and chemo weren't to blame for his restlessness.

But was it a goodbye kiss? What else could it have meant? Refocusing his attention back to his career was now the plan. If God truly had a road and a plan for him, he'd have to walk out. As for Chloe, she'd be all right. He'd already convinced himself she'd be better off without him. She was strong, spunky, and had her whole life ahead of her. Which was more than he could say for himself, as he'd leave Fleetwood with only a hope and a prayer.

A final bend in the trail and he'd arrive at the cabin, along with rest and . . . Chloe's Jeep? She hadn't mentioned she'd be stopping by. Mason searched his backpack for his phone. Battery dead. Maybe she did try to call. The kiss. Would she mention it?

A flutter of nerves invaded his stomach. Much like the evening at Chloe's shop and his all-too-late confession that had shaken her faith and trust in him. Hopefully, by now he'd put all that to rest and had restored her confidence in him.

He stopped after a few steps into the cabin. Chloe sat at the desk with his open laptop. He dropped his backpack to the floor. Why had he left it open? No. Not the email.

Chloe rose from the desk and covered her mouth with her hand, then held it out to the laptop. "When were you going to tell me about this?"

It was the last thing he'd wanted her to see. At least not like this. Her stare penetrated him, exposing his every vulnerability. Once again, he'd failed in his hopes of regaining her confidence. He stepped closer to her in a desperation to make things right. "Chloe, I can explain."

"Explain what? That you're leasing your condo and moving to California? For a year? Maybe two?" The quiver of her voice pummeled his insides. Confusion wrinkled her face. "I don't know what to think. I . . . To think, the whole reason I came here was to . . ."

To what? Explain the kiss? To say that just maybe there was a chance? "You were going to say?"

"Nothing." She shook her head. "Never mind."

What had he done? Again. What kind of person was he that he caused her so much pain? How could so many things go wrong when he was trying to do everything right. And what was it that she couldn't say?

"Chloe, it's not finalized. These were recent developments that up to now were only talked about. I haven't agreed to anything yet."

"Yet?" She glanced back to the laptop and took a deep audible breath, then exhaled. "This has always been your dream, right? Had you stayed in Boston and never came here, never met me, you'd be pursuing it, I'm sure. So what's stopping you now?" She blinked away the moisture in her eyes.

"You. Us." He blurted the words out with a shaky voice. Holding out for a last second, nonexistent miracle was stopping him.

"I am? I'm stopping you?" Her brows arched, and she placed her hands on her hips. "So this is all my fault?"

"Nothing's your fault. Not anyone's fault." He pushed down the swell emotions. He'd have to make it through this without coming apart.

"I'd never stand in the way of your dreams, Mason. And if you didn't go, would you look back with regret years from now and blame me for blowing your chance? How do you think that would make me feel?"

"No. It's not like that at all."

"I'm sorry, Mason. I don't want to be that person. I won't."

"I love you, Chloe."

Her eyes held to his. He ran his hands down her arms and took both of her hands. It was time to lay it all down. Cards on the table and accept the outcome. "You're what I've always wanted. What I've always needed. I can do without the accolades of a career and all that comes with it. I just can't do life without you. I don't want to. You're what's been missing in my life. A movie deal is what I thought I wanted for so long. But you're what I want. What I need."

She broke her gaze, then returned. "I can't do this, Mason. I can't." She took a step back.

He held on to her hand. "I'll turn everything down right now. It would only take you saying one thing and one thing alone. Just say you love me. That is, if you do. Tell me you love me, and I'll stay . . . forever." Forever? Even to himself the word came across as hollow. An echo bouncing off the walls of his heart and returning with endless unanswered questions for what the future would hold. How could he make such a foolish, ridiculous promise?

Her hands slipped from his. "We can always be friends. Can't we?"

There went that word again. As much as he'd forever value and cherish their friendship, it would always fall short of what could have been so much more. Again, he'd respect her wishes. But not without a last expression and admittance of the depth of his love for her.

He dipped his head and nodded. "You'll always be my best friend. No matter where I go. But you know as well as I do that would never work. For me at least. How do you simply like someone, when you love them more than life itself?"

Chloe's lips parted to speak, but instead she picked her purse from the hearth of the fireplace and hung it from her shoulder. "I . . . I've got a lot of orders to get out. Been a little swamped lately." She strained out a smile. "So I'd better . . . you know . . ." She thumbed toward the door.

"So that's it? It's over?" He followed her to the door. The mist in her eyes turned to tears. The only comfort that he'd derived from the conversation was that she did, in fact, have feelings for him. That he was loved by her in whatever measure she was able to offer. Through the fear. The unknowns. He was loved.

"I don't know. Maybe it should have never begun. I'll pray for you every day. I promise. I'll forfeit every prayer I'll ever pray to have that one answered. For you to be well. To live. And yes, I do care for you Mason. More than you know. But some things in life we can't plan. We can't control. I wish to God we could."

Her hand rested on the doorknob of the entry door.

"You said you'd stay forever. How long is your forever, Mason? How long? As long as Daddy's or Kristen's?" Her hand covered her mouth. "I'm sorry. I didn't mean—"

"You're right. Some things in life we can't change. And I don't know how long my forever is. But I know with God there's a chance. Isn't that what faith's about? Besides, however long it is, I want to live my life to the fullest. With you or without you. Preferably with you. But, there can be so much more for us. Who knows, maybe this whole thing can turn around. Please Chloe, don't give up on me. On us."

She nodded. "I wish I had that kind of faith. I really do. But right now, I'm all out." She wiped her cheeks, wrapped an arm around his neck, and pressed her warm face to his. "I'm sorry." With that, the door shut.

He lowered himself onto the fireplace hearth as the sound of Chloe's Jeep dissipated. What else did he, could he expect. Of all the break-up scenes he'd ever written, there was none like this. Those were simply words penned to a page with predictable happily-ever-after outcomes, as true romance stories were. But this? What had just played out was a chapter he'd never want to write. Wrecked, lonely, and soon to be for-gotten was the only way he could sum up what he was feeling.

He scanned the homey cabin that he'd soon be departing. It was quiet. Only silence. Except for Chloe's last words returning in a whisper that migrated from his ears to his heart. "I'm sorry." She wasn't the only one who was sorry. He questioned if he was the only one who ever wondered if it were possible to run out of tears. He guessed he'd find out.

Chapter 17

The treatment center bell sounded, signifying a cancer-free patient. Come to think of it, the first ringing Mason had heard in nearly half a year of his visits, and not a bell he'd be ringing. To do so would have meant he'd be cancer-free, along with the possibility of being with Chloe. Instead, five hours remained for his last treatment, and miserable Marty to contend with.

But today just maybe Marty would have a companion to his defeatist perspective. Someone to understand how the reality of truth, though dark, could drown out the voice of hope and faith. Not something one would intend to do, nor venture out in search of, but simply there. The result of life masquerading itself as a gift adorned with its wrapping and bow, only to be opened revealing the consequences of living in a fallen world. All supported by the well-known Bible verse about the rain falling on the just and the unjust. As of late, it had never rung truer.

Another sleepless night as a result of his talk with Chloe at the cabin several days prior made remaining optimistic difficult. He couldn't blame her for her decision. She was the one who stood getting hurt the most in the end and the one assuming the risk if healing didn't come. He loved her too much to allow that.

The needle pushed into Mason's chemo port for the final time. *Final* things to do seemed to be on the agenda for the week before leaving Fleetwood. Start packing. Say goodbye to friends made. A trip to Mom's in Boone for cancer-diet recipes and to drop Tabby off till he was finished packing up his Boston condo before leaving for LA. And this time taking no emotional baggage that would last a lifetime. That one being the biggest lie he'd ever told himself.

Marty pushed the roll-away partition aside, removed his earbuds, and rubbed his eyes. "Mason. Guess I dozed off there for a minute. How's it been going for you?"

"It's going." Now was as good time as any to join in on Marty's usual party of positivity, with this finale being a meeting of the minds, of sorts. But was he back to being "Mason" now? Was it out with "Mace"? And was that a sincere "How's it been going?"?

A confused look flashed across Marty's face. "Are you all right?"

"Am I all right? Look around." He motioned with his hand around the room. "Is anybody here really all right?" *C'mon, Marty.* The man who'd earned every illustrious pessimistic title known to man, at least equal to the multiplicity of titles given to boxers and pro-wrestlers, should know better than to ask a question like that. Heck, even a famous groundhog possessed the grand title of the Prognosticator of all Prognosticators.

A befuddled look and silence by Marty followed as he repositioned himself and stared out the window. Mason's assumption being that Marty must be having an off day. Then again, wasn't every day a bad day for him? Or . . . was it more like Mason having a bad day? Guilt weighed heavy on him. *God, forgive me. What am I doing? My hope and trust is in you. Let me never forget that.*

"A pastor." Marty took a sip of water from his straw.

That was all. No words to follow. "What?"

Marty broke his gaze from the window. "That's what I was. A pastor. For twenty-five years, to be exact." He rested his clasped hands on his chest. "Stood in the pulpit Sunday after Sunday, preaching the whole truth. Believed every word of it. Until I didn't anymore."

Dazed? Shocked? What was he hearing? Marty a preacher? "What happened? If you don't mind me asking."

"Life happened. Got my eyes off God and more on the circumstances around me. People sick. Dying. Started questioning God's motives of why he'd allow certain things to happen. Like, why does evil sometimes prevail?" He swallowed hard and swiped the corner of his eye with a finger. "Like why didn't he take me instead of my wife? No. Life's not fair, my friend. This isn't heaven, and it's not our home."

"Sorry to hear all that, Marty. About everything." He was right about this physical earth not being their home. They were only pilgrims passing through, as Pastor Hank had preached a few sermons back. *Pilgrim* was a fitting description to his time spent in Fleetwood. Just passing through.

Brandy removed Marty's attachments and returned to her station. He sat up and buttoned his shirt. "I understand this is your last day here."

"Yeah. It is." And it couldn't end soon enough.

"I know this might sound strange, but I'm grateful God sent you here. Not that I'm thankful because of the cancer, of course. You tried to remind me of faith and hope, and I didn't want to hear it. Too busy harboring bitterness, anger, and resentment toward life and, more importantly, toward God. Drove friends and family away as a result. Had the Lord returned or taken me with all that mess, I don't know if I would have made it to heaven."

Was being here one of God's detours in the grand scheme of things? One of Tom's "being in the right place" sayings? He replayed something Tom had said on his first Sunday visit to Fleetwood Assembly. *"You're not here by accident."* Could this have been one of those divine appointments?

Marty stood, grabbed his bag, and tossed his empty water bottle into the wastebasket.

"Hey, Marty. You take care of yourself. And about that heavenly home. One day I'll see you on the other side, right?" Another final goodbye. This time to Marty. And further confirmation of God's providence and goodness. Something else to be thankful for.

"Yeah. You will. But first, I think I'll pay a visit to my kids. I've got a new grandchild I haven't met yet. Past time to make things right." He pushed his cap onto his head and gave a salute. "See you, Mason."

Marty wasn't the only one who was thankful they'd met. Was God showing Mason a reflection of how he could have turned out? Angry? Bitter? Full of resentment? *Lord, help me not to fall into that pit of hopelessness.* A despairing place where good couldn't be seen in anything and cynicism ruled and reins.

Mason later glanced at the treatment center in the rearview mirror of his Rover one last time. He'd never wanted to erase a memory of a place more than of there. Memories to keep were the church where he'd regained a faith that was lost in his pursuit of success, and where he'd found a love that only God could have created and placed in his heart.

He dropped the church key, which he'd been given while working there, into the mail slot. A black '57 Chevy caught his eye next to the wrought iron fencing that surrounded the cemetery at the end of the block. Tom? He spotted Tom to the far side of the rows of plots, sitting on a concrete bench as Mason pulled up. Did he have family buried there? A friend?

Tom scooted to one side of the bench. "Mason. Take a load off. What brings you here?" He removed his hat and hung it on his knee.

"Saw you here and thought maybe this was where I needed to be." He smiled and patted Tom's shoulder. If anyone had any departing wisdom, it would be him. A man he'd instantly taken a liking to and considered not only a friend but much like a father.

"Right. Not worth a chance of missing what God may have for you. I reckon sometimes we'll never know what we've missed, while other times . . . well, let's just say that regret can be hard to put to rest."

Something lurked below the surface in the way Tom spoke. Could be regrets of his own that trailed his words on several occasions when they'd spoken. If he'd wanted it known, it would have come out by now.

Mason pointed toward the plots. "Family here?"

He nodded. "Started that next novel?"

He'd take it that Tom wasn't interested in giving any additional information as to his reason for being there. "Yeah. I've got a few ideas floating around in my head."

"Ever hear of K. T. Hawkins?" Tom fiddled with the rim of his hat.

Kyle Thomas Hawkins? One of the greatest novelists to ever live? "Are you kidding? Till this day I study his writing style in hopes of gleaning even a nugget from his work. It's a mystery the way he suddenly disappeared from the scene long ago. I don't think anyone knows what happened. Why do you ask? Are you familiar with his work?"

Another nod. "I am. Only one person knows the entirety of what happened to him. Some that knew of it have passed on, and a remaining few, out of respect, choose to let it lay, I suppose."

"So you know what happened?"

"K. T. was in the middle of writing a novel when it happened. It would also be his last. Never finished it. The plan was to pick up his date for a special event. The love of his life. But what she didn't know was that he'd planned to propose that night. He knew from the moment he'd laid eyes on her that she was the one. Georgia was her name."

Tom sighed and stared off into the distance. "A storm was rolling in that evening. Knocked out the power as he was writing, so he lit a candle and continued. Lost track of time and forgot the clock had stopped. By the time he'd rushed out the house, word had come that Georgia was worried where he was because of the storm. She'd sped off to his house to look for him, and that's when it happened. Her car slid off the road and . . . she was gone."

"Tragic. I didn't know any of that. You think K. T. held himself responsible for what had happened?" The story sounded like Tom's insistence of always being where you're supposed to be. "Maybe he couldn't break free from the guilt of thinking it all could have been avoided if he'd only been where he needed to be. God wouldn't hold him responsible for that."

"I know." He cleared his throat and gave subtle nod. "I tell myself that every day. But it doesn't change the fact that it shouldn't have happened. I should have been there that evening."

Wait. What did he just say? *He* should have been there? He was Kyle Thomas? *T* as in *Tom*? "Tom. Are you . . ."

"Yeah." His Adam's apple rose and fell. "I'd even gotten dressed early that morning. Eight hours early, to be exact, just to make sure I would be ready. Anxious to see her would be an understatement. Practiced what I'd say when I proposed. Had it all planned out." He pulled a handkerchief from his back pocket and wiped his cheek.

Mason put an arm around his shoulder. Regret. How it plagued so many, he supposed. Especially when tied to one of God's greatest gifts—love. Remorse, lying there dormant yet seething. Leaving one silently crying out to be released from its eating away, with its tugging of the strings most delicate to the heart. Regret for not being a better parent, husband, or wife. Regret of a grown son or daughter for not being there and for not doing more for their parents when they needed them most. A loved one having passed or missed opportunities. Only Jesus could sooth that never-releasing, ever-present hold. Jesus was also the one needed to help Mason realize that letting go of Chloe was the right thing to do. He'd never want her to live with regrets like Tom's.

The leaves of the cemetery's lone oak tree rustled from a passing gust, and the chirp of a nesting cardinal broke the silence. Two men sat hoping and praying. Maybe even pretending that everything would be okay in the face of so much that wasn't. No one ever said life would be fair. He just hadn't thought it would be so difficult. He figured given enough time, hardships from one degree to another would happen to all. But regardless, and through it all, God was still a good God. The broken are not alone. And he gave them a shoulder to cry on. All because of His love.

Tom tipped his head and put on his Stetson. He pulled out his pocket watch and flipped it open to a picture of a young lady pressed into the lid. "My Georgia. Beautiful, isn't she?"

Young. Far too much life ahead of her, and too many years of regret and tears for Tom. "Yeah. That she is."

Tom tilted his face toward the sun then returned the watch to his pocket. "Leaves should start turning soon." His voice cracked. "Beautiful day, isn't it?"

Written into a make-believe story? Sure. But in real life . . .

"Yeah." The word came out with a whisper. "Just lovely. Couldn't be any better."

Chloe dropped the box with a thud, fanned her face, and paced the floor of her pottery shop. The more she thought of it, the faster her pace and the more heat that flooded her face. Why? No, how could he do this? She gave the box several slaps with a rag sending puffs of dust floating.

Mom took her hand and led her to the couch. "All right. I know you're upset, but there must be a reason."

There was a reason, all right. Downright rude. Chloe plopped onto the couch next to Mom and jerked a tissue from the Kleenex box next to her. "He just up and left. I mean, who does that? Charlotte said he'd checked out two days ago. Two days. Did you get a call from Mason saying goodbye? Because I didn't get a call. Just left the B and B. Left Fleetwood. Left . . . me." She blew her nose and yanked another tissue. None of it made sense. Not the Mason she knew. Or thought she'd known.

Mom cupped her hand over Chloe's. "It was no secret that he wasn't here to stay."

"But not even a goodbye?"

"Maybe the last talk you two had at the cabin was a goodbye. At least to him. You said he'd opened up to you and expressed his feelings to the point of saying that he loved you. He'd even offered to stay, right?"

"Which was exactly why I couldn't say it back. I wasn't about to let him give up everything he's ever wanted for me." She tossed her crumpled tissue into the wastebasket already half-full of tissues and crossed her arms.

Mom pulled strands of hair, pasted on from tears, from Chloe's face. "It's just my guess, but I think it was too hard for him to see you again. How else would you expect him to feel? He'd put his heart out there, took the risk, and in the end lost the love of his life. It's okay to be upset with him, for now. But don't be angry. You'd only be hurting yourself."

"You're right. Look at me. Trying to place the blame on him. I messed up, Mom." Chloe wiped her cheeks and shook her head. "Why do I do that? I let fear push me away from things. Away from people. I think it always has. And now I've pushed Mason away. The most wonderful, amazing man I've ever met. I couldn't have prayed for a better man. I don't know. Sometimes I feel like I'm in quicksand, and the more I struggle to get out, the more I sink."

"Then quit struggling."

But how else was she supposed to feel when everything that had meant anything to her was slipping away? Dad. The land and cabin. And now Mason. "What?"

"Quit struggling and give it to God."

"But what if he doesn't live? Then what?"

"Let me ask you something. If he didn't have cancer, would you have loved him any less or more?"

Chloe had to admit she'd never thought of it that way before.

"Of course I'd love him all the same. But if you knew Daddy could be dying when you met have, would you have still married him?"

"Your dad was a picture of health when we first met. So it's easy for me to say yes. But I do know that once I fell in love, I never wanted to be away from him."

"Sounds like how I feel right now." Chloe fiddled with the rubber band on her wrist.

"No one's guaranteed tomorrow. Whether it's through sickness or accident, we're in God's hands. We have to trust him and cherish each day he gives us. So if I had only one day to be with your dad, it would be worth it, and I'd do it all over again. Despite the fear or heartache. Just a chance for one more day."

Chloe took it all in, considering the fear Mason was facing during his tragic ordeal. Like he'd told her, he didn't have the luxury of running from his disease. He had no choice but to face it head on, along with the children at the hospital he'd read stories to. The only hope was for a miracle.

"I hope you don't blame God for all this. Just hear me out for a second. What if all this was meant to be?"

She'd go along with everything her mom had said so far, but she'd have to explain this one. "So you're saying all this heartbreak is meant to be? And the cancer. That can't be in God's plan. Not the God I know."

"Honey, we both know sickness and disease doesn't come from God, but he can, and does, use unfortunate circumstances in life for our good. For instance, you'd never have meet Mason had he not come to Fleetwood for treatments, right?"

"I guess."

"And what were the chances of meeting him at the church? Not to mention him being the only man you ever loved."

She was right. At the altar was where the whole bizarre chain of events took place that tried her patience as never before. Mason and Tabby. Partners in crime. She nearly laughed thinking back on it, but instead cried.

That day she'd wanted him as far away from her as possible. Now that he was, she wanted him back. She wished he was back to spill marbles and glitter all over the floor. She'd gladly come back to church after an already long day in the pottery shop to vacuum and clean it all up. And the torn blouse? So what. A few clicks away and another would be sent. She longed to see him pull out his pocket calendar and watch his obsessive note-taking, which had once irritated her. But there was nothing she could do about it now.

Mom pointed to the box in the middle of the floor, which Chloe had taken down from the loft. "What's in that box?"

"Don't know. Haven't opened it yet. Looks like it's been up there a long time, with all that dust on it."

Chloe opened it and took out an old volleyball. The same one she and Sarah had played with when kids at the cabin. She cracked a smile. They'd drawn hearts, stars, and their names with markers on the ball. "Sarah loves Jeff" was written in a heart. On the other side was written "Chloe loves" followed by a question mark. Her eyes latched on to another item. She took it out.

"What is it?" Mom rose from the couch and met Chloe for a closer look.

A hat. But not just any hat. A newsboy hat, like the one Mason occasionally wore. She flipped the hat over. The initials *MC* were written in permanent marker on the rim. Mason Chadwick? It couldn't be. Could it?

"Mom, I think it's Mason's old hat. Jenny mentioned him not only losing his girl but his hat when he'd gotten the ball out of the tree." She clutched the hat to her chest.

"Maybe Dad found it and just packed it away with the rest of the outside things when we left the cabin for the last time."

This was all too much. So many signs. Admittedly, she wasn't one to believe in chance. But the way Mason showed up in town, combined with the revelations of his connection to the campground, all leading straight to her couldn't be accidental. Did it all point to divine providence? Not only was she loved by Mason since way back in their childhood, but also loved by an almighty God that cared enough to think of her future.

She pulled a sliver of paper protruding from the inside brim of the hat.

"What is it?" Mom moved behind her to read it.

"Looks like a note." She unfolded it. *April 7. Morgan Campground. The day I fell in love.* "April 7? Wait a minute. That was the day we met at the church fair. I remember because Holly's birthday was the day before." Chloe and her mom looked at each other with amazement.

Chloe knew beyond a doubt what she needed to do. Go to Boston. Not to stop him or stand in the way of his dreams. It would be strictly to tell him how much she loved him. How much she cared. To tell him things she should have said all along. Without the fear. Without running. He needed to know how much he'd affected her life. How she was now willing to face her fears, trust God, and move on from the things that were holding her back. Things that were stopping her from opening up to him. Stopping her from being with the man she loved.

·

Chapter 18

Chloe grabbed her carry-on bag from the overhead bin and made her way off the plane. She'd had plenty time to rehearse what she'd say to Mason. His refusal to answer her calls left her all the reason more to believe he didn't want to speak. If necessary, she'd beg and plead for him to listen. To simply hear her out. Then he could do what he wanted. But at least he would know how she felt. She'd say what she needed to say and apologize for the things that should have never slipped from her lips.

Her thoughtless comment at their last meeting, about how long his forever was, had singed her heart when spoken and remained with lingering regret. How would he know it was spoken out of her depth of love for him? She'd never said that she loved him in return to his declaration of love. He needed to know they were words spoken out of fear. Fear of their unknown future and the uncertainty of the number of their days together. But no more.

She'd trust God for the future, no matter how daunting. The Enemy would no longer steal her blessings and the plan for her life. Not if she could help it. Whether that plan and purpose was with Mason or without, she'd press on. It was time to stop running. Stop retreating from the hard things in life and stand, knowing God was with her and would not forsake her in her times of feeling alone.

The cab pulled to the curb and came to a stop. Chloe checked the address on her phone and the building. This was it. Mason's condo. She grabbed her bag and flung it over her shoulder. Her summersaulting insides would have normally been considered butterflies of nervousness, but instead were a resemblance of anxious anticipation. She wanted to be in the arms of the one she loved. Embraced by the man that had held her in his heart from the time of being a boy. Though far too young to know what true love was, he'd never let go of what he felt was real.

She looked for his number on the door, finding it at the end of the hallway, and drew a deep breath. Her heart pounded as she raised her hand to knock, then stopped before making contact. The sheers were drawn to narrow windows on either side of the door. She peered inside. The condo was empty? Nothing there but a lone sofa from her vantage point. He'd already left.

"No no no." This couldn't be happening. She dropped her bag. It had been less than a week since he'd left Fleetwood. Her yank of her phone from the bag sent it tumbling to the ground. She pushed down swelling emotions, sat cross-legged on the floor, and scrolled to find Jenny's number. "Pick up. Pick up."

"Hello."

"Jenny? It's . . . it's Chloe." Her voice shook. She stood and paced in front the door.

"Is something wrong, dear? You sound a little flustered."

"Have you heard from Mason lately? I'm at his condo, and it appears to be empty. I thought he wasn't leaving for another week." Another peek through the window, as though she were mistaken. At least that was what she'd hoped.

"He didn't tell you? They moved up the date for him to get to LA. You must have just missed him. He leased out the condo and got movers to get his things into storage. And what are you doing in Boston anyway?"

"I just . . ." She slid against the wall to the floor and cradled her face in her hand. "I wanted to tell him that I loved him."

Jenny's voice softened. "He knew that, Chloe. That's why it was so hard for him. It's also why he hasn't been answering your calls. But the best advice I can give is to have faith. God is in control of our lives when we turn it all over to him."

Chloe rummaged around her bag for a napkin and wiped her cheeks. "Thanks, Jenny."

"Oh, before we hang up, there's something you should know. Mason dropped Tabby off by us to take care of until he's settled. While here, he met his mom."

"Wow. That's great."

"I don't think he'd have agreed to it had it not been for you. He told me you two had spoken. He'd do anything for you. Anyway, I'll be sure to tell him you called if I hear from him."

"Thanks." She hung up and scrolled pictures of him. Of them. Would photos and memories be all that was left? And how many times had she heard that God was in control? It certainly didn't seem to be that way. At least, not the way she'd wanted things to go. Faith. *Believing in what we cannot see. Trust. I leave it in your hands Lord. It's all I can do.*

The elevator doors opened across from her. A man stepped out with a bellhop uniform and a tag that read *George*.

"Are you all right, ma'am?"

"Yeah. Just a little too late, that's all." She got up from the floor. "My friend, he already left."

He looked at Mason's condo. "Mason? You know him?"

"Yeah. I'm a friend from North Carolina." A friend. Wasn't that what she'd said was all she wanted to be to Mason? If so, then why was the word falling so short of what she knew was so much more?

"North Carolina? You wouldn't happen to be . . ." He snapped his fingers. "Chloe?"

"Yes, I am." Was he shocked? Surprised? What was that look, and how did he know who she was?

"Forgive me. I'm George, the bellman. I've known Mason for years. Since he moved here, in fact. I've always considered him a good friend. Always treated me with respect. Others . . . well, they can be a little uppity, if you know what I mean." He laughed. "But never Mason."

"Yeah, that's him, all right. A real gentleman."

"I'm really sorry you missed him, but for what it's worth, he loved you a lot."

How would he know? How much did Mason tell him? "Is that what he told you?"

"No. But he didn't have to. The way he talked about you before he left, there was no denying it. Of all his years of being here, he'd never mentioned being interested in another woman. And if I did ask him how a date went, he'd say it was nothing worth talking about. But when he mentioned you . . ."

"Thanks for letting me know how he felt about me."

"No problem. I'm just sorry things couldn't work out between you two. He did tell me that much."

"Yeah. I'm sorry too."

"Now, how about I get you a ride to where you need to go?"

Go? Where? Back home with an empty heart? Buy a case of tissues and a larger wastebasket? Make certain to never fit into her red dress again by drowning herself in pity lattes, chocolates, and danishes at Abby's? All doable. All likely.

Mason hung his leather messenger bag on the back of his chair at the conference table and sat next to Blake.

Their escort to the meeting room stopped in the doorway. "Someone will be with you shortly. Make yourselves comfortable."

"Thanks." Mason surveyed the room, with its expanse of autographed photos of celebrities on one wall and several movie posters on the other. The corner-unit exterior wall boasted floor-to-ceiling glass with panoramic views of the city.

Blake nodded and relaxed back in his chair. "Yeah. I think I could get used to this." He bumped Mason with his elbow. "So this is it, huh? Big movie deal. What you've been dreaming of. A year ago you would have never believed you'd be here in a big city like LA."

"There were a lot of things I didn't know were coming a year ago." Cancer. Chloe. And if this was his dream, why wasn't he more excited? He loosened his tie as heat flooded his face. Nervousness about signing? Or more like thoughts of not signing?

"Right. But hopefully things are turning around now. Any news on your final test results yet?"

"Should be hearing something today." Why did his dismal expectancy of the test results equal the signing of a contract resulting in a commitment of at least a year? It wasn't long ago that he'd arrived at Mom and Dad's and felt remorse for letting his career and success keep him away from the people he loved and from what mattered most. He'd vowed then to not let it happen again. But wasn't that exactly what he was doing?

And now with his reuniting of his birth mom after a lifetime of separation, would moving away make it any easier to get closer to her? She'd finally turned her life around in hopes of recovering so many lost years. He'd have thought her tears of regret would never cease with the acceptance of his forgiveness when they'd reunited. When both of their tears had subsided, she'd boasted of how proud she was for his every accomplishment. She'd read every one of his books over the years and felt worthless for abandoning such a wonderful son. How was moving away bridging the gap to a recovery of their relationship?

"Hey. Are you all right? You don't look like a man who's excited."

"I don't know. I'm just—"

A middle-aged woman carrying a folder entered the room and took a seat at the end of the table, next to Mason. "Mr. Chadwick, it's a pleasure to meet you. And Blake, nice to finally meet you in person." They stood and shook hands. "Have a seat. I'm Jacqueline. I'll be handling your contract as well as any legal matters."

The slow churning in the pit of Mason's stomach turned to knots.

"Well, Mason. We're really excited to have you come aboard. I personally have read your books. Love them all."

"Thank you, but it wouldn't have been possible without people like Blake, who took a chance on me."

"All true." Blake shook his head. "The man doesn't lie."

Mason thumbed toward Blake. "So modest."

Jaqueline laughed. "I can see that. Of course, I don't have to tell you what a fantastic opportunity this is. A chance to see your work on television, and the six-figure income doesn't hurt either. So we'll get right to it. I'm sure you'll agree that some chances only come along once in a lifetime. I can assure you—this is one of those things."

She was right about the once-in-a-lifetime opportunity. Chloe was just that, and it had nothing to do with money or success. In fact, he'd trade it all for her in a heartbeat.

"All the paperwork to finalize the deal is here." She rose from her seat. "I'll just step out for a while to give you two time to read all this over. When you're done, sign all the places I've marked, and you'll be set."

Blake pulled the stack of papers to him and fanned through them with his thumb. "That's a lot of fine print. Gonna be here awhile."

Mason reached into the inside pocket of his suit jacket for his pen, then let it remain. He needed time to think. Time to pray one final time before committing. *Lord, guide my decision and help me to do the right thing.* "I need a minute."

"Sure." Blake gave him a curious look.

Mason slid his chair back, walked to the window, and shoved his hands into his pockets. He recalled Tom's words concerning being in the right place, especially in the critical decision-making times of life. Though God didn't hold Tom accountable for his loss of Georgia, he'd lived with years of regret as a result. Was Mason about to make the same mistake? What was God's will for his life? He needed an answer now.

Blake stood next to Mason and folded his arms. They stared out at miles of buildings, streets, and cars. "And we thought Boston was big. I was thinking that after all this, we could hit that fancy restaurant down the street I'd heard about. A little celebration, you know."

Mason nodded. A celebration for someone who didn't want to celebrate and had just lost his appetite? Didn't sound all that fun.

Blake focused his gaze on Mason. "After that we could take in a comedy show somewhere. Who doesn't need a good laugh?"

"Whatever." Mason pulled the phone from his pocket and found the picture of him and Chloe at the restaurant, wearing her red dress. Amid all the decision-making he was confronted with that weighed heavily on his future, her beautiful face brought comfort and peace. She had a way of steadying his troubled waters and giving his soul rest. She was the one-in-a-million chance. She was far better than the offer currently on the table. Couldn't even compare.

He scrolled farther through numerous missed calls and messages from Chloe, to call her back. Each time he'd started to respond, he'd freeze up, unsure as to what to say. And there was no need for her to apologize again, if that was her intent.

If her offer stood for them being only friends, he'd take it. If that was all it could ever be, then it would have to be enough. He'd not live another decade or two in regret for not taking a chance. And in the end, he hoped she'd know that she had a friend whom she could count on. Someone who would always love her for who and what she was. Amazing.

He slid the phone back into his pocket, taking note of Blake's not-so-subtle peek.

"That's a new suit you're wearing?" Blake nodded. "Lookin' sharp there."

"Yeah. Still not fitting into my old ones. Got a few more pounds to go." He pulled off his tie.

Another peek from Blake as they continued their gaze out the window. "Bet Chloe would love to see you in that right now. I don't think she'd be able to keep her hands off you." He flashed his brows.

Mason quirked a smile. And there it was. Just the mention of her name and all was well.

"I think that's the first smile I've seen all day. Listen, Mason. This is your life to live. Don't worry about what people think. That's between you and God, right? You're already successful. You've got nothing more to prove."

"Yeah. You're right."

He slapped Mason's arm with the back of his hand. "You thinkin' what I'm thinkin'?"

"I don't know, but are you ready to get out of here?"

Blake smiled wide. "That's exactly what I was thinking." He grabbed him by the shoulder in a hug. "Good to have you back. We've got a novel to write."

"Oh, so now it's *we*. You're gonna help me write one? I'm holding you to that."

"Well. You know what I mean. I don't know about you, but I'm starving." Blake gave a tug to his lapel.

"Yeah. Me too."

Now there was a reason to celebrate. Mason exhaled the burdensome weight of the decision and was comforted by the confirmation of overwhelming peace that flooded him. He thought of how much clearer the important things and people became when faced with death.

Maybe this was what it felt like to experience a peace that passes all understanding. By all-natural reasoning, it was a crazy decision to walk away from such an opportunity. But what he was running to was far greater than what he was running from. Family, friends, and loved ones were waiting. There was no reason to feel alone. It was time to go home.

Chapter 19

There was no use prolonging the inevitable. Chloe, along with Mom and Sarah, would be in the county office by noon to close out their lease on the property. But first, one last trip to the cabin to say their goodbyes.

"What's a gazebo doing behind the cabin?" Chloe shut off the Jeep's ignition. Mason? Why would he . . . They pushed their doors closed and drew near for a closer look.

"Is this the same cabin?" Mom said. "Did Mason have the cabin and porch pressure washed? I can't remember the place looking this nice."

"And this looks just like . . ." Chloe stepped under the gazebo and ran her hand on the post, then took a seat on the swing. "This looks like the old gazebo in our scrapbook pictures. He must have seen the old photo of it on my shop wall. How else would he have known? But I don't know why he went through the trouble to do this. He knew we'd lose the lease."

Sarah sat next to Chloe. "You did say he needed something to do to keep his mind off things."

"Yeah, but don't you think this is a little extreme?" She shook her head. "And how did he do all this since I was here last? He must have hired a crew to get this done. I can't imagine him doing this in his condition?" She held a hand to her forehead. There was nothing he wouldn't do to see her happy. And the way he took note of the things that mattered most to her was beyond sweet. He couldn't help but be amazing.

"Maybe he wanted you to see it the way it used to be," Mom said. "I know it brings back memories for me. Your dad and I were married in this very spot. As well your grandparents. We had the most wonderful reception out here with family and friends." She leaned her head on a post that she'd wrapped and arm around and giggled. "We almost didn't want to go on our honeymoon that night. Wanted to stay and celebrate under the stars with our friends and family."

Chloe and Sarah rose and hugged Mom. "We love you, Mom," Chloe said, determined to stay strong. She'd save those tears following the signing away of the place.

They made their way onto the porch. No more loose deck boards. Chloe swung open the front door. No more squeaky hinges. The next surprise once inside was the freshly stained floors and varnished solid-wood kitchen cabinets. In fact, there didn't appear to be any area in the cabin that hadn't been fixed or improved. Chloe had no idea he'd been so busy.

Upon the fireplace mantel, as well as the hearth, were several pieces of pottery. They were her masterpieces from the craft gallery off Main Street, with one larger piece she'd sold to Charlotte for the B&B. Next to it sat a card with a message. "An amazingly beautiful creation by an amazingly beautiful creator. Love you. Mason." She held the card to her chest. He had admired and valued her giftings, and there wasn't a path he'd not found to the inroads to her heart.

On the kitchen table sat a vase of wildflowers, mostly irises and lilies, with splashes of fire pink flowers that had begun to dry out and wither. He'd evidently remembered her love for them while on their trip to the falls and had more than likely picked them from there. Something had felt extra special that day, sitting with him in her cherished spot. It had just felt right.

The baby crib in the corner of the living room caught Chloe's attention. She slid her hand across the spindles. It had been completely refinished, with even the broken spindle repaired that she'd kicked out as a baby. She'd take it back home, along with whatever contents remained by the week's end, as stated in the letter by the county. But most of all, she'd be taking the memories of the past as well as visions of the future with Mason and what could have been.

Later, entering the county office felt oddly similar to attending a funeral. The final chapter would be closed on generations of the Morgans' rights to the property. It was a place that held a lifetime of memories, not just for the Morgans but all who had visited the campground over the decades.

Between her failed attempt to see Mason in Boston and now the turning over of the property, she'd have thought it would be all too much to bear. Instead, she felt numb and jumbled with thoughts and emotions. Maybe tomorrow or the next day she'd wake up and fall apart. But for now all she could determine was that the Lord was holding her together. There was no way she could bear the weight of it all on her own.

Chloe, Mom, and Sarah took a seat in Everett Stone's office and awaited his entrance. He'd be handling the documents ending the lease. Having been a close friend to Dad for many years, Everett and his family had enjoyed the benefits of the campground. It was certain that if anyone could understand the loss for the Morgan legacy, it would be him.

"Good morning, ladies," Everett said as he took a seat behind the large desk. "Grace, I hope you and your family have been doing well. Haven't seen you in a while."

Mom nervously clutched her purse on her lap. "Well as can be expected, I guess. And how's Jane?"

"In all the years as we've been married, there's one thing that remains true. As long as she gets to work in her garden, she's happy." He laughed. "But in all seriousness, I know how hard this must be to let go of the campground after all these years, despite it not being in operation for some time. I've been around long enough to know the good it did in this community. It truly was an honor to know the entire Morgan family."

"Thank you," Mom said. "We've been blessed with the property but realize it's time to move on." She gave a faint sigh.

"On the bright side, you'll be happy to know that the east side of the property, across from the cabin, will be put to good use. The old campsite areas will be converted into walking trails and picnic areas, still benefiting the community."

Chloe fidgeted, wiping her sweaty palms on her jeans, wanting nothing more than for the meeting to conclude. To rip the Band-Aid off, then go. "Your secretary said we had something to sign?"

"Yes, of course." He spun his swivel desk chair around and removed papers from a file cabinet. "This document officially closes out the lease. All we need is a signature."

Everett slid the paper and a pen across the desk to Mom. Her hand hesitated. Then with the stroke of the pen, it was done.

Chloe felt a thud in her chest and abruptly arose to leave. There was no use lingering. It was finished. The end.

"Chloe, before you leave, I have something for you to sign," Everett said, promptly stopping her departure. "Please take a seat for a moment."

Chloe sat back down. What would there be for her to sign? The lease was under Mom's name, and she'd already signed. Grace and Sarah crunched their brows with a puzzled look.

He slid a paper over to Chloe and smiled. "It seems you've made quite an impression on someone—namely, Mason Chadwick."

"Mason?" Chloe scanned the document. "I don't understand. What is this? What does he have to do with any of this?" How many more surprises could surround the man she loved?

"In short, Mason struck a deal with the county and made an offer we couldn't refuse. It made sense for both parties. He bought the twenty-five acres on the west side of the stream. The side with the cabin. It extends from that cabin to just past the falls. He bought it all."

Chloe thought she was the only one with a jaw hanging and a confused look, until she looked at Mom and Sarah.

"But if Mason bought it, what am I signing?"

"Ownership of the property." Everett sat back and pressed his fingers together, as though praying and nodded. "You heard right."

What was happening? There had to be a mistake. It didn't make sense. "You mean, like a partnership? Me and Mason?"

"No. It's all yours free and clear. He wants you to have it, Chloe. Mr. Chadwick went through a local attorney, who drew up the papers making it all legally binding."

"So it's paid for?"

"All of it. I have to say, that in all my years on this job, I've never seen anything like this. Consider it your miracle."

Maybe it was God's way of showing a silver lining in the storm clouds that had prevailed the passing week. And though thankful for the blessing, she'd trade it all for the miracle of having Mason in her life. For him to live and a chance for her to love him. "Thank you, Mr. Stone. For everything." This must have been why Mason was with Bill the day she and Abby were at the park. And it wasn't because he'd had anything to do with taking the land from them, as Tina had insinuated. Of course, she'd never believed it to begin with. Instead, it was just Mason being Mason. Loving and taking care of her, even when he was nowhere around.

"Oh, one more thing. Mason's purchase of the land afforded the county enough money to build the walking trails and several covered picnic areas. At his request, we've named the park after your family. Morgan Park. In a way, your family's legacy continues. Have a good day, ladies."

Once again there were no strings attached. No ulterior motives. Nothing to gain for Mason, other than never letting an opportunity go by without showing how much he loved her. It was a selfless love. Maybe the only kind he knew.

Chloe broke the prolonged silence and blank stares as they took a seat on a concrete bench outside of the county office before getting in the car.

"Is any of this real? Did all of that just happen?"

Sarah leaned over with her elbows resting on her knees and her chin resting in the palm of her hand. "Closest thing to being in the Twilight Zone, if you ask me."

Chloe bumped Sarah with her shoulder. "I would say that you've been hanging around with Abby too much. But I think you're right."

Mom reached down to the ground, picked a clover, and turned to Chloe. "Do you think you can ask Mason to sign his book for me when you see him? He left before I could ask."

When I see him? Didn't she mean "if" I see him? And if there was a time she'd see him again, she'd be asking him for a lot more than an autograph. Asking for forgiveness would be at the top of the list. Asking if he'd meant it when he told her he loved her. Followed by another chance to respond to his promise of their forever.

Chloe stirred the cabin's remaining log embers with the poker and wondered if the embers of love she held for Mason would someday die out as well. She doubted it. But before it would have a chance to do so, she'd make one last effort to reach out.

She slipped a flannel shirt on, left in the cabin by Mason, and settled into his desk chair. Mason's chair. His desk. His cabin. Everything . . . his. Without his intervention, whatever items of any sentimental value would have been removed, loaded onto a truck, and followed with a final glance of the property in the rearview mirror.

She drank in a prolonged inhale of his shirt collar to savor the lingering trace of his cologne. The same scent as the day they'd met. Just as she doubted her love for him would ever fade, she questioned if the shirt would ever get washed.

With a few final strokes of the typewriter keys, the letter she'd started earlier in the morning would be done. *Love, Chloe.* This time if unanswered, she'd assume he'd moved on and was unwilling to take another chance at the risk of heartbreak. With no response to her texts or calls, it was the last thing she could do. That, and of course pray.

The late-evening chill of autumn had already settled in. She lowered herself onto the gazebo swing, clutched the pendant dangling from her neck, and marveled. How had the turning of the leaves begun without her noticing, with it being her single most anticipated time of the year? And how could she have been oblivious to the risen stream due to increased rainfall? A time when she'd pay the most visits to the falls. Falling rain, autumn leaves, and tears. A laugh attempted to escape her lips. Almost sounded like the making of a heartbreaking love song. If she were a gifted writer like Mason, she could cut an album of tear jerkers just from the past month's trials.

Which was much the opposite of her and Mason's song, "Unforgettable." Their song. Their dance. Their moment when a hint of happily ever after for the future could be possible. Unforgettable would be the way to describe his look, or rather gawk, when she'd pulled the door open sporting the red dress. Up till that point in their friendship, she'd only suspected the extent of his interest in her. But after that look . . . The corners of her mouth turned up, and this time she laughed aloud. Imagine a small-town average girl stopping Mason Chadwick in his tracks. Her smile just as quickly faded. If only she hadn't let him go.

As for revealing that she was the girl in the picture—she wouldn't. She'd want him to return because of who she was now, not then. Then, and only then, if he returned, would she tell him. Something that would be a miracle in itself. And if it was meant to be in God's plan, he'd return. Only this time she'd be the one asking him to stay and leaving that decision up to him. She took a deep breath with eyes closed and exhaled. Who was she kidding? What were the chances of him coming back? He was probably celebrating his big dream come true even as she sat there searching for the first visible stars of the evening. And why wouldn't he be? He deserved it. And so much more.

Chloe pulled the flannel shirt closed with a shiver and shut her eyes. Hopefully, God had answered her desperate plea for his health above anything else she'd ever prayed.

She threw her legs onto the swing in response to a furry rub against her ankles. "Tabby?" The cat certainly looked like him, but how would he have gotten here? The cat meowed. She picked him up and stroked his fur. "You sure do get around. You could have been . . ."

Her eyes caught movement on the porch of the cabin. It couldn't be. Mason?

Tabby's meow broke her stillness. She lowered him to the ground with her gaze riveted on Mason. Her heart might have raced before in his presence, but not like this. This time it was a heart crying out in longing. Or was it desperation? She exhaled at the realization she wasn't breathing. Not since she'd seen him standing there. But why was he here?

She slowed her racing mind. Maybe he was just passing through town on the way to see his parents and wanted to say hi. Why would it be assumed he was there for her? That he'd returned because he couldn't live without her, just as she didn't want to without him. No, too presumptuous. A setup for a huge letdown.

She met him at the foot of the porch steps. "Mason . . ." Those eyes. His expression. Neither expressed a notion of wanting to just be friends. He might have been able to keep other secrets from her, but not that one. Hiding his feelings for her was something he was not good at. It was an imperfection she prayed he'd never lose. She blinked at the moisture that had formed in her eyes and raised her brows along with a smile. He cracked a smile. Her cue.

She wrapped her arms tight around his neck, and their wet cheeks met. His lips trailed a kisses down her neck, then another tight embrace.

"I missed you," she whispered, then released him.

His hands held her face and swiped a tear from her cheek with a thumb. "Missed you too." He slid his hands down her arms and took hold of her hands. "I should have never left without telling you. I'm sorry."

"What are you doing here? What about the deal? I thought you were in California."

"Yeah, I was. Couldn't help thinking about the much better deal here. You know, about being friends. That is, if the offer still stands." He lifted her hand and kissed it.

"Friends, huh? I don't know about all that," she teased, with a sly smile and a sniffle. "I've got something to show you." Her hand held on to his, and she led him inside to the living room. She opened the lid of an old cedar trunk in front of the couch and retrieved his hat that she'd found in the pottery shop, then handed it to him.

He scrutinized it, looked on the inside, and found his initials. *MC.* "Chloe, how . . . where did you get this?" He shook his head. "It's my old hat."

"Found it in an old box at my shop. Mom thinks Dad gathered up everything he could find before leaving the cabin one day when I was young. And I found a note on the inside rim."

He pulled it out and read it. "'April 7. The day I fell in love.'"

"Mason, April 7 was the day of the church fair. The day we met. The old box that I found the hat in got pushed to the back of the loft. I only found it when looking for a carry-on bag to go see you in Boston."

He gave what appeared to be a remorseful nod. "Yeah. Sorry about that. Mom told me you'd tried to find me. It's all I could think about when I was faced with signing the contract in LA. That you cared enough to find me."

"There's something else. Something you need to know." She sighed. It was time. He needed to know. She wanted him to know. "Ever since Dad passed, I'd doubted that God really cared about the little things

219

in my life. Or anyone's, as far as that goes. What, with all the problems in the world, why would my issues matter? But after we visited your parents, I realized that I couldn't have been more wrong."

"When we visited my parents? I don't understand."

She walked across the room to the desk and pulled the chain to the desk lamp. Its light illuminated the framed photo of the girl he'd fallen for long ago.

He moved in for a closer look and rubbed the back of his neck. "Where . . . where did you get this?"

"It's a copy of the one in your room at your mom's."

His eyes held a puzzled look. "But why do you have it?"

"Is this the girl you fell in love with?"

"Yes. But that was a long time ago, and I've let go of the regrets of the past. You're the one I love."

Chloe wrapped an arm around him. "Mason, that's me in the picture. Looked different back then, but it's me. And Sarah is in the background, along with Dad's old truck next to the cabin. I wore that straw hat all summer. It was my favorite."

Mason looked at the picture, then back at her. "I've kept this picture in my phone and looked at it every day for years. I can't believe it's been you all this time." He turned to her and enfolded her in his arms.

"I love you, Mason. I have for a while but was too afraid to admit it. I'm so sorry for letting fear hold me back from what I've been wanting to say all along, and for hurting you the way I did. I—"

Mason interrupted her pleading with an embrace and a kiss. Her opportunity to cash in on a lifetime of saved-up kisses had arrived, and she'd take full advantage of it.

He stroked a hand through her hair. "I've got some good news."

"Better than the fact that you're here with me?"

"My last PET scan showed a dramatic improvement. Maybe there is a chance for our forever."

"Mason, that's . . . incredible." She thanked God for Mason's healing and resolved to never doubt God's goodness and faithfulness again.

She brushed her wet cheek with the collar of his flannel shirt. "You up to a dance?"

She flashed him a smirk. The only thing missing was her red dress and heels. But this time she wouldn't need them. The "look" was already there. She made her way to the corner of the room and slid a vinyl record from its sleeve and placed it on the turntable.

"Dance? I don't know about that." He folded his arms and teased with his eyes. "My heart belongs to someone who's utterly unforgettable. You could never steal me away from her."

"Oh, is that so?"

She dropped the needle onto the turning album. An air of nostalgia filled the serene cabin with the scratching of the needle. "Their" cabin. Her arms wrapped around his neck, and she pressed her ear to his chest. She was certain his heart had sped up. And of course, his arms were wrapped around her waist—again. They'd always made their way there somehow, starting with their first day at the fair, followed by his heroic efforts to prevent her from falling off the tall one-step ladder. Even then, she knew he'd never let her fall.

The song "Unforgettable" played. Their song. And once again their dance. She held his face, studying the depth of love his blue eyes held. Only God knew how many more kisses, dances, and I love yous there'd be. She'd leave that in God's hands. But what she did know was they had now. Their time. Their dance. Their forever moment.

"I love you, Chloe. I always have. Always will."

"I love you too, Mason. Always and forever."

As for Chloe, it no longer mattered how long forever was. If forever was for only a moment, she'd embrace it. She didn't need any more signs. He was in her arms. It was more than enough. Mason was more than enough.

www.ingramcontent.com/pod-product-compliance
Lightning Source LLC
Chambersburg PA
CBHW022141240626
47153CB00007B/2458

* 9 7 9 8 9 8 7 3 3 3 7 2 3 *